'I have been studying how I may compare
This prison where I live unto the world.'

William Shakespeare, *Richard II*

Contents

Part One

The Prison

'For who so firm that cannot be seduc'd?'

William Shakespeare, *Julius Caesar*

Chapter One

The Retreat

"Message from Brigade," Murdoch Mackintosh announced. "The evacuation is complete. GHQ is claiming over 300,000 men have been taken off. They're calling it the miracle of Dunkirk. What do you reckon, sir?"

Major Hector Brand surveyed what was left of his command. "That they'll have to stage another Dunkirk, down here, if this keeps up."

His men had been pulled out of the fighting line for a day's rest and recuperation, and were settled in the village of Hornoy. Only a few miles away to their north-east was the city of Amiens; if the houses and even the church steeples could no longer be seen the smoke clouds were clearly visible, rising into the clear June evening sky as were the aircraft wheeling above them. Amiens was being systematically destroyed. Only twenty or so miles to their west was the seaport of Dieppe. Either there, or Le Havre, farther down the coast at the mouth of the Seine, would have to be their point of embarkation. Hector Brand no longer had any illusions about their ability to hold the Germans.

It had all begun so promisingly. After a winter of waiting, and training, and champing at the bit, when Hitler had made his move, not yet a month ago, the French and British armies had leapt forward to enter and defend Belgium, secure in

3

the knowledge that the Maginot Line would guard their right flank.

The British Expeditionary Force commanded by Field Marshal Lord Gort, which had crossed the Channel so ebulliently the previous October, had had no doubts then that they could meet and match the enemy, as their forefathers in 1914 – who had included two Brands in their ranks – had met and checked the Germans at Mons and Le Cateau. There had even been the two present-generation Brands to help them do it.

Hector hadn't actually seen his cousin Harry Brand since the war had begun: their regiments had been at opposite ends of the line. Like everyone else, however, they had assumed that the British Army would fight as one force. Thus the officers and men of the Highland Division had been somewhat taken aback when they had been ordered to fill a gap in the French line facing the Saar. That separation from the main body had meant that when Gort had been forced to retreat to the Belgian coast as the German panzers had driven a wedge through the Allied line at Sedan, the Highland Brigade had been left to retreat, with their French allies, south of the Somme. Oh, to be at Dunkirk, Hector thought, now that spring is here. From everything they had heard it had been sheer hell on those beaches. But 300,000 men had been taken to safety by the Navy. His cousin Harry was somewhere up there. Hector wondered if he'd made it.

He still had a lot of fighting to do. Thus far the retreat had been carried out in a reasonably orderly fashion; bridgeheads had been established and defended, the Germans kept at bay. But thus far the Germans had been concentrating their main effort in Belgium. If the evacuation of the BEF was now complete, Rundstedt and Rommel would be seeking to clinch their victory against the remaining

4

French armies and the small British contingent, trying desperately to defend Paris. The fighting had already been severe. The 1st Battalion Shetland Light Infantry was down to four companies, and none of them was at full strength. Their colonel was dead, thus Hector found himself in command at the absurdly early age of twenty-six; he had been promoted major, again at an amazingly early age, just before the fighting had started. The responsibility did not frighten him. He was a Brand. He came from a long line of soldiers; there had been a Brand in the British Army at the Battle of Blenheim, and in almost every major battle ever since. Command was in his blood.

In the family tradition, although he was of the Scottish, subsidiary, branch, Hector Brand was a tall, strongly built man, if by no means a giant like his cousin. Like all his family he had yellow-brown hair and blue eyes, with craggily handsome features. But again unlike Harry, he had been a soldier since entering Sandhurst straight out of school eight years before; Harry had been a reluctant soldier, had even dreamed of becoming a doctor before being caught up in the war euphoria of 1939. Hector had no extreme feelings about the course his life had followed; it had seemed the only natural thing to do. And for a Brand it had all been very easy: Fettes, Sandhurst and a Scottish regiment. His own father had been killed in the Great War, and thus he had grown up under the aegis of his famous uncle, Brigadier George Brand, who was presently serving in Norway in a peculiarly futile offshoot of this war. Hector's holidays had been spent as often with the English Brands, his cousins Harry and Louise, as with his mother's family in Scotland.

Equally had he early accepted that he would one day have to repay his training and place in society by fighting for his country. It had been a concept which, glowing in his late teens and early twenties, had lost a good deal of its appeal over the past few years. This was partly because of the disillusionment felt by so many officers and men of the professional British Army that they were *ever* going to be allowed to fight, as their political masters seemed to be bending over ever further backwards in their determination to keep the German dictator happy. Equally partly had it been caused by the appearance of Jocelyn in his life. With due permission from his superiors he had married the lovely redhead as soon as his promotion to captain had made it possible, and they had had two glorious years together before the call had come. Now she was safely with her mother in Edinburgh, and herself mothering his now three-months-old child. He wondered if he would ever see the babe?

Brigade came through that evening on the field telephone, seeking information as to the Battalion's exact strength and position. "Can you hold where you are?"

"That depends on how long and against what," Hector replied.

"A few divisions, old man. And as long as possible."

"Then I won't talk about more than hours, without reinforcements."

"The good news is that it will be mostly infantry, according to our reconnaissance. This isn't very good tank country, you know."

"Point taken." Hector looked out across small fields, broken with hedgerows and sunken lanes. It was called bocage, looked very romantic in the glow of the setting sun, but must be a tank commander's nightmare. "What's the bad news?"

"There are no reinforcements."

"Keep in touch," Hector suggested.

"All those bloody anti-tank guns," Mackintosh grumbled.

Murdoch Mackintosh was the senior remaining officer; he was the only remaining captain, and thus found himself, at an even more absurdly early age – he was only twenty-three – second in command of the battalion.

"We can use them against infantry," Hector said. "Dig in. Here is where it all stops." Them and us, he thought.

The Highlanders were happy to stay put for another few hours; they had done nothing for the past week but march and take shelter from marauding Stukas. They were a mostly unshaven, unwashed, uncouth lot, bare knees bony beneath their kilts. But they were still full of confidence; born fighting men, their real concerns were their next meal, their next drink, and their next home leave, in that order. They had no idea of the force that was moving against them. Mackintosh did. "Do they really mean us just to stay here and be overrun, sir?" he asked.

"They'll think of something," Hector promised him. "Where's dinner?"

He was no cleaner and hardly smarter than his men, and at that moment his interests were the same as theirs, with the added reflection that he had to inspire them, yet again. "Someone coming, sir," called Sergeant Major Boyd.

Both officers stood up. There were no civilians left in Hornoy, the village's inhabitants having joined the great exodus of French men, women and children, and animals, all moving to the south in their effort to escape the fighting. "Riding a bicycle," Mackintosh remarked.

"He's one of us," Hector said, seeing the kilt flutter in the evening breeze.

A few minutes later the corporal stood before them. "Message from Colonel Wemyss, sir." He held out the piece of paper clearly torn from an army-issue notebook.

Hector read: *Am holding Poix with insufficient force. Can you extend your right to cover open country between us?*

7

Consider it important to maintain line if possible. Reply with available strength. Urgent. Wemyss.

Hector raised his head. "Has the Colonel lost his radios?"

"Jerry is too close, sir," the corporal said. "He'd overhear."

Hector supposed the Gordon Highlander was right. Thus he should reply in kind. He studied the map. Poix was a few miles away to the south-east, actually on the main road leading south-west from Amiens. It certainly lay in the direct line of any German advance from the city. But he couldn't help without contravening his own orders. He tore a page from his own notebook. *Effective three hundred and seventy-two,* he wrote. *Insufficient to hold Hornoy if attacked in strength, but am commanded to do so. Is there no reserve?* He folded the paper and handed it to the corporal. "Good luck."

It was now almost dark. Hector surveyed the country through his binoculars. It undulated, but the village was sufficiently elevated for him to pick out a glint of steel in the last rays of the sun, some distance to the north. Mackintosh had also been using his glasses. "Think they'll come in the night, sir?"

"My bet would be first light. But double your sentries, Murdoch."

Hector did not suppose he was going to sleep. But in fact he did not wish to sleep. If he carried out his orders to the letter, as he had every intention of doing, this time tomorrow he would probably be dead. There was so much to be thought about. Jocelyn, of course. And the boy he had never seen. But he was as much in love with his wife now as the day he had proposed. He could remember every nuance of her body, her movements, her somewhat uncertain attitude to life. As, for example, she had never got over the disaster of her introduction of one of her closest friends, Constance Lloyd, to Cousin Harry. Harry was one of those men who found all women irresistible and, amazingly, most women seemed to find him irresistible in return. Even Constance Lloyd, so determinedly anti when they had met, had succumbed, with the result that Harry had found himself on the end of a shotgun wedding. Had *he* survived? Hector did not suppose he would find out until he got back to England himself. Supposing he was going to do that.

How the hell had he, and so many thousands of others, got themselves into this mess? Poor leadership, certainly. Or to be precise, lack of leadership at every level. He had always considered there were three layers of government. At the bottom was politics, which involved the placing of party before country, or, to put it another way, the continuance in office above every other consideration – presumably in the belief that one could do the job better than anyone else. Hector had always voted Conservative, because that was what he had been brought up to do. His family, his class, had an inbred antagonism to anyone wearing a cloth cap. Or they had. When he looked around him at the very gallant men who were preparing to die at his behest, not one of whom – and he suspected this included Captain Murdoch Mackintosh – would ever have voted Tory in their lives, he could only realise, a trifle late, how mistaken he and his forebears had been. It had been the Conservative leadership, as typified by Stanley Baldwin's refusal to impose the necessary taxation to raise the country's defences to a state where it could compete with Nazi Germany – purely from a fear of losing the next election – that had exemplified politics at its worst.

The second level was diplomacy. Diplomacy presupposes that one can argue with the other side without either losing its temper or resorting to force. It also presumes a certain amount of honesty, on both sides. In each of those regards Neville Chamberlain, so upright, honest and sincere, had been like a rabbit confronted by a king cobra when attempting to negotiate with Adolf Hitler.

The third, and most important, aspect of government was statesmanship. This assumed two presumptions. One was an ability accurately to foresee the results of your, and your opponent's, actions, to form judgements as to where those actions were likely to lead – as opposed to waiting for things to happen and then making desperate arrangements to follow. The other was an ability to make the harsh decisions that were often necessary to influence the future. On that basis there had only been one statesman in England during the ten years just past. That he was now in charge might save the country. But it was not going to save those men pre-committed to hopeless tasks, made hopeless by their masters' ineptitude. Hector reckoned he was quite entitled to feel bitter.

Hector was awakened at three by his batman, MacLean. "They're out there, sir."

He sat up, rubbed his eyes, and reached for his binoculars. It was just getting light, and he could see movement, perhaps a mile away. "Stand to," he told Mackintosh. To their right there was a crackle of gunfire; Wemyss was under attack.

"Breakfast, sir." MacLean appeared with a tin tray. The corned beef and bread was cold, but he had managed two cups of coffee on his primus.

Hector drank thirstily, chewed greedily. "Take the right, Murdoch," he told Mackintosh. The captain finished his coffee, and disappeared into the gloom. "We'll need you as well, Mac," Hector said.

"Yes, sir," MacLean agreed, putting away his cooking utensils in favour of a rifle. "I could rustle up some water for shaving, sir."

"I'd keep it for drinking," Hector said. "It could be a long, hot day." He continued to study the fields in front of him. "Sergeant Major Boyd," he said quietly. "Get your guns ready. Range a thousand yards. We want to make each shot tell."

"Yes, sir," Boyd said.

A glimmer of brilliant light appeared out of the east as the sun emerged. It immediately picked out a thousand pinpoints gleaming in the fields, as well as revealing fresh clouds of smoke rising from Amiens, and from Poix as well. Hector opened his mouth to give the command to fire, and was beaten to it by the Germans. A ripple of red scorched the dawn and a moment later the first shells struck the village. They had the range to perfection. Houses exploded, masonry sang through the air, walls collapsed, dogs barked, and men screamed as they were hit.

"Fire!" Hector shouted, and his anti-tank guns opened up. They also had the range, and for several hours the artillery duel raged; the riflemen could only keep their heads down while the sun and shells soared overheard, the heat of the day being accentuated by the clouds of dust and smoke rising out of the village, which was now on fire in several places.

Yet the expected assault did not come. "The bastards seem to think they can blow us out of existence," Sergeant Major Boyd remarked. "You'd think they'd have learned that isn't on from the last lot." It was, however, a pretty depressing experience, especially as Hector knew his men were being killed and wounded, and there was damn all he could do about it. It became even more depressing when Boyd reported that he was just about out of ammunition for his anti-tank guns. But with projectiles designed to pierce tank armour rather than destroy men, they were, in any event, no match for the German field artillery.

It was late in the afternoon of the long, hot day that Hector had prophesied before the German firing died away. "Casualties," he said, having to work his tongue to get his saliva going before he could speak. Sergeant O'Brien, the sole remnant of the medical unit attached to the battalion, crawled away, while Hector wondered, not for the first time, how a man with a name like O'Brien had found himself in a Highland regiment. But there were more important matters to be considered; the Germans would be coming now. Or would they? There was no movement from in front of him.

MacLean touched his arm, and he swung the glasses. Away to his left men were moving forward, seeping like water into a broken dam into the gap between him and the next strongpoint. "Shit!" he muttered, and looked to his right. There too the Germans were moving through the gap.

"Hutier tactics, sir," Boyd said. He had been in the Army a long time. "They used them in 1918. Caused no end of panic."

Hector chewed his lip. He had been ordered to hold the village, no matter what. Even if he was being surrounded? O'Brien re-appeared. "We have thirty-two dead, sir. And fifty-seven wounded, but only twelve seriously."

That still left him with fewer than 300 effectives, Hector thought. "Captain Mackintosh?"

"He's slightly wounded, sir."

"Brigade, sir." Corporal Mearns was writing vigorously as he listened to his earphones. Then he held out the slip of paper.

Brigade weren't bothered about the Germans overhearing

12

their command; this was serious. *As soon as possible, fall back and across River Bresle. Use bridge at Inchville.*

"Map," Hector said.

Boyd spread it before him. "We won't get to Inchville, sir," he remarked. "That's damn near thirty miles away, and due west, across the enemy advance."

"While the river runs only five miles away, south-west," Hector said thoughtfully. "We'll make for the nearest point, Sergeant Major." He grinned at Boyd's expression. "We'll worry about how we cross when we get there."

Mackintosh joined him, his right arm in a sling. "Shrapnel," he explained. "Do we have a plan?"

Hector indicated the map. "A five-mile hike."

"There are Germans down there."

"There are Germans there, and there, and there as well," Hector pointed out. "It'll be dark."

He summoned all the surviving NCOs, told them to keep their men close, told O'Brien to assemble a party of strong volunteers for stretcher-bearing. "But every man who can walk must do so. Remember, no talking, no noise at all. Every man follow the man in front. Real Indian stuff. Captain Mackintosh, you're the rearguard. No stragglers."

"And you, sir?" asked Sergeant Major Boyd.

Hector grinned at them all. "I'll be the man in front."

Such transport as they had managed to save on the retreat was virtually out of petrol. In any event, using transport would have involved too much noise, even supposing they could drive their trucks across country. "Immobilise them," Hector told Boyd. "And the guns. We can't burn them or blow them up, because we don't want Jerry to realise we've left for as long as possible."

The demolition work was carried out quickly and efficiently by removing distributor caps and firing pins, which were light enough and small enough to be carried in haversacks; the vehicles were then booby-trapped. "Now," Hector told his men. "You all know what we have to do. There'll be no stopping until we reach the river." He took off his steel helmet and put on his glengarry, gave the thumbs-up sign. "Let's go."

He set off, using his compass. MacLean and Mearns followed, carrying the portable radio. O'Brien came next, with his seven stretcher cases; the more seriously walking wounded followed. Boyd led the main party, and Mackintosh brought up the rear, with a volunteer rearguard. There was as yet no moon, although one was due later, but if the intense darkness concealed them from the enemy, it also concealed many of the obstacles that lay in their way. There had been no opportunity to reconnoitre the ground, and Hector had to follow his compass. This led him in and out of hedgerows, across fields from which the cattle had only recently been removed, leaving their cowpats behind, and through ditches, mainly dry but nonetheless obstructions which caused him and his men to trip and stumble and mutter curses.

The wounded were heroic in their determination to keep quiet, even as the jolting and the occasional dropping to the ground of their stretchers must have been excruciating. Hector estimated they had covered about a mile when Boyd came up to join him. "To our right, sir," the sergeant major said. Hector turned his head. The night was still very dark, but he saw what the sergeant major meant; only a few hundred yards away was another body of men, proceeding in the same direction, with slightly more noise. "Do you think they're ours, sir?" Boyd whispered.

"We can't chance it," Hector said. "Stop the column."

The word was passed back, and the weary men, especially the stretcher-bearers, sank to the ground in relief. Mackintosh came up to join Hector. "We'll just let them get clear," Hector said.

"What happens if they're occupying the river bank when we get there?" the captain asked.

"Let's cross one bridge at a time," Hector said.

After about fifteen minutes the Germans disappeared into the gloom, apparently unaware how close they had been to the Scots. Hector sent the word back, and they resumed their retreat. Half an hour later they had to halt again as another column of men loomed on their left. Once again the temptation to contact them was great; they could have been Wemyss's people retreating from Poix. But once again Hector decided not to take the risk; his business was to get *his* people out, not go down in a death or glory firefight with vastly superior forces. But it was uncanny to be moving in the midst of a victorious enemy.

Towards dawn the noise behind them increased, and he assumed the Germans had at last moved on the village. That meant there would soon be a pursuit. But in front of him Hector saw the gleam of water. He made the column halt, and crawled forward, accompanied by Boyd and MacLean. The banks were wooded, and they were well concealed as they stared at the obstacle. "Not more than thirty yards wide, sir," Boyd said. "Wonder how deep it is?"

"It's running pretty hard," MacLean commented.

Hector didn't doubt his men could get across, providing

they weren't attacked in the process. "Send up Captain Mackintosh," he said.

Mackintosh arrived a few minutes later. "Now there's a pretty sight!"

"How's your arm?" Hector asked.

Mackintosh had discarded his sling. "Just a scratch. Water will do it good."

"We have to assume this is a crossing in the presence of the enemy," Hector said. "But they don't know we're here yet. I want you to get across, Murdoch, with four machine-guns. We won't move until you are emplaced on the far bank, and we will cover you until then. Then you have to give us covering fire."

Mackintosh gulped. "Yes, sir."

"You can have forty men. They all have to be swimmers. And quiet as mice. You'll use whatever ropes we have left."

"Yes, sir."

"Pick your men." Mackintosh crawled away again, while Hector endeavoured to listen. But in addition to the general racket behind them, the constant whisper of the water was making it impossible to discern any movement close to them. "I need forty men to act as a rearguard on this bank, Sergeant Major," he said. "Volunteers. We'll keep the last machine-gun, and cover from this side."

"Permission to command the rearguard, sir."

"Sorry, Boyd. You're in charge of the crossing. I'll take the rearguard." Boyd didn't attempt to argue; he hadn't expected anything different. "But I want forty of your best riflemen," Hector told him.

Boyd nodded, and crawled into the darkness. "And me," MacLean said. Hector didn't argue about *that*; because he had expected nothing different, either.

The riflemen assembled under the immediate command

of Sergeant Dewar. By then Mackintosh's crossing party had also assembled and Private Webster, who claimed to be the strongest swimmer, had stripped to his kilt and was tying the rope around his waist. Then he slipped into the water and started across. The river swept him sideways, but he went steadily, and quietly on his way, using a breaststroke. In the middle, he stopped swimming, and went down, hands held above his head. He sank until only his wrists were showing, then surfaced and resumed swimming. "Say nine feet," Hector muttered.

A few minutes later Webster was clambering up the far bank, and making the rope fast to a tree. Mackintosh and his men pulled it taut and secured it on their side. "Permission to cross, sir."

"You have it," Hector said.

Mackintosh went first. Like his men, he was laden with equipment, parts for a machine-gun, spare magazines; they had hardly any food left apart from the iron rations in their haversacks, so that wasn't a problem. Slowly, man after man went in, and made the crossing. Using his binoculars in the darkness Hector could just make out the first machine-gun being reassembled and set up. "Piece of cake, really," Boyd remarked.

MacLean touched Hector's arm, and pointed behind them. Hector peered through the trees at a sudden glow, still just below the visible horizon, away to the north-east. "Shit!" he muttered. But all the advance guard were now across. "All right, O'Brien," Hector said. "Get your wounded moving."

He looked back at the moon again. But he dared not tell them to hurry. Every man knew he had to move as fast as he could, and to chivvy them might lead to mistakes and catastrophes. Ferrying the wounded was a long job, as two men had to accompany each stretcher case, and as the stretchers themselves could not be used

– they were sent across separately – the minders had to support the helpless men, which involved slow and careful movement. By now the entire command had become aware of the rising moon. "How long do you think we have, sir?" Boyd asked.

"All night, if there are no Germans about," Hector told him. "Not more than an hour, if there are." Finally the last wounded was safe on the south bank. "All right, Boyd," Hector said. "Quick as you can."

"Smartly, lads," Boyd told his men, and they began slipping into the stream. This went well, as the main body had only their own weapons to carry, and the men made the far bank in a steady stream. Then to their great relief some clouds appeared behind them, and the moon only glared at them for a few seconds before being hidden in an even greater blackness.

The last twenty men of the main body were still in the water when the moon reappeared, huge and round and yellow, almost turning the night into day. "Jesus!" MacLean muttered.

But for the moment there was no fresh sound, and the last of the men were crawling out on the far side. "Prepare to cross," Hector said. "By sections."

He would leave the machine-gun, its firing pin removed, as he did not know if he might need it before the end. And as the first man entered the water, a star shell burst high above them. Presumably it was to alert other German units in the vicinity, as no one nearby could have any difficulty seeing them.

Instantly Mackintosh's machine-guns opened fire from the far bank. Hector could not for the moment locate an enemy, although there was a good deal of firing from his side of the river. The first men of the rearguard, already waist deep, but still in the shadow of the trees, looked back

18

at their commander. "You have to go," Hector told them. "It's that, or a Nazi prison camp."

The men went, sinking down to their shoulders even before they reached the deep part of the stream, swinging along the rope. For the moment the Germans were concentrating on the opposite bank, and half of the rearguard were across before the firing was turned on the river. "Jesus!" MacLean muttered again, as several men released the rope and were carried away by the current.

Hector dismantled the machine-gun. Now shots were crackling through the bushes around him, as the Germans realised there were still British troops on the north bank. But he was now down to four men. "In you go," he told them.

MacLean was last. "You *are* coming, sir?"

"I'm going to be right behind you, Corporal."

MacLean slid into the water. Now Hector could hear crackling sounds from the west; the Germans were advancing towards him, behind a hail of fire. He lay on his belly to slide down the bank into the water, looked across the tantalisingly narrow stretch to the far bank. As he watched one of the last of the rearguard let go the rope and disappeared, and the water was dotted with little spurts of white foam. But MacLean was still crossing, with the utmost resolution. Hector drew a deep breath and went in. He had taken off his glengarry and stuffed it into his belt. Now he put on his steel helmet, sank right down until only the top of the helmet was showing, one hand grasping the rope, the other, with his feet, propelling himself forward as he reached the deep water.

Now there were men on the bank behind him, firing, but Mackintosh had spotted them and had directed one of the machine-guns to pour fire into the wood, so that the enemy shooting was wild. Hector was through the deep middle and his feet had again touched the bottom when he felt a jolt.

Shit, he thought; I'm hit. But for the moment he didn't appear to be immobilised, and he kept going forward, to feel another jolt as he reached the bank. MacLean was one of the men who pulled him out, while bullets thudded into the bank to either side. Then he was dragged into the shelter of the bushes. "Where is Corporal Mearns?" he asked.

"Here, sir."

"Is your equipment intact?"

"Yes, sir."

"Then make to Brigade: *First Shetlands across the Bresle, due south of Hornoy. Await orders.*" Mearns began sending.

"You're hit, sir," MacLean said, watching the blood welling out of Hector's tunic.

"Just a bruise," Hector assured him. "Come with me."

The firing had died down as the Germans realised the Scots were now installed on the far bank. Mackintosh had also called a ceasefire, and the predawn darkness was intensely quiet. "Am I glad to see you, sir," Mackintosh said. "How many did we lose?"

"Not more than a dozen," Hector said. For the moment he could think of the dead men in no other way; only the living mattered until they were out of this mess.

"So what happens now?" Mackintosh asked.

"We wait for orders from Brigade," Hector said, "I've asked for them. Until then we hold here. But . . ." he realised the morning was going round and round, the ground heaving beneath him as if he were on a ship at sea. "You'll have to take command, Murdoch," he said, and fainted.

Chapter Two

The Surrender

Memory peered through a sea of pain. There was a great deal of noise; none of it seemed very coherent. But through both the noise and the pain there was a face, peering at him. In the circumstances, Hector thought, a very pretty face, even if the hair was totally concealed behind and beneath the starched white hat. "Who are you?" he inquired.

"Staff Sister Janet Wilcox, sir."

"And where am I?"

"It's a place called the Forest of Arques. Not far from Dieppe."

Hector tried to envisage the map, and succeeded; he had spent too many hours studying that map. "Where are my men? The 1st Shetlands?"

"They're here, sir. The whole Brigade is rendezvousing here, preparatory to moving down to Le Havre. There we'll be taken off by the Navy. Meanwhile we hold here until they're ready."

"I must get to my men." Hector tried to sit up, and fell back again; the pain had returned.

"I don't think that's practical, sir, right this minute," the nurse said. "You've been hit twice."

"I remember," Hector said. "Where?" For the first time he looked down at himself, but he was wearing some kind of nightshirt and could only feel.

"One in the back and one in the shoulder, sir."

"Am I dying?"

"Good lord, no! Neither hit was life-threatening."

"And I was not hit in the legs. Therefore I can walk. Help me up, and fetch my uniform."

Gently the nurse pressed him back onto the cot. "You lost a lot of blood, sir. You really must rest. Promise me you will, or I will have to give you another sedative." Her face screwed up into a most attractive smile. "And there's not much of that left. There are men who need it more than you."

Hector realised that he was actually surrounded by men, some smoking cigarettes, some lying still, most groaning, one or two occasionally screaming. He sighed. "I'll be good. But for how long?"

"Dr Mallin will be along soon, sir. He'll tell you how long."

Hector lay back and closed his eyes; he could still smell her perfume after she had gone. But he had already forgotten her name. Janet something or other.

He was overwhelmed with the sense of catastrophe. Of course, the catastrophe had happened days, or even weeks ago. Perhaps it had happened even before the war had begun, as the British Army had blithely set off to continue where it had left off in November 1918, totally unaware, it seemed, that the entire concept of warfare had changed in the intervening twenty-one years. But despite the disasters of the retreat, he had felt he had his men in hand, that they were doing their bit, and would remain a fighting unit to the end. Now his end had come far sooner than he had expected. Like hell it had, he told himself. He summoned an orderly. "I've been shot in the shoulder," he said. "So I need some kind of sling. Will you arrange that, please."

"Yes, sir." The orderly looked doubtful. "You've also been hit in the back, sir. There's a broken rib."

"So? Check that I'm properly bound up."

The orderly obliged. "You're tight, sir."

"Well, then, get me that sling, and my uniform."

"I'll need permission, sir."

"From the doctor? What's his rank?"

"Captain, sir."

"Well, I am a major, and I have given you an order."

The orderly gulped. "Yes, sir."

Before he returned, the entire field hospital clicked into as near attention as anyone could manage: the brigadier had arrived. He was accompanied by the doctor, and by Janet Wilcox.

"I do apologise for this, sir," Hector said.

"You got your men across the river. That was a great job, Brand."

"I'm sure I'm fit enough to take them out, sir. At least back to Le Havre."

The brigadier grimaced. "We're not going to Le Havre. The Germans have got round behind us. Dieppe is out as well. We're going to fall back on St Valery. The Navy will try to get us out of there. It's a small harbour, but there's a lot of beach."

"St Valery," Hector said, remembering pre-war holidays. It certainly was a small harbour. But . . . "Isn't that the place where there's a Benedictine Monastery? Where the monks actually manufacture the stuff?"

"Absolutely," the brigadier said. "We must try to pick some up as we go. Take care, Brand: you're now Colonel of the 1st Shetlands."

"Thank you, sir." The brigadier grinned at him, and passed on. It was not until he'd gone that Hector realised he had not actually given permission for him to rejoin his men. On the other hand, he hadn't actually said no, either.

On the *other* hand, Staff Sister Wilcox had hung behind. "I gather you are being a naughty boy, Colonel," she remarked. "Or trying to be."

"I have given an order, which I expect to be carried out," Hector told her.

"Well, sir . . ." there was the wail of a siren, followed by several other screams. "Jesus!" she muttered.

"Haven't we marks?"

"Oh," she said. "A bloody big red cross on top of the tent. Do you suppose that'll make any difference?" It obviously didn't; even as she was speaking there was a howling sound, and a huge explosion. Hector found himself lying on the ground on his face, with his cot on top of him. And a weight on top of the cot, pinning him down. The air was filled with the chatter of machine-gun fire from the swooping Messerschmitts that had been accompanying the Stukas. "Stay down!" Nurse Wilcox was shouting. "Stay down!"

He gathered she was the weight on top of his cot, but thought it would be a good idea for her to come down with him. And a moment later she did, tumbling off the cot to lie beside him. "Sensible move," he remarked, having a strong desire to kiss the nose which was now only a few inches from his own. And then realising that the nose, and the lips and the eyes, had changed character. The eyes were the worst as they stared at him. She had been such a pretty woman. She had also contained a great deal of blood, which was pouring everywhere. Hector sat up, painfully, and saw that her entire back, from neck to buttock, had been ripped open by a bomb fragment. He reckoned she had died instantly.

Around him was pandemonium. The bombers had passed on, but some of the hospital tents were burning, all had been knocked down; men were screaming in pain or shouting incoherent orders, hurrying to and fro. There was, for the moment, no order and no discipline, and a lot of white nightshirts. That Hector's was stained with Janet Wilcox's blood merely made men more anxious to get out of his way. He staggered through trees, one hand pressed against the quite sharp pain in his back, the other tucked into the collar of the nightshirt to provide a rest for his injured arm. A man hurried by, wearing uniform, and the kilt.

"Soldier!"

The man snapped to attention. Even wearing a nightshirt Hector's aura of command, together with his voice, was unmistakeable. "Where are the 1st Shetlands?" Hector asked.

"Ah . . . over there, sir." He pointed.

Hector didn't know whether the man had just pulled something out of the air or not, but he staggered in the indicated direction. He was surrounded by burning vehicles and more dead and dying men. But also by the living, who were being marshalled into some kind of order. "What the hell . . . ?" an officer peered at him. "Brand!"

"Wemyss!"

"My God, man, we heard you'd been hit. Do you realise you're bleeding to death?"

"Not all mine," Hector explained. "Where are my men?"

"Just behind mine. But . . . you can't walk around in that thing?"

"I look worse without it," Hector said. "Thanks, old man. See you in St Valery."

Wemyss, a soldier of the old school who wore a moustache, scratched his head as Hector staggered away.

Hector had to go through it all again with Mackintosh and MacLean and Boyd. But here he was in command.

MacLean, Hector knew, had a spare uniform for him, and soon he was looking almost as good as new, even if he did not feel anything better than second-hand. "You just caught us, sir," Mackintosh said. "We're under orders to move back to the coast. Some place called St Valery-en-Caux."

"I've been there," Hector told him. "It's rather nice. How many effectives?"

"Two hundred and seventy-three, sir. With twenty-five walking wounded. The others were taken to the field hospital."

"Yes," Hector said grimly. "We'll have to hope they get out."

Mackintosh was looking doubtful. "We've no transport, sir. And it's a fair old walk."

"I'll make it," Hector told him.

The 'fair old walk' was actually something like forty miles, across country, heading just about west. The entire remnants of the Highland Division, sadly reduced in strength, were retreating in this direction, several thousand men who knew they had been defeated, but were not yet prepared to give up. They moved in a series of leap-frogging rearguard actions, retiring from one established position, past another manned by other Scots, to a third which they set about preparing themselves, before the next group came back to them. This kept the Germans at bay, but Hector was disturbed to note that the enemy were not pressing them all that hard. Either they did not care if what was left of the Division was taken off *à la Dunkirk*, or they knew that wasn't going to happen and saw no reason to expend men and materiel to overrun a force they already regarded as being in the bag.

Hector had sufficient problems of his own. In addition

to the weakness caused by the loss of blood, the pain, in both his arm and his side, was considerable. O'Brien insisted upon remaining at his side, feeding him just enough analgesic to sustain him without having him pass out. While overhead the German Stukas and Messerschmitts ruled supreme in a clear June sky, every so often dipping down to deliver a frightful attack upon the retreating army, sending men diving for cover in the ditches and hedgerows, and always managing to inflict a distressing number of casualties.

At least they were not hampered by any refugees; as with farther north, the inhabitants had fled, taking what they could with them. The battalion passed through several villages, most in flames, with only a few terrified animals to be seen. "Do you reckon we've lost the war?" Mackintosh asked, as he and Hector lay beside each other on a grassy embankment beside the road, while the bombers raged overhead.

"This war," Hector agreed. "But I still don't think Hitler can ever get enough men and guns across the Channel to conquer England. One thing is for sure: it'll be a right old punch-up!"

"If only because we have nowhere to run, once we're home," Mackintosh suggested.

The final stage of the retreat were the longest two days of Hector's life. The pain seemed to increase with every step, and blood was again starting to seep from his wounds, even though O'Brien restrapped him every morning. There were occasions when he was almost delirious. His brain became filled with images which bore no relation to time and space. He would awake sweating because Janet Wilcox was lying dead across him, and then her face would be replaced by that of Jocelyn, so real that he wanted to scream in mental agony.

27

But then O'Brien and MacLean would help him up, and he would grin at his men, and say, "Only a bit farther."

And they would grin back. And on the second evening they topped a slight rise and looked at the sea.

"I thought the Navy was waiting for us," Mackintosh said.

"They'll be along," Hector assured him. "That's St Valery."

The little seaport was almost entirely man-made, and it was also shallow. Offshore, her sides marked with huge red crosses, lay a hospital ship to which men were being ferried in a series of small boats. There was no other ship in sight.

"That's where you belong," Mackintosh said.

"Bugger that," Hector said. "I stay with the regiment. I expect your full support in this, Murdoch. I have a few slight wounds, that's all."

"You're probably going to get a gong for all this," Mackintosh said. "But it's not going to do you a lot of good if you're dead."

"Let me worry about that! Let's get down there."

However exhausted they might be, the Shetlands were invigorated by the sight of the sea, and they were quite happy to march all night. They arrived at a scene of ordered chaos, spreading far beyond the little town itself, where various units were making camp, and a perimeter was being set up. The Shetlands occupied their allotted space and found themselves re-equipped with machine-guns and anti-tank guns. There was even a squadron of tanks that had come through and was positioned in a dip to their left. "Counter-attack," said the colonel. "When the bastards get close enough."

Hector slept heavily, at last accepting a sedative dose large enough to knock him out; he reckoned he had done all he could. But he awoke to loud gunfire and bursting shells. The Germans had moved up their artillery and were systematically blowing St Valery out of existence. The troops sat it out for the rest of the day, praying for the sight of something to shoot back at. The Division's own guns, such of them as had been brought this far, replied as best they could, but they were far out-gunned. "Where the fuck is the Navy?" McLean inquired. "Begging your pardon, sir."

The hospital ship was now fully laden and was pulling out. Men stood on the quay to wave her away. "Lucky bastards," Dewar growled. "They'll be home in a couple of hours."

Hector preferred to watch the rolling fields in front of him, the puffs of black smoke that indicated the enemy shell fire. Then Mackintosh said, "Oh, Jesus Christ!"

Hector heard the whine of the planes at the same time, and looked up. But the Stukas weren't attacking them. Another belting for the little seaport, he thought. But neither were they attacking the seaport. He turned on his knees, beside Mackintosh, to gaze out to sea, and the hospital ship, now about two miles off. Even at this distance he could see the huge red cross painted on her side. Therefore surely the Stukas could see it too. But they were hurtling down behind their screaming sirens, and the sea around the ship was pitted with pluming columns of water. "Can't the bastards see what she is?" Mackintosh asked.

The ship was struck several times; the watchers on the shore could see the curling brown and red of the explosions rising amidst the white of the spray. She lost way and turned aside, almost as if her captain was contemplating a return to St Valery. Then she was hit again, by a new wave of bombers. For a few seconds she was entirely smothered in

Alan Savage

smoke, before the skies cleared as the bombers swung away
for their base.

The hospital ship was not going to regain St Valery.
Burning fiercely, already she was listing steeply. Most of
her boats had been shattered; only one or two had been
let down. Men and women were throwing themselves into
the water, while boats were putting out from the shore in
the hopes of rescuing some of those who had survived the
bombing. But for the large number of seriously wounded,
lying in bunks or cots below decks, there could be no hope at
all. "Bastards!" Mackintosh rasped. "Where is the Navy?"

Apart from the sinking ship and the drowning soldiers
and nurses, the sea remained empty.

The brigadier visited them that afternoon. He was a big
man, a true Highlander, who leaned on his crook as he
surveyed the entrenched men; as with so many of his
officers, including Hector, he had been wounded in the
retreat. "How is morale?" he asked Hector.

"Low, I'm afraid."

"If you had obeyed orders, you'd have been on that ship,"
the brigadier said. "Thank God you weren't, Hector. But . . .
I'm not bringing any good news."

"No Navy?"

"Can't be done. The Navy has taken too many losses. And
after all, we're only the remnants of a single division, not
an entire army. So . . . obeying orders from London, I've
sent out for a parley. Do you wish me to tell your people,
or will you?"

"I will tell them, sir," Hector said.

The brigadier nodded, peered at the blood seeping through
Hector's tunic. "I am going to recommend you for the DSO,
Hector."

"All of these men deserve a medal, sir."

"I know you're right. But your leadership has made them deserve it. I am also going to make representations to our captors to have you taken to a military hospital. I'm amazed you're still on your feet."

Hector grinned. "I spend as much time as possible off them, sir."

The brigadier held out his hand. "Good luck, Colonel Brand."

Hector waited until the final message arrived from Brigade, then he summoned his men. It was just on dusk, and the firing had dwindled to the odd crack of a rifle. "I'm sorry to have to tell you," he said, "that the Germans have accepted the surrender of the Highland Division. This takes effect at eight a.m. tomorrow."

He paused and looked over the faces in front of him. Some showed surprise, some anger, some disgust. Most showed only exhaustion. "As you will have gathered," he said, "the Navy has been unable to come to our rescue. The exercise would simply be too costly. There is no point in feeling resentful about this. You have fought long and well, and with exemplary courage and discipline. Your efforts in this war will never be forgotten."

Another pause, another look over the stricken faces in front of him. He did not think many of them had actually taken in what had happened, what was in store for them. "Now," he went on, "according to the usages of war, Captain Mackintosh and I and the lieutenants are going to be separated from you and placed in a different camp. Sergeant Major Boyd will then be in command. I know that you will preserve your discipline, and your identity as a unit, in the trying months that may lie ahead as much as you have

31

done on the field of battle. I can only say that it has been an honour and a privilege for me to have served with you, and to have commanded you. My only regret is that we shall be prevented from seeing our loved ones again for some time to come. God bless you all, and may He go with you wherever the paths of war take you. Thank you."

"Three cheers for the colonel!" cried Sergeant Major Boyd.

The response was muted.

"So, what do you reckon?" Mackintosh asked.

Hector was lying down, utterly exhausted. He had not realised how much the responsibilities of command, the exigencies of battle, had been sustaining him over the past couple of days. He should, of course, have been in hospital long ago. But he was even more reluctant now, especially as it was going to be a German hospital. "I'm afraid it's going to be a rather boring war for us," he said.

"But we'll escape, of course," Mackintosh said. "It is our duty to do so. Isn't it?"

"It is our duty to attempt to escape, certainly, if the possibility arises," Hector agreed. "But I imagine the Germans have that point much in mind as well."

"We'll make it!" Mackintosh said confidently.

"I'll wish you all the luck in the world."

"Oh, I'll wait for you to rejoin me, sir." He frowned. "You will be rejoining me?"

"I'm afraid I don't know, Murdoch. Anyway, it may take a little time. I wouldn't wait. If you see an opening go for it."

Mackintosh considered this for some minutes. Then he said, "Damned bad show, really. For you more than anyone. Being wounded, I mean."

"Well," Hector said. "I could be dead."

Once again they lay in silence for some minutes. Then Hector asked, "What's the situation with your family?" He knew Mackintosh wasn't married.

"Dad and Mother will be happy to hear I'm alive," Mackintosh said.

"Is there anyone else?"

"Well . . . I have an understanding. Or I did. Haven't heard in the past few weeks."

"I'm sure there are letters knocking about somewhere," Hector assured him. "They'll turn up in due course."

Mackintosh considered. "Does she have any rights? I mean, supposing something were to happen to me?"

"Are you engaged?"

"No. The fact is, my parents don't approve. So we were rather letting things slide. But we were quite close. I wouldn't like her just to be shunted aside, if . . . well . . ."

"Sadly, that's very likely to happen," Hector told him.

"Shit!" Mackintosh commented. "What a fucking awful war!"

Hector lay back and closed his eyes. Both his parents were dead, so there was nothing to worry about there. George and Julia Brand had always treated him as a son rather than a nephew, and would be suitably concerned, but they would have their own son, Harry, to worry about. At least there was no chance of Jocelyn being shunted aside; she was as much a part of the Brand family now as if she had been born one. But she was going to be very lonely. As, he reflected, was he.

Next morning, at five to eight, the battalion piled their arms and awaited the Germans. All around them the rest of the division was doing the same. The firing had stopped and the silence was uncanny, the only sound being the whipping of the wind. Behind them St Valery burned. A Mercedes open tourer bumped over the road towards them, followed by several truckloads of soldiers. "Battalion! Atten-shun!" Mackintosh bawled. He was in charge of the parade; Hector was now too weak to stand.

The Highlanders came to attention, trying to stare straight ahead, to ignore the jubilant grey-clad figures who surrounded them. Hector looked up at a surprisingly kindly face, frowning in concern. "You are very badly hurt, Colonel." The German colonel spoke perfect English.

"Just a couple of scratches," Hector assured him.

"This is not what I have heard, and what I now see." He gave a succession of orders, in German, then stooped beside Hector. "Permit me to introduce myself. I am *Standartenfuehrer* Joachim Baron von Patten. Have you heard of this?"

Hector frowned, trying to collect his thoughts. "I have heard the name," he said, uncertainly.

"That is good. My father fought against yours, twenty-five years ago. Is not the world a small place?"

Of course, Hector remembered; Uncle George had spoken of it. "That was my uncle, not my father," he said. "And yours . . . ?"

Patten smiled. "He was taken prisoner, badly wounded, by your father. He never forgot the kindness that the then Captain Brand showed to him. Neither has the family. You will permit me to repay that kindness, now."

"I ask for no better treatment than any other prisoner, Baron," Hector said.

Patten continued to smile. "But you are in my hands now, Herr Colonel."

*   *   *

How brilliant the sun, how intense the heat. Had there ever been a June so magnificent? And so disastrous.

Jocelyn Brand pushed her pram over the undulating road, hardly pausing for breath while going up hill, feeling no strain on her muscles when the road dipped down. She was a tall, slender young woman, her flowing red hair, restrained by an Alice band, indicative of her personality. She was angry. The news seemed emblazoned on her forehead, immediately in front of her eyes.

"Yesterday, 12 June 1940," the impersonal voice had said, "the Highland Division, evacuation from the small seaport of St Valery-en-Caux having proved impossible, surrendered to superior German forces, commanded by General Erwin Rommel. This morning the German Army entered Le Havre. There are now no British combatant forces on the continent of Europe." The voice had almost sounded relieved, that the ordeal, in which some considered Britain should never have embarked in the first place, was finally over.

But what of the individuals who had had to undergo that ordeal? The announcement had been four days ago. Jocelyn did not yet know whether her husband was alive or dead. Surely she would have heard if Hector was dead? Or were the Germans still counting?

She pushed open the garden gate, while little Alan watched her with enormous, anxious eyes. Obviously he could not understand anything of what had happened. But he could feel his mother's unhappiness. Jocelyn rubbed her nose vigorously, before reaching the front door, well aware that she was being watched from behind lace curtains. All the lace curtains in the street, no doubt. Drumbooee was only a few miles from Edinburgh, although north of the Firth; some considered it almost a suburb. Indeed, with its well-to-do houses and its green acreage it was a popular area for middle-class businessmen to have their homes; that it was on the railway line made commuting easy.

Jocelyn and Hector had bought here as the ideal spot in which to bring up a young family. They had not, then, thought in terms of a single child who had never seen his father. Might never see his father. They had, however, considered the future sufficiently, in 1937, to allow for the fact that Jocelyn's dad was ailing. Thus they had chosen a cottage with a dower, into which her mother could conveniently be installed, whenever it became necessary. It had become necessary two years ago.

Today was the first time Jocelyn had regretted their generosity. Mother was normally a splendid companion, but she was inclined to go over the top. She had been over the top for the past four days, weeping and consoling her only daughter, and thus needing consoling in turn herself, when Jocelyn had wanted only to be alone with her grief. She drew a deep breath as she wheeled the pram up to the front door, then looked up in surprise as it was opened for her. "Lou?" She couldn't believe her eyes.

Louise Brand was her husband's cousin, and a very typical member of the family, large and blonde, face friendly rather than pretty, looking surprisingly trim in her ATS uniform, which went ill with the hair she was wearing loose, tumbling in golden profusion around her shoulders. "Joss!" They were in each other's arms. "And Baby!" Louise released Jocelyn to lift the bewildered child from the pram, and hold him close. "Oh, he looks fine!"

"He is fine," Jocelyn said. "But . . . what are you doing here?"

"I got leave. Daddy got me leave, to come up and see you. I have the most tremendous news."

"Is there such a thing as tremendous news?" Jocelyn asked. But her heart was starting to pound.

"Oh, yes! Come inside."

"You take Alan, I'll manage the pram." Jocelyn waited for Louise to take the baby into the house, then lifted the pram up the few steps into the front hall.

Her mother hovered in the sitting-room doorway. "Jocelyn! Have you heard?"

"Not yet." Jocelyn closed the door behind herself. "Tell me."

"Daddy's heard that Hector is alive," Louise said. Jocelyn clasped both hands to her neck. "He's a prisoner of war," Louise said. "And . . . well . . . he's wounded, apparently. But they think he's going to be all right."

"Think!" Jocelyn's legs would no longer support her, and because the sitting-room doorway was blocked by her mother she sat on the steps.

"He's going to be all right." Louise handed the baby to Mrs Macartney, sat beside her friend. "It's going to be all right, Joss." She put her arm round Jocelyn's shoulders, and Jocelyn began to sob uncontrollably. She had not wept when she had been told of the surrender. "Listen," Louise said. "I want you to have dinner with me, tonight." Joselyn raised her head, frowning through the tears. "I'm staying at an hotel in Edinburgh," Louise explained. "Well, I didn't want to impose on you here. I'd like you to come in and have dinner."

Jocelyn looked at her mother. "I think you should go, Jocelyn," Mrs Macartney said. "I mean, isn't the news wonderful? I think you should celebrate."

"But . . ." I can't go out to dinner, without Hector, Jocelyn thought. She had not, in fact, been out to dinner since just before the war had begun, nine months ago. That had been the night she and Hector had gone out with Harry Brand and Constance Lloyd, a dinner that had been at her instigation, as part of the family effort to find a wife for Harry . . .

and which had turned out very oddly indeed. "Harry," she muttered. "How is Harry?"

"Harry's in hospital, down in Somerset," Louise said. "He's even more badly wounded than Hector. Oh! I didn't mean that Hector is badly wounded. Just that . . . Do come to dinner! We have so much to talk about." The cousins-in-law had not seen each other since the war had begun.

"But . . . Edinburgh? How would I get back?"

"You could stay the night, and come back tomorrow. It'll do you good, really."

Again Jocelyn looked at her mother. "I think it would," Mrs Macartney said.

Louise accompanied Jocelyn upstairs. "What am I to wear?" Jocelyn asked.

"Something smartish."

"What are you wearing?" Jocelyn looked at Louise's uniform.

Louise giggled. "Oh, not this. I've got something smart, too. Joss . . ." she glanced at the door, then closed it. "There's someone with me." Jocelyn raised her eyebrows. "It's a secret," Louise said. "It has to be, a secret."

The penny dropped. "You don't mean a man?"

Louise nodded, her head jerking up and down as if someone was pulling a string. "Oh!" Jocelyn didn't really know what to say. Somehow she had never really associated Louise, who was only just twenty, with men. Her cousin-in-law was a big, jolly girl, with a somewhat over-large figure, which was no doubt attractive to some men, but she was no beauty. "Well . . . what fun!"

Louise licked her lips. "The thing is . . . we're registered as Mr and Mrs Smith." Jocelyn's jaw dropped. "Well," Louise said. "I think the hotel people are a little suspicious.

So . . . you were at our wedding, see. You're an old friend of Jimmy's, as well as being my cousin. You'll greet him as an old friend. OK?"

"Jimmy?" Jocelyn asked, faintly.

"That's his name." Louise hunted through the wardrobe. "This is ideal." She took out the pale green chiffon cocktail dress. "Oh, yes! You always look good in this one. Now, what do we need? Toothbrush."

"In the bathroom," Jocelyn muttered.

Louise bounced into the corridor, returned a moment later. "There was only one tube of paste, so I left it for your mum. You can use mine. Or Jimmy's. He won't mind. Well, we're all set. Let's go." She looked at her watch. "The train leaves on the hour."

Jocelyn was trying to think. "Lou . . . you are actually, well . . ."

"I have given Jimmy my virginity," Louise said, with dignity. "Well, somebody had to have it: there's a war on."

They caught the train without difficulty, but it was crowded, and they had to stand. Jocelyn was in any event feeling extremely odd; this was the first time since he had been born she had left Alan for more than a single hour while she went shopping – and now she was leaving him for a whole night. Of course Mummy was perfectly capable of looking after him; she had been delighted at the prospect. But it still felt strange. Because for all of those six months she had not been invited out. Nor would she have gone out now if invited by a man. She was Hector Brand's wife.

Now she was going out with a fallen cousin! If Jocelyn was not the most regular kirk-goer in the world, she nonetheless adhered to the high moral values of Presbyterianism. She had enjoyed sex enormously since her marriage, partly because she had never had any before her marriage. The thought of allowing any man, and that had included Hector, getting too close outside of marriage had just never crossed her mind; well-brought-up young ladies did not do that sort of thing. As for actually going off to an hotel with one and pretending to be his wife . . . she had always supposed Louise was as moral as herself.

On the other hand, Louise's brother Harry was supposed to have seduced Constance Lloyd out of wedlock. Well, he must have done, as Constance and Harry had only been married a few months and Constance was apparently about to give birth. The exigencies of her own pregnancy, not to mention the difficulties of wartime travel, had prevented Jocelyn from attending the hastily arranged wedding, but she had been as shocked as every other member of the family at the idea that Hector's favourite cousin should have behaved like that. Of course, the English Brands had put a very good face on the matter; she wondered what kind of face they were going to put on *this* matter.

"There's something I should tell you," Louise said, staring at her from the opposite seat as the train crossed the bridge over the Firth.

"Oh, good lord!" Jocelyn said. "Not something else?"

"Well, you see," Louise said, and Jocelyn got the impression that she was far more concerned about this indiscretion than about being in the midst of an affair.

"Don't tell me," Jocelyn said. "The man is married."

"No, no," Louise said. "Nothing like that. But he's an American."

"A what?" Jocelyn didn't know any Americans, and from what she had heard and read she didn't think there was any possibility of her liking one: the Americans weren't exactly being helpful in the struggle against Hitler.

"You'd hardly know it," Louise said. "He comes from

New England, a place called New Haven, has only the slightest twang, dresses properly . . . and he's a newspaper correspondent."

Jocelyn didn't know what to say, except to ask the obvious question. "Is he going to marry you?"

"We haven't talked about that. I mean, there's a war on." Presumably she felt that in such circumstances moral values were old-fashioned. "You are going to like him," Louise said.

Jocelyn couldn't be sure whether that was a statement or a question.

It was just six when they arrived at the station in Leith, a splendid June evening with hardly a cloud in the sky. Jocelyn wondered if it was a splendid evening in France as well. Or Germany, or wherever Hector now was. And if he could see it.

"Let's walk," Louise decided. "It's not far and we'll never get a taxi. Would you believe," she said chattily, carrying Jocelyn's valise, "that this is the first time I have ever been to Edinburgh since your wedding?"

"And have you come up here to have your affair, or to see me?" Jocelyn could not resist that question.

"Well, to see you, of course. But when Daddy wangled it so that I could have a furlough, to tell you about Hector, I got hold of Jimmy . . . we've been dying to get away together for ages, but it simply hasn't been possible. Whenever I've had a night out of barracks the folks have expected me to go home."

"Have they met Jimmy?"

"Oh, no! Oh, no, no, no! Remember, it's a secret. Here we are." The hotel was down on the front. It looked a highly respectable place, but a glance into the lounge as they approached Reception suggested that it was popular with military personnel.

"Good afternoon, Mrs Smith," the clerk said, and took a key from one of the cubbyholes behind him. "Your husband has stepped out. He asked me to tell you that he'd be back about seven."

"Oh, right," Louise said. "Have you arranged that room for my cousin, Mrs Brand?"

The clerk looked at Jocelyn, apologetically. "I'm afraid that has not proved possible, madam. There is simply not a room available."

"I think I had better be getting home," Jocelyn murmured.

"Absolutely not! You can sleep with us."

"Eh?" Jocelyn asked.

"Madam?" the clerk inquired.

"You can put a cot in our room," Louise said. "You do have such things? Cots?"

"Well, yes, madam, we do. But . . . er . . ." he was clearly scandalised at the idea of two women and a man sleeping in the same room, even if two of them were married. "I'm not sure the manager would agree to that. Propriety, you know."

Jocelyn felt equally scandalised, at the idea of sleeping in the same room as a total stranger. But Louise had the bit between her teeth. "Listen," she said. "This lady, my cousin, Mrs Brand, is the wife of Colonel Hector Brand of the 1st Shetland Light Infantry. She has just learned that her husband, instead of being killed, as she had supposed, is alive and a prisoner of the Germans. Thus she and I, and my husband, are going to celebrate tonight. Because we may not see each other again for a long time. Now, are you intending to stand in the way of such a celebration? You go and speak with your manager, and tell him I expect a cot in my room in fifteen minutes. Got it?"

The clerk gulped. "Come along, Joss," Louise said, and marched for the stairs; there did not seem to be a lift. "We're on the first floor," she said over her shoulder.

"Do you think we should really be doing this?" Jocelyn asked.

"Of course we should be doing it. Nothing annoys me more than stuffy hotels with stuffy rules and stuffy clerks."

"Yes, but suppose the manager refuses?"

"He won't," Louise said. "If he does, Jimmy will probably punch him on the nose, and refuse to pay the bill."

"Oh! Right." Jocelyn was wondering what on earth she had got herself into.

"Here we are." Louise opened the door. "Would you believe this is the first time I have ever stayed in an hotel. With a man who wasn't a close relative, I mean."

"I should think so, too."

"It's the best room in the hotel," Louise explained. "It's the only one with its own bathroom." She opened the door. "*Voilà!*"

But the room itself was far smaller than Jocelyn had anticipated. "Where could they put the cot?"

"We'll sort things out. Here they are," she announced, as there was a knock on the door. And then gave a squeal as it opened. "Jimmy!"

Chapter Three

The Prisoner

Jocelyn found that she had backed against the wardrobe. She had not formed any mental idea of what the famous Jimmy might be like. But the man framed in the doorway was certainly nothing she could have imagined. For one thing he was quite old, at least by the standards of a twenty-three-year-old; she reckoned he might be forty. Which ruled out any faint hope that Louise might have seduced him, more likely the other way round.

But he was also very handsome, in an aquiline fashion, and although there were grey wings to his thick black hair, his body looked lithe and strong, with no trace of a paunch. She would have known at once that he wasn't an Englishman, at least, the sort of Englishman with whom a Brand woman might have been expected to associate, for he wore a sports jacket, unbuttoned, giving him a somewhat rakish air; for all that his shirt and tie were both silk and his shoes handmade; Jocelyn had been associated with the wealthy Brands long enough to spot these things at a glance. Nor did he look the least embarrassed by her presence. "This is Jocelyn," Louise was saying, proudly.

He came into the room. "James Davison, Mrs Brand. Lou didn't tell me she had a beautiful cousin!"

Jocelyn opened her mouth and then closed it again, while

she glanced at Louise. "Jimmy has a great line with the ladies," Louise said. There was another knock on the door. "That'll be the cot," Louise said. James Davison raised his eyebrows. "There isn't a bed in town," Louise explained. "You don't mind, do you?"

James Davison looked at Jocelyn. "I couldn't possibly think of a better arrangement."

He embarrassed her, but Jocelyn decided that was because of what she knew of him, and the fact that she was going to know a lot more of him, willy-nilly, after dinner. But he was also splendid company, knew his wines as well as any Brand might do, and himself showed not a trace of embarrassment. And besides, "I'm going to Germany next week," he remarked, casually, over coffee in the lounge.

Jocelyn gazed at Louise in consternation. "Oh, I *knew*," Louise said. "But I wanted Jimmy to tell you himself."

"But . . . just like that? How do you get there?"

"Via Sweden."

"Isn't there a chance you may be torpedoed or something?"

"I suppose there is. But the U-boats are more interested in English than neutral shipping at the moment."

"Why are you going?"

"It's my job. I'm a correspondent, remember. Inside stories, and what have you. My paper is trying to arrange an interview with one of the big boys. Probably Goering although we're aiming at the man himself."

Jocelyn shuddered. "I don't see how you can want to. I mean, all those stories about atrocities . . ."

"Are, at the moment, just stories," James pointed out, gently. "It's up to people like me to find out if they're true or not. But that's a sideshow. I might be able to find out something about your husband."

"Would you? Could you?"

"I can and I will."

"Oh, that would be simply splendid! Do you think you'll be able to see him? Speak with him?"

"I can't promise. But I'll surely try."

"Oh, James!" Instinctively her hand crept across the table to squeeze his fingers. Louise smiled indulgently.

After that, going to bed was even more embarrassing. James gallantly remained downstairs having a smoke while the two women undressed and used the bathroom. By the time he came up, Jocelyn was lying in the cot with the blanket pulled to her chin. She closed her eyes when the door opened, and rolled on her side, away from the bed and the bathroom door. But she could still hear, and she couldn't stop herself listening. They definitely had sex when he got into bed, even if they were as muted as it was possible to be. But Louise's great shuddering sighs were unmistakable. Jocelyn wondered when, if ever, she would have sex again. Not being a terribly earthy woman, and not having had anything for so many months, she had almost ceased missing it until she listened to those two.

But she couldn't resent James's presence. Not if he might be able to find out something about Hector, reopen contact. She awoke bathed in sweat. The room was quiet, save for the sound of breathing from the bed. It was also very hot. Jocelyn threw back the blanket and got up, tiptoed into the bathroom and had a glass of water. But she knew she wasn't going to sleep again; the time was five past three.

Very cautiously she parted the black-out curtain and opened the door onto the balcony, stepped outside, and closed it behind her. The sea was like a vast dark cloud, but already there was movement behind her in the city, milk floats, refuse lorries, and a cool breeze sweeping up the Firth, cutting through her nightdress to bring her flesh out in goosepimples. She turned to go back inside, and the door opened. She stepped back, and felt her hips against the balustrade. "Couldn't sleep?" James asked.

"It's so hot."

"Cooler out here." They gazed at each other. Jocelyn had never been in such close proximity to any man, save her husband, while wearing only a nightie. And he was wearing only pyjama bottoms. He had a thick mat of hair on his chest. "I hope we didn't disturb you," James said.

"Are you going to marry Lou?"

"It's not very likely. Does that make me several kinds of a louse, in your eyes?"

"I'm afraid it does. Does that mean you're not going to see if you can get in touch with Hector?"

"Oh, I'll see what can be done about your husband, Jocelyn. I'm not that much of a louse."

"Then why won't you marry Lou?"

"Simply because I'm not in love with her. And she isn't in love with me. We have good sex together, and she wants good sex."

"Don't you think that's rather primitive?"

He smiled. "Beasts in the field. That's what we are, basically, Jocelyn. Because we occasionally have high-flown thoughts doesn't mean that at bottom we're not primitive. What's happening in Europe right now proves that."

Jocelyn shuddered. "I'm going in. I'm feeling quite chilled."

He touched her arm as she went to pass him. "Supposing I manage to find out something about your husband, would you like me to come and see you, when I return from Germany?"

She looked up into his face. Beasts in the field, he had said. And now he wanted to mount her. He *was* a louse. But he was a most attractive louse, and if he could bring her news of Hector. "Yes," she said. "Please come and see me, when you get back."

James Davison remained outside long enough to allow Jocelyn to get back into bed. He was afraid that if he followed her in now he might get in beside her. Afraid! There was a laugh.

James had never been able to forget that he came from the wrong side of the Boston tracks, or that he was in Boston at all because his forebears had preferred to emigrate in 1846 than starve. He thought they had done the right thing, but that had not in any way changed his resentment, both of the British and of those born to better things in the States. His built-in resentment against so large a proportion of Atlantic mankind had turned out to be an asset. Coupled with his gift for words and his utter fearlessness of such things as slander or libel, it had earned him the reputation of a hard-hitting journalist that had very rapidly taken him to the top of the tree. Or near enough.

Once he had fulfilled his various assignments in Europe there was an editor's chair waiting for him – if he chose to take it. There was also his vocation as a confidential roaming reporter for the State Department, which could lead to higher things when the truth could eventually be told and which, in his opinion, excused almost everything he chose to do. Because success had not alleviated his resentment. His articles on how England was managing to lose this war were very popular; when he got back from Germany, ready to write articles about how the Germans intended to win it, he would be more popular yet. Except with the British Establishment. Which made the fact that he had been able to seduce the daughter of a prominent member of that Establishment the more enjoyable. But that had been a job of work, so to speak. Now he was suddenly confronted with something different, an intensely attractive, intensely vulnerable girl. That she was already a mother, according to Lou, merely made her the more vulnerable. So, would he be able to seduce her, as well? If only by marriage, she also belonged to that Establishment which had ruined his family a hundred years earlier. To feel sympathy, much less gallantry, towards her would be a betrayal of his antecedents. Yet he did.

That wasn't cowardice. That was weakness. And when he returned from Germany with news of her husband – he had no doubt he would succeed in obtaining that – she would be like an apple waiting to drop into his hand. An even more successful instrument of revenge.

Having been delivered into the hands of the German Red Cross, Hector rather lost track of events over what seemed the next few days but it was actually much less than that. He was in a great deal of pain, which was alleviated by the analgesics he was fed, which in turn made him even more uncertain of time and place, and he had to undergo two more operations because there were still metal fragments in his wounds. But no people on earth could have been more kind or solicitous for his well-being and eventual recovery than the doctors and nurses who attended him. He could only hope his men were being equally well treated. But when he thought that, he would remember the Stukas dive-bombing the hospital ship. There was a paradox here which his drugged and exhausted brain could not fathom.

He was aware of being moved, of travelling in a train.

Presumably he was on his way to Germany. There were other wounded on the train, but Hector did not know if any of them were British; he couldn't communicate with them as he was kept in a separate compartment. He dreamed of Jocelyn, and awoke in an erotic haze to find himself being wash-bathed by two nurses. Neither was very young, nor very attractive, but they were women, with breasts and lips and thighs, and they were handling him intimately and with the utmost gentleness.

When they saw that he was awake they smiled at him, and one made a remark in German, at the same time giving him a gentle squeeze. The other woman said, in English, "Gerda thinks you are recovering."

After that he thought about Jocelyn a lot, dreamed of her, wanted her so desperately. "What is happening in the war?" he asked the English-speaking nurse, when it was her turn to attend to him.

"The war is over," she said. Hector moved so suddenly he gasped in pain. "You must not do that," she said severely. "You will open the stitches."

"But, over?" he asked, incredulously. "We have made peace?"

"You have surrendered," she said. "Yesterday. Now the fighting has stopped." He lay silent for a few minutes. He simply could not believe that had happened. "Now," the nurse went on, "if that madman Churchill would also surrender, or if your people would come to their senses and overthrow him, you would be able to go home, Herr Colonel."

"You'll have to explain that," Hector said. "You just said we *had* surrendered."

"I was speaking of the real enemy, the French. We have

50

no quarrel with England. The Fuehrer has said so. You only entered this war as allies of the French. Now that the French have been defeated, there is no point in your continuing the fight. There is nothing you can do to harm Germany, and there is a great deal Germany can do to harm England."

"Ah," Hector said. How he wanted to go home, and have the reality of Jocelyn instead of mere dreams. But how happy he was, and proud, that Great Britain had not surrendered. He knew enough history to recall that she would probably go on fighting forever. He was proud of that too.

But where did that leave him?

The train stopped regularly. At some stations a few of the wounded left, at others more wounded came on board. But that was only while they were in France. Once they crossed the border into Germany there were no fresh wounded. Hector would have liked to have been able to see out, to glean some idea of where they were and thus where they might be going, but the blinds in his compartment were kept drawn, and he was no longer very keen to engage his two attendants in conversation. It was very obvious, from the complete freedom with which the train travelled, in broad daylight, from the total confidence of the women, and the surgeon who examined him that evening, that the war *had* ended, at least in Europe. He felt he could do without any more lectures on Churchill's, and therefore British, senseless intransigence.

The train followed the same pattern throughout the night, and into the next day, at some time bifurcating following a station stop. Hector felt that he had advanced, in that he was to some extent now able to follow the passage of time – they had taken away his watch. But he remained in considerable pain and discomfort, and he knew he was terribly weak, while his brain, clouded with the drugs they were feeding him, kept drifting away into fantasy-land. It was the following afternoon, when the train made another stop, that the nurses came into his compartment accompanied by four men with a stretcher. "Is this where I get off?" he asked.

His English-speaking friend smiled. "*Ja, ja.* This is where you go. You are special, eh?"

"Am I?"

"*Ja, ja.* We say *auf Wiedersehen*, now."

He was lifted onto the stretcher and carried off the train on to the platform; waiting for him was an extremely handsome woman, dressed in the height of fashion and wearing a huge picture hat with a drooping ostrich feather, and two younger women, who from their facial resemblence were both sisters and daughters of the older woman. The stretcher-bearers placed Hector on a trolley, while the woman approached, to stand above him and smile at him. "I am Thelma von Patten," she said in English.

"Colonel von . . . ?"

"Is my husband. You have been placed in my charge."

"I don't understand."

She squeezed his hand. "We will speak of it later. I wish you to meet my daughters. Agnes." The girl was about eighteen, he estimated. Like her mother she was tall and slender, with splendid features and flowing dark hair. She actually gave him a little curtsey. "Charlotte." This girl was younger, only recently a teenager, Hector suspected. But if she was more plump than her sister, she was also even prettier. And she had red-brown hair. Jocelyn had red hair, although of a lighter shade.

"I also have a son," Thelma von Patten remarked. "But he is with the *Wehrmacht.*" She gave instructions to the attendants, and Hector was half-wheeled and half-carried down the steps at the rear of the station. Here there waited a very large Mercedes saloon. With great care Hector's stretcher was laid on the back seat, the doors closed. The three women got into the front, the mother behind the wheel. She turned her head to look at him. "Around now you are supposed to give me your parole. Do you feel like doing that?"

"I'm afraid not," Hector said.

She smiled. "No matter. We will talk about it again when you are up and about. You realise that may not be for some time."

"I understand that, Frau von Patten. And I wish you to know that I am most grateful for your kindness."

"It is no trouble at all," Thelma von Patten said, and drove off. Hector still had no very clear idea where he was, but there were mountains away to the south, and he reckoned he must be in the vicinity of Munich. But they were not driving into the city; rather the road was climbing away from the railway line and station, and into the foothills to the south-west. "This is our summer place," Thelma von Patten explained. "You will be comfortable here, and Agnes will look after you. She has been training as a nurse. She also speaks fluent English." She smiled into the driving mirror. "Do not be alarmed. Dr Vogel will come in every day."

The girl turned her head to smile at him. Hector thought being looked after by Agnes von Patten, on the scale of the two nurses on the train, might be a memorable experience. But what was he thinking? These people were his enemies, whom he had to destroy if at all possible. That they were being extremely kind to him was in expiation of the past, and perhaps some guilt for the present and the future. He could never consider them his friends.

They drove for perhaps an hour, then stopped so that the girls could give Hector something to drink and make sure he was comfortable. "What I really need . . ." Hector ventured.

"Of course. Agnes." A bedpan was produced, and attended by the two girls. They did not seem the least embarrassed as they untied his bedgown, and were overseen by their smiling mother. Hector could not escape the feeling that he was some kind of guinea pig to help in the training of the two budding nurses, and was very relieved that in his pain and drug-clouded state he showed not the slightest response to their ministrations, even the touch of Agnes's fingers as she held him to direct the flow.

"I hope that is more comfortable for you, Herr Colonel," she said, rearranging his bedgown.

"Very much so, and thank you, Fräulein."

He was curious to find out if he was the first man she had so handled, but decided against asking her at this moment. He was sure he was a first time for Charlotte, whose eyes were as big as saucers. Another hour and they pulled into the courtyard of a small *schloss*, which was still larger than the average country mansion. Their summer cottage!

Here there were several servants, male and female, directed by a butler whose name, he gathered, was Johann, waiting to lift his stretcher from the car and carry him into the hall, a place of high ceilings, parquet floors, and suits of armour amidst the potted plants. Thelma von Patten gave orders, and he was lifted up the stairs, the servants sweating and straining to keep the stretcher level, the two daughters fussing, one at each side.

Definitely, he thought, I am to be their toy. At that moment he did not find the thought unappealing. The journey had made him very tired and he remained in considerable pain, while he was still not in full control of his thoughts. He was taken into a large and airy bedroom, the windows wide open to allow the breeze to come sweeping down from the mountains, which were now much closer; even though it was late June the peaks were still covered in snow.

Hector tried to envisage a map of central Europe. Those mountains were actually offshoots of the Alps, he was sure. Therefore, just on the other side, lay Switzerland! Something to think about, when he was stronger.

But for the time being, rest and relaxation, and recuperation. Though he was nothing more than a toy to the two girls, he was apparently a treasured toy. One of them was in his company day and night; they took alternate nights, sleeping in a chair by the window. He had but to stir for his attendant to be at his bedside. The bedding was changed every day, as was his bedgown, by whomsoever of the girls might be present; they supervised the work of female servants, who he reckoned varied in age, from fifteen to fifty. They chattered to each other in German, a language he was only slowly picking up, but he did gather that a good deal of it was both earthy and teasing of his two young captors, especially among the older women, one of whom delighted in holding his penis and extolling its virtues, or, in its limp state, he supposed, his weaknesses, to the girls.

For their part they blushed prettily but engaged in the general laughter. After that first morning Agnes made no further attempt to touch him; Charlotte never had, although she always looked more closely than her sister. He wished she could speak English as fluently, but she was clearly learning. Certainly their laissez-faire attitude to sex was outside his experience in young gentlewomen – but all the more fascinating for that. "It is the fashion in this new Germany of ours," Dr Vogel explained. "Matters of the flesh are to be treated openly, provided the flesh is, shall we say, wholesome. Anyone can see that you are an Aryan. But the girls are really very fond of you." He was an earnest little man who wore a pince-nez and an intense look, and spoke excellent English.

"I am grateful for that," Hector acknowledged.

"You are a fortunate man," Vogel remarked, a trifle enigmatically. "I would not get well too soon, if I were you, Colonel."

"Tell me how well I am," Hector suggested.

"The bullets obviously hit nowhere vital," Vogel explained. "But apart from the broken bones there was considerable tissue damage, as there was severe blood loss. These were both accentuated by the fact that you did not receive immediate treatment, as I am sure you understand."

"I was receiving treatment," Hector could not resist pointing out, "when you fellows came along and blew up the field hospital."

"The fortunes of war," Vogel said equably. "Now we must do the best we can to patch you up. And when you are well you will soon be going home."

"What did you say? I thought Great Britain had refused to surrender."

"That madman Churchill did so, certainly, after the catastrophe of Dunkirk and the fall of France," Vogel agreed. "He made all manner of hysterical speeches, about fighting on the beaches, something that has not been successfully achieved by any army in history. It is possible to say that when an enemy force gets as far as your beaches, you are beaten."

"But you are not there yet," Hector riposted.

Vogel shrugged. "It is a matter of time. It is simply a business of attaining air superiority. This is the vital fact of modern warfare. And it is an immutable fact. We proved this in Poland, and again in France. Air superiority means victory."

"And you assume you are going to achieve air superiority over England?"

"My dear Colonel, that is not an assumption. It is another fact. The *Luftwaffe* possesses more than twice the number, both of planes and trained pilots, of the RAF. The result is not in question. Of course, we salute the courage and the daring of your pilots, but it is not possible to win at such odds."

"I seem to remember that at Arbela in 331 BC, Alexander the Great and his Macedonians defeated Darius III and his Persians at odds of three to one," Hector ventured.

Vogel chuckled. "Ah, those were the days, eh, Colonel, when one man's courage and leadership could transform a battle. Sadly, they are history. What can your Air Marshal Dowding do? Leap into a Spitfire and shout over his radio 'Follow me, chaps, we shall attack the enemy!' Would that not be romantic? But it is not practical. By the time he could be airborne the tactical situation would have changed beyond recognition. In modern warfare, Colonel, numbers and materiel are what matters. Sadly, leadership is no longer important, at a tactical level. At a strategical level, of course, it is still of vital importance. That is why we are the victors. The Fuehrer controls events because of his strategical genius. Your Mr Churchill can only attempt to plug the gaps. You must have heard the legend of the Dutch boy who put his finger into a hole in the dyke and saved his country from inundation. That is that Mr Churchill is trying to do. Unfortunately for him, there are too many holes, and he has only so many fingers, eh? Soon even he will have to accept that fact, or if he does not the nation will, and throw him out, and put someone in his place who will have the sense to understand that Britain's future lies as a partner of Germany in the new world order, not in hopeless opposition. Now I must give you a sedative. You

57

are becoming agitated." Indeed he was, Hector realised; it was all he could do to stop himself from punching the fellow on the nose.

Trying to deduce what was actually happening was Hector's main concern, in the beginning. He was surrounded by total confidence, among both his hostesses and their servants, but he did discern an absence of that euphoria he had observed immediately following his capture. Then, of course, he had been perhaps unnaturally depressed. But there was also the total absence of the Baron, or indeed, any word of him. When the Baroness came to visit him, as she did most days, he would invariably inquire after her husband's health. And she would invariably give her gentle smile and say, "He is very well, thank you, Colonel."

The two girls never mentioned their father, or their brother, nor did they show any anxiety about them, as would surely have been the case were they embarked upon an expedition as hazardous as invading England – or, indeed, in action anywhere. Meanwhile, their attractiveness grew as the pain began to fade and he began to regain his strength – and as the sedative doses were reduced and his brain and body began to function properly. This was not merely because he had become virtually as intimate with them as he was with Jocelyn, more so, in fact, as both he and Jocelyn were intensely private people and by mutual agreement had refrained from intruding upon one another more than was necessary. These two young girls had obtained access to his every physical secret. The difference was that – as yet – he had no access to theirs.

But now he had to consider ways of using their obvious pleasure in him. He told himself this had nothing to do with sex, although he would have had to be a eunuch not to

appreciate their sexuality. But as he grew stronger, the time
when he would have to be transferred to a prison camp was
coming closer, and he would never have a better opportunity
of escaping than from these apparently unguarded surroundings, with the knowledge that Switzerland was only a few
miles away. But as one of the girls was always with him, his
escape would have to involve either the destruction of one
of them – an utterly abhorrent thought – or the seduction
of one of them. That could never be an utterly repellent
thought, however much of a cad he might have to be.

Thus he studied them carefully, while always appearing
to be weaker than he actually was. He could fool them
easily enough, because they were concerned only with his
welfare. Dr Vogel was a less simple matter; the doctor fell
to muttering that now convalescense was well advanced it
was the will that mattered, the determination to regain his
strength. But he also instructed the Baroness to feed him as
much milk and meat as possible. There did not seem to be
a shortage of either.

Hector's first task was to determine which of the two was the
weaker, and in this regard he very rapidly selected Charlotte.
Agnes was already a woman, with a woman's instincts. She
also had a boyfriend who wrote to her regularly, a lieutenant
in a panzer regiment which was stationed in north-western
France, awaiting the order to cross the Channel. Agnes did
not speak of him much, simply because she did not wish to
distress her guest, as her Willi was inclined to write in a very
triumphalist vein, but she was clearly well suited regarding
men. More than that, she was a dedicated Nazi, and while
she did everything she could to make Hector comfortable
and even happy, at the first suggestion of criticism of the
regime she would retire from his bedside to her seat by the

window, and read her book, and for at least the next hour would leave him in no doubt of her displeasure. She also undoubtedly regarded him as old enough to be her father, even if he was less than ten years the elder.

Charlotte, who, he had learned, was fifteen, was a bundle of animated happiness. Of course she should, and with even more reason, consider him too old to be a sex object, but he did not think this was altogether the case, simply because he was the first potential sex object with which she had ever come into contact. Equally, she too was a Nazi through and through, but again the emphasis was different; where Agnes had been presented with the Nazi image and agenda and seemed to have determined it was for her, Charlotte was almost young enough not to remember any other form of government. She was a member of the Nazi Youth Movement, as had been her sister, and looked forward to the following summer when she would be able to go camping with her friends; she did not appear to have any doubt that she *would* go camping next summer. "The war will be over by then," she asserted. Hector's German was now quite passable.

Hector had no intention of earning *her* displeasure by disputing that point. "What do you do when you go camping?" he asked.

"Oh, we walk a lot, and we swim a lot, and we have sing-songs every night. But we have lectures, too. There is always a party member to tell us things."

"Sounds like fun," Hector said. "What do you wear when you swim?" He had heard rumours.

"Oh, we don't wear anything," she said, not apparently the slightest bit embarrassed by the confession.

"That sounds like even more fun," Hector said. "Then I imagine you have a boyfriend."

"Me? What do I want with a boyfriend?"

"Well," Hector said. "I can tell you, Charlotte, that if I ever went swimming with you in the nude I should want to be your boyfriend."

She giggled. "You mean you would want to have sex with me?"

"Isn't that the same thing?"

"Well, of course it is not. Having sex is fun. Having a boyfriend is serious."

It occurred to Hector that he might be wading in deep water, but she remained his best prospect of getting out of here.

"So, you have sex with these boys, but you don't actually have a boyfriend," he ventured. "What do you do when you do have a boyfriend?"

"Well . . ." for the first time she flushed. "We can't go all the way. Not until we're sixteen. If we go all the way and are found out we're whipped. And if any girl were to get pregnant, oh, she'd be sent to prison or something. Our leaders are very strict." She gave another little giggle. "It's safer to have sex with another girl. Until you're sixteen. That's just as much fun, and there's no risk." She frowned at him. "Would you like a sedative?"

"Do you think I need a sedative?"

"You're becoming restless. Is it hurting?"

"As a matter of fact, yes."

"I'll call one of the maids to change you."

"Can't you do it?" he asked. "You've seen it done, often enough."

Charlotte licked her lips. "I might hurt you."

"You could never hurt me, Charlotte." He released the ties for his bed robe.

Charlotte hesitated a last time, then opened it, and carefully untied the bandage, which was secured across his chest.

"Does Agnes have sex with her boyfriend?" he asked her.

Her face was serious as she extracted his right arm from the sleeve, and then carefully rolled him onto his side; the sheet was still folded across his thighs, and she had not yet uncovered the effects of their conversation. "Oh, yes," she said. "She's over sixteen." Now she was breathing very quickly, but this was because she was unwrapping the bandage, and uncovering the pad of lint.

"How does it look?" he asked. He could feel her peeling away the lint.

"There's an awful scar!"

"What about the rest of me?" Her head came up as she gazed at him. There were little pink spots in her cheeks. And from the way his heart was beating he suspected there might be pink spots in his own. "Just an idea," he said. "I've rather lost touch with down there." Literally, he thought. "As you said just now, it might be fun. And it would tell us both how well I actually am."

Still Charlotte gazed at him, and he wondered if he had tried too much too soon. Her tongue showed between her teeth as she gave a hasty glance at the door, then left the bedside to close it. She came back and eased the sheet down past his buttocks, then rolled him on his back. "That must prove something," he said, as her eyes widened at his erection. "It's the conversation, and my returning health, I suppose. Does it bother you?"

"Why should it?" she asked. "All the boys I bathe with get those, all the time." But she was breathing quickly again as she pulled the sheet back to his waist. "I meant to ask you," she said. "How come both wounds are in your back? Were you running away?"

"Let's say I was retreating in a hurry."

"This looks much better," she said, examining his shoulder. "We'll soon have you up and about."

"Don't you think you have already done that?"

She was rebandaging him with quick, deft fingers. "I thought you were a married man," she remarked, with considerable composure.

"Who is not likely to see his wife again for some considerable time. Anyway . . ." he drew a deep breath. But Jocelyn would forgive him, when he got home. "It's not much of a marriage."

Charlotte's tongue was between her teeth again as she tied the last knot. "Do you know," she remarked. "I am going to be sixteen next month." She raised her head, her cheeks suddenly entirely pink.

"That's tremendous!" he said. "Perhaps you and I could have a party. Of our own. A private party."

She was standing immediately beside him, and he slid his hand up her arm and then let it drop from her elbow onto her hip, to move back onto her buttocks; she wore both dress and petticoat, but he could feel the flesh move beneath his fingers. "Would you like that?" he asked.

Her practicality continued to astonish him. "If you got me pregnant," she said. "You would have to divorce your wife and marry me. Papa would insist on it."

"Even if I am an enemy?"

"You're an Aryan," she pointed out. "Anyone can see that. That's what really matters."

"Of course," he agreed. "Well, I think I would like to be married to you."

"Just like that?" she asked. "You hardly know me."

"I think I know you very well."

"Not enough to love me."

"Enough to know that I could love you." What an incredible conversation, he thought. But it was actually working. "Do you think you could love me?"

She studied him. His hand was still resting on her buttocks, and now he started to move it to and fro, gently. "I think you are the nicest man I have ever met," she said. "Do you know that you have never kissed me?" She lowered her head, and their tongues sought each other. The things I do for England, he thought. The very pleasurable things, in this instance. She was an absolutely entrancing child, made the more so by her utter amorality. He needed to think.

But that was not practical until she had been replaced by her sister, later that day. By which time he was more than a little agitated. He had deliberately set a ball in motion, but it had immediately started travelling far more quickly than he had supposed possible. He knew he would not be capable of the excessive activity needed to make his escape across the mountains for another several weeks. He had estimated it would take him that time to make an impression upon Charlotte. Now he was faced with the necessity not only to keep her happy but to keep their secret for that time.

He also as yet had no guarantee his plan was going to work. Charlotte might find him a delightful riposte to her sister's amatory successes, but there could be no doubt about her loyalty to the Nazi regime. He had, somehow, to make her fall so completely in love with him that she would be prepared to abandon Hitler. Well, he thought, after her birthday and hated himself. But if it was taking him to Jocelyn . . .

Both Dr Vogel and Agnes were also observant enough to realise that Hector was beginning to regain his strength. Fortunately, their ideas on how to handle the matter agreed with his. Vogel prescribed regular exercise, and Hector was duly dressed in clothes borrowed from the Patten son, Rudolph – they were much of a size – and paraded in the paddock behind the *schloss*, watched by the curious horses, as well as the sisters and their mother. Agnes, an enthusiastic photographer, took snaps of him with her box camera. This had to be a team effort, and indeed he was appalled at his physical weakness, especially in his legs, after several weeks in bed. Climbing a few mountains was going to be quite out of the question until he had some real strength back. His problem was that as soon as they were sure he had got his real strength back they were going to pack him off to a prison camp.

But he had Charlotte. Not only was she eager to attend to him whenever they were alone together, but she was also determined to keep him as her lover. "They can't send you to prison," she declared. "I won't let them. Not for ages and ages." And she kissed him, long and passionately. She had developed a quite exceptional crush.

Then what of him? He stroked her back and her bottom and her breasts, feeling more and more criminal. She had not as yet removed a single garment in his presence; but she meant to do that. And he had to encourage her. Meanwhile the situation was changing. Or had changed. It was into October, and there had been no invasion. He asked the Baroness about it. "You English," she said contemptuously. "Do you not know that the Fuehrer has more to do than waste his time on you? He has offered you peace. Peace with honour. And you have refused. Well, then, he will let you stew in your own juice, become what you have always been, in reality, a small offshore island which is of no importance whatsoever to the rest of Europe."

"Am I to understand, Baroness, that the projected invasion has been called off?" Hector asked, innocently.

She glared at him, then smiled. "For the winter, Hector. For the winter. By next spring, when you have spent the winter starving, as our U-boats are entirely cutting off your overseas trade, your lifeblood, eh, you will be more amenable to reason. I am only sorry for you, that this miserable business drags on, entirely due to the intransigence of Mr Churchill, and that you are prevented from being reunited with your family. However, I have good news for you. You know that next week is my daughter Charlotte's birthday? I am sure she has told you of it."

"She may have mentioned something," Hector murmured.

"She will be sixteen. She will be an adult, all but. An important age, perhaps more so for a woman."

"Absolutely," Hector agreed.

"Normally we would have a big party in Berlin for such an occasion. The Fuehrer himself came to Agnes's sixteenth birthday party." She paused to allow Hector to understand the significance of that, and he murmured appreciatively. "Sadly, we do not feel that a big party would be appropriate, in the present circumstances," the Baroness went on, her tone leaving no doubt that she placed the entire blame for the situation at the door of Winston Churchill. "We shall, of course, have a party, but it will be strictly family. You'll be pleased to know, I am sure, that my husband will be joining us, as well as my son Rudolph, and Agnes's young man, Wilhelm. Charlotte does not have a young man. But you are of course invited, my dear Hector." She gave an arch smile. "I suspect Charlotte regards *you* as her young man." Hector swallowed; this was coming uncomfortably close to the truth. "Do say you will attend," the Baroness pressed.

"I should be honoured, Baroness," Hector said. "Do I have any clothes to wear?"

"Oh, you shall have clothes," the Baroness assured him. "I have had your uniform laundered and entirely repaired."

"That was very kind of you," Hector said, feeling that the entire heaven was falling into his lap.

"And will you escort Charlotte? She has especially asked that you do this."

"I should be honoured to escort Charlotte, Baroness."

"I am so pleased. But . . ." another arch smile. "I also have a surprise for you. A present, if you like." Hector could only wait, wondering. "We have had a letter from a friend of your family. An American gentleman, named Davison."

Another pause. Hector knew he had to respond, and quickly. Davison? He knew no friend of the family named Davison. He took a stab in the dark, picking a name out of the blue. "Not old Jim?"

"Why, yes! He signs himself James, but that is often called Jim, is it not?"

"Yes," Hector said. "Good old Jim. Whatever does he want?"

"Well, he's here in Germany, doing his journalism," the Baroness said. "And he has found out that you are our guest, and he has asked if he can call and see you. You will not object to this?"

"I should love to see Jim again," Hector said. Who the hell was he, and who had sent him? He did not doubt that he had been sent.

"I am so pleased. Because I felt that the least I could do was invite him to join us for the party. He is arriving next week."

"What tremendous fun," Hector muttered. But perhaps he had found another string to his bow.

Chapter Four

The Prisoner

Jim Davison. An old friend of the family. Hector had last seen the family in the late summer of 1939. That was only just over a year ago. There had been no one named Davison around then, or even heard of. So just what was up? He would have to play whatever was going to happen by ear. He reckoned Charlotte was still his best bet.

But now he encountered an unexpected problem. Agnes had as usual supervised his walkabout in the paddock, together with two of the maids and two grooms, had photographed him, and then returned with him to his room, while the maids drew a bath for him; the slightest exertion brought him out in a sweat. "I think you are doing very well," she said.

"Thank you. I still feel a bit weak."

"Well, of course. But you are on the mend. That is the important thing." She helped him out of his robe and into the tub, while the maids stood by, to help if needed. As usual, the three of them treated him as if they, and he, were totally disinterested in sex, and again as usual, Agnes soaped his back. "Are you looking forward to the party?" he asked.

"Oh, yes. Because Papa and Rudolph will be home."

"I'm looking forward to seeing your father again. And to meeting Rudolph. And Willi, of course."

"You will like them." Agnes pushed him back to lean against the porcelain, while she soaped his legs. Her face was, as always, serious as she concentrated. She appeared to be totally asexual, at least where he was concerned; but he had Charlotte's word that she was by no means asexual with some men. "Are you going to speak to Papa about Charlotte?" she asked, casually. "Or would you prefer to speak to Mama?"

"Eh?" He attempted to sit up, and she gently pushed him back. "You know sudden movements are bad for you," she said severely.

"Explain what you mean," he said, and glanced at the servants.

"They do not speak English," Agnes said reassuringly. "Charlotte has fallen madly in love with you. Well, that is obvious to everyone."

"That's nonsense! I'm old enough to . . ."

"Be a very romantic figure to a fluffyhead like Lottie. Don't tell me you haven't realised it."

"Well . . . I know she's very fond of me. But then, so are you. Aren't you?"

Agnes raised her head to look at him, a most unusual expression on her face. "Yes," she said. "I have grown very fond of you, Herr Colonel Hector."

"I'm the family pet?" he suggested.

She moved her hands slowly up his thighs. Although she had bathed him on innumerable occasions since he had come into her care, there was suddenly more to it today than ever before. This might have been because of his erection, but he had had those before, during the past few days, and it had not seemed to bother her. "Yes," she agreed. "The family pet. But Lottie does not think of you that way."

"I shall bear that in mind."

She handed him the cloth to wash his genitals and stood

up, watching him as he finished his bath. "I have considered speaking to Mother about it."

"Eh? Oh, please don't do that."

"Why not?"

"Well . . . I wouldn't like Charlotte to be punished. It can't be anything more than a schoolgirl crush. Surely?"

"I do not think she would be punished, for falling in love," Agnes said. "But Mother probably would not let her attend you any more. It is dangerous. Do you not agree?"

"Well . . . in what way?"

"Has she ever touched you?"

"Good heavens no! She doesn't bathe me. You do."

"I am not talking about bathing."

"Well, there is no other reason for her to touch me, surely?"

"There is every reason," Agnes said, again severely. "Charlotte is a girl of very lax morals. This is the trend in our country. It is no longer immoral to wish to have sex. It is only immoral to have sex with someone of the wrong race."

"Absolutely," Hector agreed. "But I do assure you that while Charlotte may be old enough to have crushes on men, she certainly isn't old enough to know what to do about it." Had he spoken too glibly? Agnes was frowning again, as she held the bathrobe open for him. Clearly he couldn't leave things as they were; if she were to have Charlotte barred from his room all his plans would have crumbled. Besides, he was a man who had always followed his instincts. Agnes was far too upset by what she had deduced from her observations. He allowed her and the maids to lay him on the bed, and she covered him up. Almost as if absently, he caught her hand. "And are you, also, a very moral person, Agnes? Sweet Agnes?"

She stared at him, nostrils flaring. But she was making

no effort to free her hand. Instead she spoke to the maids, dismissing them. They left the room. And still she had not freed her hand. "Charlotte is such a child," he said.

She had the most exquisite features, which became more so as a variety of emotions chased across them. But now at last she freed her hand, and stepped away from the bed. Dammit, he thought. I've blown it. "Sickness, pain, induces many strange sensations," Agnes remarked. There was fresh colour in her cheeks.

"And you are both my nurse and my saviour, as well as betrothed to another man," he said. "I know these things. As I am a married man. But perhaps that is a part of it. For the past weeks I have done nothing more than lie here, watching you, watching your movements, drinking in your beauty. You are right, pain and drugs affect one's sensations. But often they induce the truest of sensations. I know that I have never beheld a more wondrous creation than yourself." Actually, in the coldest of physical terms, that was by no means a lie. But once again he was fishing in the dark.

She came back across the room, sat on the bed beside him. "No one has ever said anything like that to me, before."

"Are you offended?"

"How could I be offended by such sentiments?" She held his hand between both of hers, raised it to her lips, kissed it.

Where Charlotte was all for reality, here he had the ultimate romantic. He allowed his other hand to flop onto her thigh. "I could love you," he said. "I think I already do."

"Gratitude."

"No. Believe me." What a monster he was becoming.

"As I could love you," she said. "But . . . your wife!"

"Is nothing, compared with you." Once again, Jocelyn would have to forgive him.

"And Willi?"

"Is a boy," she said. "But. . . ." she got up again, restlessly, moved to the window to look out, came back to the bed. "You are an enemy of my country."

He caught her hand again. "I could never be an enemy of you, Agnes." He brought her hand to his lips to kiss it. How sweet smelt her flesh. "What worries me," he said, "is that as soon as I am strong enough they will take me away from here, and I shall never see you again."

"No," she snapped.

"How can you stop it, Agnes, dearest Agnes?" He still held her hand, and now he drew her down onto the bed beside him.

"If. . . if you were to resign from the British Army, swear an oath to the Fuehrer, become a German . . ." her eyes were gleaming with excitement. "You could join the *Wehrmacht*! You could divorce your wife . . ."

"And Willi?"

"Oh, don't bother about Willi! We are not actually engaged. There was an understanding between our families. Nothing more."

"Could you possibly love a man who turned his back on his country?"

"Of course I could!"

"Would you turn your back on Germany and Hitler, if it could happen?" She stared at him, while his heart pounded. Had he, once again, galloped too quickly for her?

"Hitler is the hope of Europe, perhaps of the world. It is his mission to save the world from Communism." she said quietly. "I could never abandon that dream."

"But you expect me to abandon Great Britain and all that she has stood for throughout the centuries."

"If you really love me."

"And if you really love *me*?" Another long stare, then

72

she got up and left the room. He could only wait and see what turned up.

But he felt obliged to warn Charlotte, when next they were alone. "She's just jealous," Charlotte said. "Why should she have everything, and me have nothing?"

"Is that how you look at me, as nothing."

"No! Of course you are not nothing. You are everything to me, Hector, dear Hector." She kissed him, But she could do nothing more because Agnes suddenly appeared. Agnes now developed a habit of dropping in quite regularly when Charlotte was sitting in. And when she was alone with him, she did not return to the subject of their love. She was obviously thinking. Hector wished he knew in which direction.

"Hector! Jim Davison!" Thelma might have produced the American out of a hat.

"Jim!" Hector cried. "How good to see you again!"

Davison at least had quick wits to go with his handsome face and somewhat florid appearance. "And for me too, old son," he said, coming forward to shake Hector's hand. "Boy, you look done up."

"You should have seen him a month ago," Thelma said. "Now we are working on getting him well again."

"How're the folks?" Hector asked.

"In the pink. Joss sends you her love, and a hug from the boy." Joss, is it, Hector thought. Or was that all part of the game? "So do your mother and father, and Lou, of course."

"And Harry?"

"Ah, well, he's not too good. Got himself all shot up at

Dunkirk, and is in hospital. Could be there for some time. But they reckon he'll pull through."

"That's great," Hector said.

"Well," Thelma said. "I am sure you two have a lot to talk about. I will see you later. Joachim and Willi are arriving this evening, so we will have a family get-together."

"And tomorrow's the birthday party, eh? I'm looking forward to that." Davison pulled a chair to sit beside the bed, waited for the door to close. "Seems to me you've fallen on your feet here." He grinned. "Even if you're lying on your ass, eh?"

"I've been lucky," Hector said. "My uncle saved the life of the Baron's father, and he's out to repay that debt."

"And he can? In this Germany? Must be a pal of the Fuehrer's. Well, I guess your people will be happy to hear that you're on the mend."

"Will you be able to tell them that?"

"Sure. Soon as I get back."

"Which will be when?"

"I aim to be in England for Christmas."

"What are you doing here, anyway."

"In Germany? Interviewing people for my paper. Here, finding out how you are."

"Well, perhaps you can tell me exactly what is going on. I get a somewhat slanted opinion here."

"I'll bet! Well, I suppose the big news is that Roosevelt has been re-elected for a third term. Some are questioning whether that's legal. But it's what the people want."

"Do you reckon that's good for us?"

Davison shrugged. "Seems Wilkie is just as keen on you guys as he is opposed to Hitler's lot. But there's no way we're gonna come off the bench. The people simply wouldn't stand for it."

"I'm not sure we can do it without your help."

"Well, you sure ain't lying down. Only a couple of weeks ago your navy sank three Italian battleships."

"You mean there was a battle?"

"Not at sea. Your planes did it. Caused quite a stir. Oh, and Chamberlain has died. Cancer. Seems not many people knew he was sick."

"What about the invasion?"

"Well, after the *Luftwaffe* got such a bloody nose . . ."

"Say again?"

"You didn't know? Well, I guess they haven't been shouting it from the rooftops over here. Sure, the RAF took on the *Luftwaffe*, and won. Seems they shot down about two Germans for every one of their own. So Hitler called off the invasion, until next spring. But I have my doubts he'll ever try it now. Like Napoleon, he'll turn elsewhere."

"Well, glory be! Napoleon went to Egypt."

"And got beat there too, eventually. So there we are, up to date. Now tell me, what are your prospects?"

"The moment I am fully fit again I'll be sent off to a prison camp." He gazed pointedly at the American. "That is, supposing I'm still here."

Davison returned the gaze for several seconds, then got up and went to the window, looking out at the mountains. "Switzerland? You stand a chance of being shot."

"Is that supposed to bother me?"

"No. I guess not. Can you do it?"

"I'm working on it. I need to be fitter. But that's happening. And I imagine I'll need some help."

"You thinking of me?"

"As a matter of fact, yes. If you really are a friend of the family."

Davison made a face. "I hope you won't make this personal."

"But you're going to continue sitting on the bench, or fence, or whatever."

Davison came back to the bedside. "I'd be putting my head on the block, Colonel. Not only physically, but work wise. I'm getting on, thanks to being a reporter people trust. Break that trust and I'm on the breadline."

"Well, it was only an idea. If you're a reporter people trust, can I trust you not to tell anyone what I have in mind?"

"You can count on that. You . . ." he checked as the door opened and Agnes came in.

"Mother is expecting you downstairs for lunch, Mr Davison."

"I'll be right down."

Agnes came up to the bedside, smoothed Hector's forehead. "You really mustn't overtire the colonel," she said. "I'll see you later, Herr Colonel Hector."

The door closed behind her. "Now there is a looker," Davison remarked. "And, you know, she seems quite fond of you. Herr Colonel Hector! You given that any thought?"

"She is a fervent Nazi, and she is engaged to be married," Hector said. He had no intention of letting this rather unhelpful American know anything of what he had in mind in that direction.

"Tough," Davison agreed. "Well, I'll see you later."

"Wait! Will you at least take a note for my wife."

"Surely."

Hector went to the table and wrote hastily. "As I imagine you intend to read it anyway, I shall read it to you," he said.

Davison merely smiled.

"Dear heart," Hector read. "This will be delivered by James Davison, who I imagine you already know. I am well on the way to recovery, and have every hope of being with you again soon. Until then, I love you. I wish you to be certain of that, no matter what happens, or you may hear. Hug the lad for me. Yours always. Hector."

"That's real sweet," Davison commented.

Davison was intrigued, both by Hector's plans and by his relationship with Agnes von Patten: if the big Scot was having it off with the beautiful German girl, he, Davison, need have no conscience at all about seducing Jocelyn. He was not overly concerned at having to refuse to help in the proposed escape. No matter who helped him, Brand was extremely unlikely to make it, and whoever did help him was likely to wind up in deep shit. His business in life was far too important to risk that.

But he had every reason to find out just what was going on between Agnes and Brand, and seized his opportunity after lunch when Agnes announced she was going for a ride. "Mind if I tag along?" he asked.

Her gaze was cool. "If you can keep up, Herr Davison."

It was a pleasure to impress her with the quality of his horsemanship, while admiring hers and the delightful flow of black hair flooding out from under her hard hat. It was she who drew rein first, taking off her hat to fan herself while their horses steamed. "I love this country," she said.

The mountains were still several miles away, but they were in the foothills, surrounded by autumnal colours. And she had given him a cue. "But you can also love someone who intends to destroy it."

She shot him a glance. "What a strange thing to say."

"You telling me you don't have something going with the Brit?"

She replaced her hat and adjusted her hair, then turned

her horse. "You are a romantic, Herr Davison. Shall we go back?".

She had come close to him, and he caught her sleeve, his desire for knowledge caught up in the scent of the chase, something he could never resist. "If it's a foreigner you're looking for, I'm on your side."

She gazed at him for several seconds, her eyes cold. "Isn't that lucky for us, Herr Davison!" she commented, and kicked her horse forward.

The Baron and his son duly arrived that evening as promised, and both came up to visit Hector. "I can see you are on the mend," Joachim von Patten said boisterously. "I am glad about that."

"And I want you to know, Baron, that no matter what happens, I shall always be intensely grateful to you and your family for the help they have given me."

"We could do no less. But you will soon be going home. The Fuehrer has made a last, and truly impassioned, appeal to Churchill to call a halt. Only a fool would refuse the terms offered. And we all know the British are not fools."

Rudolf was a very stiff young man, who obviously did not care for having an English prisoner of war as a guest in his parents' house. But he remained polite.

Decisions, decisions, Hector thought. If he carried through his plans for escape, he would not only be risking his own life, but almost certainly he would disrupt and perhaps destroy this happy if wrong-headed – at least to his way of thinking – family. Of course it was his duty to escape, if he could. But if there was a chance of Churchill making peace . . . Now that he was so much stronger and able to do things for himself, Hector was left to himself at night, although a manservant dozed in a chair outside his door, ostensibly in case he needed assistance but in reality, as Hector well understood, to make sure he had no rash thoughts of escaping. His window was not barred, but it was some 40ft from the flagstones of the yard, and there were no convenient ledges or drainpipes; leaving that way could only involve, at best, a few broken bones. It was up to the girls. But which one?

He awoke with a start as his door opened, very softly. He slept with his curtains drawn, but he could tell from the chinks of light coming through that it was dawn, and he didn't have too much doubt as to who was approaching his bed. "What happened to my watchdog?" he asked.

"I sent him off."

"You don't suppose he'll gossip?"

"Oh, pooh! Servants' gossip? Nobody pays any attention to that. Aren't you going to wish me many happy returns?"

"Many happy returns."

She kissed him, then lifted the covers and slid into bed beside him; she was wearing both nightress and dressing gown, but he suspected they were not going to stay in place for very long. "Sixteen," she said. "I have waited too long for this moment." She snuggled against him. "You could be more enthusiastic!"

"You took me by surprise." He put his hand inside her dressing gown and caressed her breast. "It'll happen. But are you sure?"

"It's happening," she said happily, and then rose on her elbow. "What do you mean, am I sure?"

"Well, as you say, if you become pregnant, . . ."

"You'll divorce your wife and marry me."

"That's not going to be easy to do if I'm in a prison camp."

"I told you, I won't let them take you away."

"How are you going to stop them, my dearest girl?"

"You don't want to marry me at all," she said, sitting up, half-turned away from him.

He put his arms round her waist. "Of course I do, sweetheart. I want to be with you, forever and ever and ever. But if I can't do that, I think it would be better for us to wait until the war is over."

He was gambling here, but the odds were all in his favour. Charlotte threw herself full length again, on her face. "We can't wait. Mother is already muttering about finding me a husband. If we wait, it'll never happen."

"Then we must make it happen. You and me. That's all that matters. You and me against the world, and to hell with Hitler and Churchill and the lot." Her head turned, and he kissed her. "That's what I want. Don't you want that too?" Her mouth puckered; he wasn't sure whether she was about to smile or cry. Then the bedroom door opened.

"Shit!" Charlotte muttered, and buried her face in the sheet.

Agnes closed the door behind her. "You little slut!" she snapped.

Charlotte rolled over and sat up. "That bastard Hans . . ."

"Did what he was supposed to do." Agnes turned her glare on Hector. Like her sister she wore a dressing gown over her nightdress. "You are a bastard," she said. What a mess, Hector thought. In the seduction stakes he really was a tyro. Lack of practice, he supposed. Agnes was pointing at her sister. "You! Out!"

Charlotte pouted. "So you can get in bed here, you mean?"

"I am going to take the skin from your arse," Agnes said. "And if you don't get back to your room immediately, I

80

am going to tell Mother. And Father!" she added for good measure.

Charlotte got out of bed. "I hate you," she said. "I loathe and despise you!"

"Get out," Agnes said again. Charlotte glanced at Hector, then left the room.

Agnes closed the door behind her. "Did you have her?"

"No, I did not."

"You expect me to believe that?"

"Have Vogel examine her."

"And inform the world that I have a slut for a sister? What were you doing?"

"We were celebrating her birthday. She is very enthusiastic. But you know that."

"I still think you are despicable to allow her into your bed at all. I warned you about her."

"What was I supposed to do? Scream for help? She was quite safe, believe me. I don't think I could have made it, no matter how hard she tried."

She glared at him for several more seconds, then suddenly burst out laughing. "That would be hilarious! English war veteran raped by sixteen-year-old schoolgirl."

"As you say, hilarious. What happens now?"

"Promise me this won't happen again."

"I can't keep her out of my room."

"I can," Agnes assured him. "I will send the maids in to help you dress."

"And us?"

She had walked to the door. Now she paused, and looked back at him. "I am considering it. I didn't tell you before, but Willi isn't coming to the party after all. The swine has gone off to Berlin. Orders, they say. Orders!" She closed the door behind herself, leaving Hector in a very uneasy frame of mind. It was all happening too quickly. He had

81

worked on an agenda that he would seduce Charlotte on her birthday, and then slowly bring her round to agreeing to help him escape, coming with him if necessary, while he regained his full strength but before Vogel decided he could leave. That would all have required very careful working out with regard to timings.

Now . . . he had not yet seduced Charlotte, but he was sure he could have her agreeing to his plan with a little persuasion. But to get together with her again, and again be discovered by Agnes would blow the whole thing. If he didn't get together with her she would almost certainly go off the boil. Therefore it would have to be done over the next twenty-four or at most forty-eight hours. The trouble was, he did not think he was yet strong enough to cross those mountains. Shit, shit, *shit!*

That left Agnes. Agnes was more beautiful than her sister, more desirable, more sophisticated, and Hector didn't doubt she was also more steadfast, once her mind was made up. But he had no idea in which direction her mind would go. There was also that remark about her boyfriend not coming . . . or had she merely been put out?

The servants arrived to help him dress in his uniform, for the first time in several weeks. It somewhat hung on his underweight frame, but it had been mended and laundered and he felt much better to be in it, even if below the kilt his legs were painfully thin and bony. They had also, he discovered, taken away his skein dhu. Dressed, he went downstairs for his exercise. The entire family, as well as James Davison, turned out to watch him, with Charlotte looking very disgruntled, but Agnes totally calm. Dr Vogel also arrived, accompanied by a Major Luttmann, a heavy-set man in a splendid black uniform, who Hector gathered was the local police chief. He said little, but looked a lot, and was clearly there to find out just how well the English prisoner was.

"Is the colonel not doing well, Herr Baron?" Vogel asked. "I think we will soon be able to take him off your hands."

"Oh, but . . ." Charlotte bit her lip.

"I think Charlotte would like Colonel Hector to stay with us for the duration," Thelma remarked jovially. Charlotte flushed.

"I'm afraid that is not possible, my dear," the Baron said, glancing at Luttmann. "Not even as a birthday present. It seems this war is going to drag on for some time yet. You will have to make do with your new pony." Charlotte pouted.

"Do I gather Mr Churchill's reponse to your Fuehrer's peace feeler was negative, Baron?" Davison asked.

"Yes," Joachim said. "It really is a great pity."

"I don't think we should talk about the war any more," Thelma declared. "This is a happy occasion. I think we should watch Charlotte ride her present." Charlotte was already wearing jodhpurs and a hard hat, and they assembled in the paddock while she put the pony through its paces. She rode very well, if not as straight as her sister.

Champagne was served, and then they lunched, a meal which lasted until five that afternoon. Innumerable toasts were drunk, mainly to the Fuehrer and the future of Germany. As it was the end of November it was already growing dark before they left the table, and with a huge fire burning in the grate in the drawing room to accompany their brandies they were all fairly somnolent. Agnes played the piano and sang in a high, clear voice, and Hector nudged Davison to stop him snoring. Dinner was a quiet affair; even the servants looked sleepy and Hector surmised that they had been doing their share of drinking in the kitchen. He excused himself immediately after the meal. He was genuinely exhausted by the sustained effort of being on his feet, and he felt he needed his rest, as he had no idea what the rest of the night was going to bring.

One thing seemed obvious. Were he fit enough, this would be the night to make his break, when the entire *schloss* was sunk into a drunken stupor. In which case Christmas, now only four weeks away, was the time to aim for. But at Christmas there would be snow on the ground, and thick on the mountains.

"I will take my leave now, Baron, Baroness." Luttmann kissed Thelma's hand, and then did the same to the two girls, lingering over Agnes's knuckles. Then he shook hands with Davison, who had woken up, looking meaningfully from the American to the girl – Agnes had not been able to resist taking a photograph of Davison while he slept, despite a whispered admonition from her mother.

Vogel also shook hands and Joachim himself showed the doctor and Luttmann out; the servants had all gone to bed.

"I think I'm for the sack as well." Davison stood up. "Thanks for including me in, Baron; I've had a great day. Trouble is, I'm not sure I can remember where my room is."

He looked at Agnes, who obligingly escorted him up the stairs. "That guy Luttmann; he's Gestapo, right?"

"No, SS."

"The real tough guys, eh. Do you think he suspects?"

Agnes had reached the door of his room. "Suspects what, Herr Davison?"

"It's my opinion you people are running a very great risk, sweet Agnes. But if you want a hand . . ."

"You, Herr Davison?"

He grinned, rested his hands on the wall, one on each side of her head, and kissed her, lightly. "I'd chance my arm for you."

Agnes ducked under his arm. "I still have not the slightest idea what you are talking about, Herr Davison. Have a good night."

Hector dosed, and awoke at the sound of his door opening. He had not really expected her to come, for she had appeared to drink quite as much as any of the adults, in strong contrast to Charlotte, who had drunk hardly anything at all. She closed the door behind herself, moved beside the bed, a long sliver of white nightdress, topped by the flowing dark hair. She put her hand on his shoulder, and he caught it and squeezed it. She freed herself and lifted the nightdress over her head. He slid across the bed raising the covers, and she lay beside him. He dropped the covers over them both and took her in his arms. Her kiss was deep and sensuous, and she moved her body against his, then reached down to hold him. He slid his hands over her buttocks, and she caught one of them and placed it between her legs, then moved to and fro, achieving a very quick climax which left her shuddering gently. "I love you," she whispered. "I adore you. He's hard, Herr Hector! Can you lay on me, or is it better on your back?"

"I think on my back." Was it really going to happen? After so very long? It was not merely the feel of the girl, the grip of her thighs on his as she straddled him and rose above him, the feel of entering a woman after so long. When she contracted on him he seemed to feel it in his toes, and he climaxed almost as quickly as she had done, his body continuing to jerk for several seconds.

She lay on him. "Now we are one."

"And Willi?"

"Fuck Willi." Her breath rushed against his face as

she smiled. "I will let someone else do that. As for that American . . ."

"He didn't make a pass?" Hector was appalled.

"Don't worry, I slapped him down. But Davison suspects our plans . . ."

"I don't think he'll betray them."

"I hope you're right. Now listen. After you went to bed, my parents discussed you."

"In front of Davison?"

"He was there. I don't know how much he heard, though. He appeared to be asleep. But Luttmann was there."

"What did your parents say of me?"

"Papa has arranged with Luttmann that you will remain here until after Christmas. Then you will be sent to a camp. In the New Year."

"Five weeks, maybe. Will you tire of me in five weeks?"

"Never! Will you love me, for ever and ever?"

Hector took a deep breath. "Yes." He thought that might very well be true, even if not quite in the sense she was hoping for.

"Then I will help you escape."

"Oh, you darling girl!" He held her close, crushed her in his arms, while she squirmed appreciatively on his chest. "When?"

"In another month you will be strong enough to travel. Vogel says this. That is why you will be sent to a prison camp. But before then there will be Christmas. There will be a great celebration. That will be the time."

Two minds with but a single thought, Hector thought. "To do what, exactly?" he asked.

"I will take you to Switzerland. That will mean crossing the mountains. Do you know mountains?"

"There are a few in Scotland, where I was born. But, at Christmas, we will need warm clothing."

She nodded. "I will attend to that. Oh, it will be so exciting."

He did not dare ask her what she wished to happen after they reached Switzerland. "And until Christmas?" he asked.

She threw her leg across his thighs. "I shall come to you every night."

He wondered what Charlotte would make of that?

"Telephone for you, dear," Mother said.

Jocelyn ran into the hall, where the phone was situated. "Yes?" Her heart was pounding.

"Hi!"

"James? James Davison? When did you get back?"

"Couple of days ago. But I had things to do before I could get up here."

"Where?"

"I'm in Edinburgh."

"Did you find out anything about Hector?"

"I had a couple of meals with him."

"Did you? But . . . ?"

"It's a complicated story. Dinner?"

"Is Lou with you?"

"Ah . . . no, she's not. She doesn't even know I'm in Scotland. I'm at the same hotel. Shall I expect you, say about six?"

Jocelyn hesitated. She had no doubt he would be looking for some kind of reward for his efforts; she had known that from the beginning. But in an hotel, all she had to do was say no. And she did so want to hear about Hector. "Six-thirty," she agreed.

*   *   *

Mother didn't like the idea, even if she didn't know what the idea was. She just didn't like the idea of Jocelyn going out at night. "But he has news of Hector, Mother," Jocelyn explained, and caught the train.

It was all so familiar; even the clerk on the desk looked familiar. And James was in the lobby waiting to give her a hug, and a kiss on the forehead. "You grow more attractive every time I see you," he told her as he ushered her into the bar.

"You've been working too hard." She accepted a scotch, trying to keep her nerves under control. She had to be patient. "Did you have a successful trip?"

"Oh, sure. Saw all the right people." He touched her glass with his. "Including your husband."

She leaned forward. "How is he?"

"Recovering well."

"And you saw him . . . in prison?"

"Would that everyone could be so lucky," James said. "He's in what you might call paradise. A private castle, in the bosom of the family, cared for by two young girls who are absolute knockouts!"

"You can't be serious!" Jocelyn protested. "These people are our enemies."

"I can tell you this," Davison said. "They're not Hector's enemies right this minute. Let's eat." Over dinner he told her everything he could remember about the Patten *schloss* and the family, and how Hector was being nursed. "The younger daughter, Charlotte, well, she's going to be a looker, in a year or two. Right now she's a little plump. But the older one, Agnes, could have walked straight out of a bathing beauty parade. Not that I ever saw her in a swimsuit, worse luck. But I have an idea Hector may have, or less."

Jocelyn drank some wine; over the long year she had been separated from her husband and the rest of the Brands she hadn't done much drinking Mother was a teetotaller and her head was starting to spin. But less, she felt, from the alcohol than from what this man was telling her. "What do you mean?" she asked.

"Well, it seemed to me that they had something going for each other."

"You said she was eighteen."

"Sure. But she's his nurse, see. She . . . well, she bathes him. Among other things."

"An eighteen-year-old girl?"

"She's a trained nurse, see. Well, just about. So they reckon on letting her complete her training on your husband. Like I said, lucky for some. Heck . . ." he leaned across the table to squeeze her hand, "I didn't mean to upset you, Joss. I was just trying to put you in the picture."

"Yes," she muttered. "Thank you. Why doesn't he escape if he's not in prison?"

"Yeah. Well, I have to say I asked him that same question. Where he is, Switzerland is only a few miles away and getting out of that house is surely just a matter of opening a couple of doors. He says he means to, when he's fit enough. Claims he still hasn't regained his strength. But, well . . ."

"Say it. Please."

"I can't help wondering if he really wants to try. I don't blame him," he hastily added. "I'm not sure I would, in his position. But of course, time's running out. As soon as he is fully fit they're going to shift him to an officer's prison camp, and that will be that for the duration."

"Yes," she said absently. "I should like to go home now, if you don't mind."

"So early?"

Jocelyn looked at her watch. "It's gone ten. And the last train is at eleven. I really should."

"I was hoping you'd stay a while."

"Why?" She looked straight into his eyes.

"Actually, I've something to give you. Hector gave me a note for you. It's in my room."

"Oh! I wish you'd given it to me earlier."

"Well . . . come on up, and I'll give it to you now."

She frowned. "To your room? When your 'wife' isn't here? I'm not sure the management would like that."

He grinned. "The management isn't going to say a word. I've greased a few palms. Coming?"

He stood up, and after a moment's hesitation she did also. Now her brain was definitely in a spin. She wasn't at all sure of her feelings, her emotions. Only that she was both upset and angry. The thought of Hector cheating with an eighteen-year-old girl . . . but Hector would never do something like that. Save that he seemed to have done it. Perhaps the note would explain it, somehow reassure her.

They were alone in the lift. Davison stood against the far panel, gazing at her, and she gazed back. "Ever had sex in an elevator?" he asked.

"Oh, really, James!"

"Those who have say it's some sensation," he remarked. She was interested, despite herself. "Have you done it?"

"As a matter of fact, yes." But the lift was stopping and he held the door for her. The corridor was empty. "Just across here." He unlocked the bedroom door, switched on the light. "We're a floor higher than we were last time, so there's no balcony."

The room was smaller, too. But it had its own bathroom. Davison closed and locked the door. "We don't want anyone prowling around. Brandy?"

"I really need to catch that train, James."

"There's time." He poured two glasses, handed her one. "Should be champagne, eh?"

"What have we got to celebrate?"

"I meant, if I intended to seduce you. You think I am going to, don't you? I can see it in your face, your every movement."

"It occurred to me that you might try," Jocelyn said. "May I have the note, please?"

"Ah! Yes." He took it from his bureau drawer, handed it to her, watched her expression as she read it.

She raised her head. "No matter what happens," she said, quoting from the note.

"Obviously he expects something to. Something of which you might not approve."

"Perhaps." She folded the note and placed it in her handbag, stood up. "Thanks very much for the dinner. And for everything, I suppose."

He stood in front of her. "You do realise, Joss, dear, dear Joss, that it's liable to be quite some time before you see Hector again?"

She nodded. "That seems likely."

"And that in the meantime, how shall I put it, he is finding out how the other half lives?"

"And you think I should do the same, is that it?" She shook her head. "I'm sorry. It's not on."

"Listen," he said. "You asked me to risk my neck to find out about your hubby. And you asked me to come and see you when I got back."

"Did you seriously suppose that was an invitation to my bed?"

He grinned. "I'm inviting you into mine."

"And I am declining. Again, thank you very much." She went to the door, half turned her head. "I'll tell Lou we had dinner together. I'm sure she'll be interested."

"Be reasonable," he said, and caught her shoulder to spin her round with such force she stumbled and lost her balance. One shoe came off, and before she could recover he had seized her round the waist and laid her across the bed. He came down on top of her, and although they were both fully dressed she could feel his erection on her thigh, while his hand was already pushing her skirt above her knees. "You really turn me on," he said.

Jocelyn was a big, strong woman, and the alcohol had removed most of her inhibitions. She still held her handbag, and with this she struck him twice across the head. He grunted, and pushed himself up. "You know you really want to, you silly little girl," he said. "Why fight it?"

Jocelyn got her hands on his chest and pushed him over, struggling to her feet, regaining her shoe. He reached for her again, and she heard something rip. Oh, hell, she thought. But she was already swinging the handbag again and Davison fell over to avoid it. Then she was at the door and turning the key. "You are the most ungrateful woman I have ever known," he muttered.

She had the door open. "I'm not really going to tell Lou about this," she said. "But I am going to tell her that I don't think you're very suitable, as a man or a lover. And I don't want ever to see or hear from you again." She closed the door behind herself, but leaned against it for a few moments, getting her breathing under control. But getting her emotions under control was going to take much longer.

Hector, seducing, or being seduced by, an eighteen-year-old beauty! Living in the lap of luxury in some German castle. While she . . . Of course it was all going to end, for Hector, in the New Year. So Davison had said. But could she believe anything Davison said, when he so obviously only wanted to get her into bed? Illogically, she believed everything he had told her about Hector.

She rode down in the lift and hurried into the lobby. "My coat, please," she told the hat-check girl, who promptly produced the garment. "Excuse me, madam," she said. "But do you know your dress is torn? At the back." Other people had noticed it too, and were staring at her.

"I know," Jocelyn said. "I caught it in a door."

"Oh dear, madam! Would you like me to call the house-keeper to stitch it for you?"

"I'll manage, thank you." Jocelyn covered the offending rent with her jacket and hurried down the steps into some very cold night air. The station was a quarter of a mile away, and she almost ran towards it, jacket held close, while her brain continued to seethe. The dress seemed to be the last straw: it had been her favourite, now it was ruined. She knew it could be mended to look as good as new, but she would never wish to wear it again. She hated all mankind. All womankind, too. She felt quite suicidal. Of course, she had to live, for Alan. Not for Hector. Never for Hector again.

The stationmaster peered at her ticket as she reached the door. "It's gone, miss."

"What do you mean, gone?"

"Last train left five minutes ago, miss."

"Oh, shoot! What time is the next one?"

"Next stopping train is four o'clock tomorrow morning, miss."

"Oh, dear God!"

"Don't you have anywhere to stay, in town?"

Oh, certainly, Jocelyn thought bitterly. I can go back to that hotel and knock on Davison's door. He'd let her in, she had no doubt at all. Apart from that, she had only £2 in her purse. Presumably that might buy her a room for the night, but she didn't suppose it would be in very pleasant surroundings, and in any event she had no idea where to find a cheap hotel. "Couldn't I stay here?" she asked. "In the station?"

"All by yourself, miss? You don't want to do that. It'll be freezing cold by morning. I'm just about to lock up."

"And there's no other train to Drumbooee until four o'clock? What about out of Central?"

"Well, you could go along there, miss. But there won't be another train stopping at Drumbooee tonight, ye ken. They're all expresses."

But Central would at least be open all night, she thought. Surely. She could spend the night on a bench. "Thank you," she said, and hurried into the night.

She didn't know Edinburgh all that well, and her instincts were to keep away from the vicinity of Davison's hotel, just in case he had decided to come looking for her; she didn't think she could face another confrontation. She had a general idea of where Central Station was, but having made a small detour she suddenly found herself beside the water. It was utterly dark, because of the blackout, and there was no moon, but she could make out the shapes of the ships farther down the Forth. Behind the bridge was the naval base of Rosyth, of vital importance in the war against Germany. Even as she watched, she thought she could make out the dark shape of a destroyer nosing its way up to her berth. War was great for men, she thought bitterly. They fought it, and they became heroes, or they died. In the eyes of his superiors, Hector was a hero, who had done his best to lead the remnants of his battalion to safety, and been seriously wounded doing so. She had been informed that he was to receive the DSO. That he was now a prisoner was a cause for regret, never condemnation.

And she knew that were the exact terms of his imprisonment known, his fellows, and his superiors, would say 'Lucky Devil'. Make the most of it while you have it? She might have said that herself, about someone else's husband.

But for her . . . she stared down at the rippling water

94

beneath her, and once again felt a tremendous urge to end it all. She had been so in love with Hector. She *was* so in love with Hector. But when he returned, some time in the distant future, after having shared his bed with a member of the German nobility, was there the slightest chance she could still love him? More important, perhaps, was there the slightest chance that he would still be in love with her? Why, oh why, had she allowed herself to become pregnant? When it had happened it had been the most joyous event in the world. It had cemented their marriage. But Hector had never even seen the boy.

She sighed, and turned, and was surrounded by laughter. "What's this, then?" someone shouted, and put his arm round her waist.

Sailors, returning from a night ashore. All drunk, all happy. "Let me go," she snapped.

"Now, darling," said the man holding her. "You're just what we're looking for."

She slapped his face, and to her amazement he slapped her back. She had never been hit before, and saw stars while her legs seemed to turn to jelly. "We'll have her over there on the grass," someone said. "Don't worry, darling, we'll pay for it."

"She's not a tart," objected someone else.

"And what do you know about it, boy?"

"Just look at her," the boy insisted. "Look at her dress."

"If she's not a tart, how come she's here on the waterfront at this hour?" someone asked.

"Let me go!" Jocelyn shouted again.

In response, the man holding her round the waist slipped his hands up to grasp her breasts. She struck at him again, this time with her nails, and he gave a cry of pain and anger as he stumbled back. Jocelyn gazed at the shadows around him. She could make out none of their faces, but she did know that she had only one friend in that crowd – and she couldn't make out his face either. The men surged forward; she turned away from them and leapt over the wall.

Part Two

The Escape

'We shall escape the uphill by never turning back.'
Christina Georgina Rossetti

Chapter Five

The Tragedy

"Well, Herr Colonel," Vogel said, putting away his stethoscope. "You are now entirely fit again. Oh, you will carry those scars for the rest of your life. And perhaps you may even get the occasional twinge when it rains, eh? But were I a British Army doctor, I would recommend your return to duty."

Hector buttoned his shirt. "However, Herr Doctor, as you are not a British Army doctor, but a German one . . ."

Vogel chuckled. "I can recommend your removal to more proper surroundings, eh? To the company of your comrades. You will enjoy that, eh? Oh, it will not be so comfortable as here, and the food will not be as good, and of course there will be no beautiful young ladies to wait on you, but there is nothing like being with one's comrades, is there, Herr Colonel?"

"Nothing at all," Hector said pleasantly. "You are not intending, I hope, to interfere with the Baroness's Christmas arrangements?"

"Oh, I should never do that." Another chuckle. "I am invited to Christmas dinner. But I am afraid, once we enter the New Year, I will have to make my recommendation."

"Of course," Hector said. "Will you be in again, before Christmas?"

"Perhaps once. You really do not need me any more. I will say '*auf Wiedersehen*', Herr Colonel." He went to the door, opened it, and checked. The Baroness stood there. "Forgive me, Baroness," he said. "I did not know you were waiting."

Thelma inclined her head, and he sidled past her. Then she came into the room and closed the door. "What does he say?"

"That I am well enough to leave you, in the New Year."

"Hm," she said. "I am sorry about that. Truly. I am even more sorry about what I have to tell you." Hector frowned. But Great Britain could not have surrendered or made peace, or he would not be going to a prison camp. "It is about your wife," Thelma said. "Sit down."

Hector sank into a chair, his heart pounding painfully. "What about my wife?"

"She fell into the Firth of Forth."

"Fell into . . ." he could not believe his ears.

"Fell, or was pushed, or jumped, it is very confused. It happened in the middle of the night."

"That's impossible."

"I'm afraid it did happen. The information was conveyed to me by the local Gestapo commander in Munich, Major Luttmann. You met him at Charlotte's birthday party. There can be no doubt."

"My wife is dead?"

"No, she was rescued. But she is in hospital."

"But . . . ?" What on earth could Jocelyn have been doing in Edinburgh by herself? And falling into the Forth? Or jumping? That meant she had actually been in Leith. No, that had to be ridiculous!

"They say she will be all right," Thelma went on, anxiously watching him.

"Thank you. And my son?"

"There was no report about that. You do not think . . . ?"

"No, Thelma. I do not suppose he went in with her," Hector said. "He will be with his grandmother, I imagine. May I write to my wife?"

"Of course. Write your letter and I will mail it. I don't know how long it will take to reach her."

Hector nodded, and sat at the table. Thelma went to the door. "I am most terribly sorry about this," she said. "Please don't let it spoil your Christmas."

"I'm sure it won't." Hector assured her, and picked up the pen Agnes had offered him.

But what was he to write? Commonplaces, because the letter would certainly be read by the German censors before being forwarded? Loving commonplaces, of course. And he could say that he was about to be moved to a prison camp; that might put anyone reading the letter off the track. Except that they would know it was a lie long before the letter reached Jocelyn. If only he could work out what she had been doing in Edinburgh, at night, by herself.

He heard the door open, but did not need to turn his head; he could recognize her footsteps by now. Agnes stood at his side and rested her hand on his shoulder. "I wish to say that I am sorry." He put his arm round her thighs and rested his head on her hip. "But Mama says she will recover."

"Yes."

She leaned over to see what he was writing. "Do you love her that much?"

Hector took a deep breath. "I do not love her at all, Agnes. But I must appear to do so."

"Then this will make no difference to our plan?"

"None at all."

She kissed the back of his neck. "It is all set," she whispered. "I have spoken with Vogel and he says you are totally fit."

101

"He told me that, too."

"Well, listen. We will escape on Christmas night. Here is what we are going to do."

No more than a few days. Perhaps Jocelyn's escapade – whatever had been involved – had actually been a stroke of fortune, for him if not for her. As a result of the news no one expected him to be quite normal; it *was* quite normal for him to start whenever anyone came near him, as if they might be bearing more bad news. Even Charlotte showed a great deal of sympathy. But it was obvious she was still in a tremendous sulk. If she was to betray them . . . "She knows I'd never forgive her," Agnes assured him. "And I'd make her life hell."

She lay as she liked best, naked in the crook of his arm just before dawn. "Tell me about what happens after we reach Switzerland," she said.

"Well, I may be interned for a while. Until my people can get me out. Will you be all right?"

"Of course! I will wait for you. I will claim political asylum."

"You'll need money to live."

"I will have money. I have everything prepared."

"I am sure you do. But . . . everyone will know you helped me."

She giggled. "They will be furious!"

"Do you think they may be in trouble with the authorities?"

"Papa? Of course not. He is a friend of the Fuehrer. And he is not responsible for what I may do." Hector had a terrible suspicion the matter might be taken out of Papa's hands. What a weight he was going to have to carry for the rest of his life. "And after you are released from internment?" she asked.

"Well, we'll go to England."

"And be married."

"As soon as it can be arranged." What a cad he had become. But in this instance it was his duty to be a cad.

"I am so excited," she said. "And so happy."

Hector sat in a corner of the withdrawing room while the family opened their presents, accompanied by a great deal of laughter and shouting. They were so happy. Even Agnes appeared totally happy, although this was the day she would betray them. They were also somewhat hungover, for the Baron and Rudi had arrived the previous night and the champagne corks had popped before the entire household, servants included, had gathered in the courtyard to sing 'Silent Night' with that emotion so definitively German.

Never had Hector felt so guilty, so regretful of what he had to do. But then he recalled that these were the people who had strafed the hospital ship outside St Valery and bombed the clearly marked hospital tents in the Forest des Arques. As for being hungover, that was all to the good, as today they intended to put a great deal more alcohol on top of the fumes already roaming about their brains.

"We have not forgotten you, Hector," Thelma said archly, and handed him a large parcel.

"But . . . I have nothing to give you."

Charlotte gave a loud snort as if to indicate that in her opinion he had already given one member of the family a present, if not several. "You will give us all presents when the war is over," Thelma said.

They were all waiting for him to open his gift, so he untied the ribbon and took out a splendid silk dressing gown, black decorated with golden dragons. "This is quite magnificent," Hector said.

"It will remind you of us when you are far away," Thelma told him.

"Are you allowed to wear dressing gowns in prison camp?" Charlotte inquired, and received several censorious glances.

"Now I think you should kiss us all," Thelma said. "Or at least the ladies."

Pre-lunch drinks led into lunch itself. They listened to a speech by Hitler on the radio, in which he assured them that the triumphs of 1940 would be nothing compared with the triumphs coming in 1941. As for England, he compared it with a chicken with its head cut off but which is still rushing around the yard. It would soon cease squawking, the Fuehrer said, with a sad lack of logic. "You'll note he did not mention Musso and his lot," Rudi remarked, pouring some more champagne.

"He could only be rude about them," Thelma declared.

"Is there something wrong in Italy?" Hector inquired, as ingenuously as he could.

The Germans exchanged glances, then the Baron shrugged. "One would never suppose the present-day Italians are the descendants of the Romans, the greatest fighting nation the world has ever known. They have tried to conquer Egypt and been beaten to bits by your army there. They have tried to conquer Greece and been beaten to bits by the Greeks. They are totally inept."

"When you think that a few years ago the Fuehrer looked up to that man," Thelma commented.

"He still does, for some reason of his own," her husband said. "Not to worry. Musso's antics at least divert the British from their real business, defending Britain. With respect, Hector."

"Point taken," Hector said, sipping champagne.

His task was to appear to drink as much as anyone else while remaining reasonably sober. Agnes kept a careful eye on him, and it was her suggestion, when lunch finally ended, that their guest should lie down. "You are looking most awfully tired, Hector," she admonished.

Hector was happy to obey, returned to his room, and was fast asleep in a matter of seconds. As always just before going into action, once he had received his orders and made his dispositions he was utterly calm. Whatever would be, would be. He awoke with a start, to find Agnes drawing the curtains; it was already dark out there. "Is it time?" he asked.

"We have not yet had dinner."

"More drinking?"

"You must try to keep a clear head. But in any event, you will be very tired, and retire early. Make a joke about it. Tell them that as you soon will no longer be sleeping in a soft bed you wish to make the most of it while you have the opportunity. I will come for you as soon as the coast is clear."

"If we leave it too late, we will not make the border by dawn."

"I know that. But this is the safest way. Tomorrow they will all sleep in. They always do on Boxing Day. They will not stir before twelve, not sufficiently to notice that I am not here, anyway. Only then will they come looking for you."

"But that means we will cross the border in daylight."

"That is the best time. We must see where we are going, and we do not want the Swiss to start firing at us. I have thought it all out, Hector. Believe me."

"I do believe you, Agnes. But . . . are you sure. Certain, absolutely, sure?"

"I am more sure than I have ever been in my life," she said, and kissed him. "Now get dressed and come downstairs. They are opening more champagne."

Hector wished he had the ability to see the future. This girl was so confident, but also so trusting. Obviously, if her plan worked, they would have a long time together before they actually regained England. Time in which they would grow to love each other, instead of just wanting each other? Or grow to hate each other? Much depended on when he told her the truth. Common sense dictated he should not do that until they reached England. Honesty, and indeed honour, demanded he do it as soon as they were out of Germany. But what would her reaction be?

The house held a hum of excited merriment as preparations were made for dinner. Hector had supposed lunch had been the main meal of the day; they had finished with brandy-soaked plum pudding. But dinner was an even larger meal, punctuated with the inevitable toasts. The girls wore evening gowns and looked beautiful; even Thelma looked beautiful on this occasion. The Baron, Rudi and Vogel wore stiff collars and white ties, having discarded their uniforms for this occasion. Hector felt like a tramp. But as usual he was treated as a member of the family in everything.

After the meal, while it was still too early for him to retire, he was invited into the study for a smoke by the Baron. "I want you to know, Baron," he said, as he clipped his cigar, "how much I appreciate everything you have done for me over the past few months."

Joachim waved his hand. "It began as a duty. But now, we are really very fond of you, Hector. We shall be very sorry to see you go. All of us."

"As I shall be sorry to go. But maybe one day, when this

is all behind us, we will meet again and drink champagne and laugh at the memory."

"I should like that," Joachim agreed. "Tell me, has there been any more news of your wife?" Hector shook his head. "But you presume she is all right?"

"I can only hope."

"Of course. You and she . . . this is a delicate question, to which I hope you will not take offence. May I ask how long you have been married?"

Hector's cigar had gone out, and he carefully relit it before replying. "Three years."

"That is not very long, eh? When last did you see her?

"I had leave in January."

"Then you have now been separated for almost a year. You must still be very much in love."

"I think so. I hope so."

"Of course. You have children?"

"I have a son, who I have not yet seen at all."

"This damnable war, eh?" The Baron flicked ash, and regarded it for several seconds. "You realise that Agnes has developed a considerable affection for you?"

"I realise she has a schoolgirl crush on me, yes," Hector said.

"It is more than that, I am afraid. Agnes is no longer a schoolgirl. Did you know that she has broken off her engagement?"

"I didn't know she was engaged."

"Well, it had not yet got around to rings. But it had been a long-standing arrangement between our two families." The Baron shrugged. "It is not your fault. If there is a fault, it lies with my wife in permitting Agnes to be your nurse. But she was so keen. However, what's done is done. But I am sure that you, an officer and a gentleman, as well as a married man and at the moment an enemy of our people, deplore the situation as much as I do. Now, obviously you are about to be removed from Agnes's life. I would like the removal to be permanent. I would ask you not to write to her or make any attempt to contact her, from your camp. Without the physical presence of you, and without any communication, we may hope that the infatuation will dwindle and in time disappear. Will you assist me in this matter, Hector?"

"Of course, Baron. I give you my word that once I am transferred to prison camp I shall make no further attempt to contact Agnes."

"She may well attempt to write you, at least for a while."

"I shall not read her letters."

"Good." The Baron held out his hand. "I think we shall be friends, you and I, when this was is over."

If only that could be so, Hector thought.

As arranged, Hector retired reasonably early, and reasonably sober as well. He had in fact been as much disturbed at how much more sober the Baron had been than he had supposed, as by what he had had to say. He *was* going to destroy this family. Therefore, at the very least, he had to find some way to make it up to Agnes, without destroying his own marriage! That, he reckoned, was going to be a more difficult task than actually escaping.

Despite himself, he nodded off, but awoke the moment his door opened. He still did not have a watch, but it was totally dark, and he reckoned it had to be some time after midnight. The house was also utterly quiet. "Are you awake?" she whispered.

He put out his hand to touch her. She was very heavily dressed, in what he estimated to be a skiing outfit; both jacket and pants were quilted. He swung his legs out of bed and she kissed him. "Let's go."

"My boots."

"Leave them. I have better boots downstairs." She held his hand, led him from the room. They crept along the gallery and down the stairs. The silence was oppressive.

On the lower floor she led him past the dining room, which looked like a battlefield, and into the front lobby, off which opened the big cloakroom. Here she switched on the light, and he discovered that she had laid out ski boots, and a pair of thick pants as well as a quilted jacket, all belonging, he guessed to Rudolph, and big enough to be worn over his uniform; they had already discussed and rejected the idea of using skis; most of their journey would be uphill, and he was not very experienced, anyway. There were also two back packs, each of some size and weight.

"That is yours," Agnes said, helping him into it and strapping it into place. "It contains food and water, mainly. And some brandy to keep out the cold." She put on her own. "Mine has maps and a change of clothing and money." She was about the most efficient woman he had ever met.

There were hats for them each, caps of the kind the Germans called *kuptstopfers*, shaped like an English deerstalker with flaps to cover the ears. With these were scarves, to wrap around their faces, and snow goggles. Finally, she had equipped them each with an alpenstock. She adjusted her scarf. "All set?"

He nodded. "The dogs?"

"I will see to them." They tiptoed back into the hall. Hector would dearly have loved to ask where the Baron and his son kept their weapons, either their sidearms or the shotguns he knew were somewhere in the castle, but as Agnes had not raised the matter he decided against it; obviously she would not want him shooting at her own people. They stepped outside, into an immediate drop of some forty degrees, he reckoned. "Count up to sixty," Agnes said. "Then walk to the gate, slowly and quietly. Do not hurry. When you reach the gate, stand absolutely still."

Hector nodded, drew a deep breath. He reckoned this was the most dangerous moment of the escape. He began counting, while Agnes moved away from him, along the wall, to the dogs' enclosure. They began to growl as she approached, but quietened the moment they heard her voice. She spoke to them softly, enticingly; Hector could not hear what she was saying. He reached sixty, and moved away from the wall. Not looking round, he walked steadily to the gate. Behind him the dogs were giving little yelps of pleasure as Agnes spoke to them and apparently fed them. He reached the gate and, as instructed, stood absolutely still. Then he heard her coming towards him across the yard, also moving very quietly and slowly. She reached him, thrust the key into the lock. It had been freshly greased and there was no sound as it turned and the gate swung open. "What do you English say?" she asked.

"Piece of cake."

They crossed the other courtyard to the main gate. Here Agnes also had the key to the postern, and then they were outside the castle itself. Although it remained very cold, probably just below freezing, Hector thought, it was not snowing, and what had fallen earlier had hardened into ice. Yet their footsteps would be obvious enough. "The forecast is for more snow by dawn," Agnes said. "That will be good for us, eh? We may as well use the road for the time being. It is six miles to the border."

"Is that all?"

She smiled. "I am speaking of the border with Austria. Do not worry, it is no longer guarded."

"Austria?" he asked in consternation. "Then where is Switzerland?"

"Beyond Austria," she explained patiently.

"You mean there is no common border between Germany and Switzerland?" His head was spinning.

"There is. But it is all the lake, the Bodensee. We cannot cross the lake, so we must go round it, and that is through Austrian territory. Do not worry, it is only a few more miles. But it is through the mountains."

Hector swallowed. "Then let's go."

They followed the road, skirting the village, and walked steadily into the freezing night, their breaths clouding before their faces. Agnes was clearly a fresh-air fiend, as were so many of the German youth, who did walks like this all the time, but Hector soon became aware of how unfit he was, and they had to stop every hour to allow him ten minutes rest. But she never revealed the slightest impatience. Then she said, "We must go up, now."

Above their heads the mountains were starting to tower. "You mean we're in Austria?"

"We have been in Austria for some time. I told you it would be easy. But now we must climb."

"What time is it?"

"A quarter past four. We have a good three hours of darkness left. We follow this road." It was hardly more than a track, leading away from the main road. For the first half an hour it ascended slowly and there was no difficulty, although Hector made the disagreeable discovery that he was even less fit than he had supposed; soon his thighs were burning and his ankles paining. His pace slowed, and Agnes came back to him. "Are you all right?"

"I need to rest."

"Then rest. We have time." He sat at the roadside, oblivious of the cold seeping up through his backside.

111

Agnes squatted beside him. "It is hard, after several weeks in bed," she commented.

"Tell me how far we have to go."

"We climb another two hundred feet, then we level off for perhaps half a mile. That will be easier, eh? Then we climb again to the next pass. That is about four hundred feet above the plateau. That will be hard. Then we descend into a valley, two hundred feet. That will be good going. Then we climb again, five hundred feet."

"That means we'll be over a thousand feet up."

She nodded. "But that is as high as we need go. The border itself is in the next valley. That is far down, several hundred feet. That is actually the most difficult part, because it is quite steep. But we will make it."

"And the border? Is it fenced?"

"No, no. It is patrolled. But by the time we get there it will be light and we will be able to see, and choose our moment to cross." She had the immortality complex of youth, when there are no obstacles worth considering.

"Let's go," he said, and stood up.

By sheer determination he kept going to the top of the first level, but it was slow work, and often Agnes held his arm to help him on; her own fitness was phenomenal. Then he had to rest for some twenty minutes before he was able to continue. As she had promised, the walk across the plateau was a great relief after the climbing, but they had not got half way when the first snowflakes drifted past them. "This is good, eh?" Agnes asked. "They will cover our tracks."

Not, he supposed, that anyone would have any doubt where they must have headed, when they were found missing. By now the path had long disappeared, but Agnes knew where the good ground was, and crossing the plateau was actually easier than he remembered the going between Hannoy and the Bresle. But then the mountains loomed above them again. "Rest here," she said. "It is a steep climb."

They sat down, slapping their hands together, although it seemed less cold now that it had started to snow. "It is half past five," she said. "We are making good time."

He was glad she thought so. And the next climb was steeper yet. The snow was falling harder now and several times he slipped and came down heavily. So did she. But the exertion kept them warm and eventually they reached the pass. The mountains reared to either side, now brilliant white even in the gloom, where they could see; the snow flurries came thick and fast, driven now by a rising wind from the south, out of Switzerland. "They will never find us in this," Agnes shouted, her mouth against Hector's ear.

They descended into the next valley at a good speed, and here they were somewhat sheltered from the wind, but ahead of them loomed the last climb to the high pass. They sat with their backs to it while Hector rested. His entire body was a mass of pain and discomfort; his legs ached and his ears sang. Agnes seemed to know exactly how he felt; no doubt, for all her fitness, she had her discomforts as well. She hugged him. "Think of Switzerland," she shouted. "Ready?"

He heaved himself to his feet and set off after her, driving his alpenstock into the ground, and forcing his feet forward; the snow was now several inches deep, and seemed to be clawing at his boots. But the heavy darkness had actually begun to lighten. He concentrated on the quilted thighs moving in front of him. All the sexual happiness in the world lay between those thighs, and when he reached Switzerland it would again be his. So much for being a married man. Or for being an honourable man. Because all of the beauty, all of the passion, all of the *lust*, which he knew also lay between those thighs, would have to be betrayed, and for what? So that he could go on fighting and killing for King and Country. But really, he told himself, be logical. Where does the betrayal of a pair of thighs, however magnificent, compare with taking a man's life? And he was sworn to do that as often as he could, until the war was won. He slipped and fell with a thud. Instantly Agnes was beside him, lifting his head from the snow. "My darling," she said. "Are you all right?"

"Yes," he gasped. "Yes, I'm all right."

Thighs had nothing to do with it. This girl was a heroine who had to be destroyed simply because she believed in a madman's dream. "This snow is heavier than I had thought it would be," she shouted. "We have to shelter."

"Where can we shelter?"

"Near here. Can you make it?" He struggled to his feet, and she led him onwards. But after another few feet of the ascent she turned off onto a parallel path, along the cliff face. "Don't slip," she warned. "It's a long way down."

Hector had never suffered from vertigo, and looked down into the steadily lightening gloom. The floor of the plateau was some 200ft below them, only occasionally visible through the snow flurries. He put his shoulder against the rockface and followed the girl, wherever possible placing his boots in her footsteps. They followed the ledge for about a hundred yards, then the cliff face receded and they were in a gully, where there was a wooden hut. The door was unlocked, and a moment later they were out of the snow and feeling momentarily warm. "You knew this was here?" Hector asked.

"Of course. I have climbed in these mountains all my life. There are several of these shelters. They are constantly re-equipped." She pointed at the neat pile of logs and kindling beside the fireplace. "Unfortunately, we cannot light a fire, or they will come here first when they start looking for us. But . . ." she opened the cupboard, took out some tinned food and milk. "We can at least eat,"

He was surprised at how hungry he was. They sat at the table, facing each other. "How long do we stay here?" he asked.

"Until the snow eases off. I do not think it will be long. Do not worry, they are all still fast asleep." She blew him a kiss. "I love you. Now, let us warm each other up, as we cannot light the fire."

It was daylight before the snowstorm ceased. "Now we must hurry," Agnes said. "But be careful." Hector saw what she meant when they got outside; the cliff edge was almost entirely obliterated by the packed snow, while to the north there was nothing but white, covering the plateau, smothering the hills beyond. "A good day for staying in bed," Agnes said. "Let's hope they do."

As usual she led the way, and again he used her footsteps. He was feeling much stronger now, more confident that they would make it. They reached the path up the hillside without difficulty, and began to climb. Because of the snow this was harder work than during the night and his fingers began to freeze through his thick gloves. But they went steadily upwards until Agnes suddenly paused. "There!"

Hector stood beside her, looked down the long, steep slope at the valley beyond. At the bottom there was a stream, but he reckoned that was frozen over. To the right there was a huge body of water, stretching out of sight – the Bodensee, its waters choppy from the wind. And beyond . . . "Switzerland," Agnes said. "Not more than an hour away. And do you know what is over there?" She pointed. "Berchtesgaden." She laughed. "But the Fuehrer is not in residence. Now be careful, going down."

She set off herself, testing the ground before her with her alpenstock, choosing her way. Hector followed. They were halfway down when they heard a shout. "Shit!" Agnes commented, but she stopped and looked round and up.

The man was several hundred yards away and farther up the slope, but even at a distance they could see he was wearing a uniform greatcoat and carried a rifle. "They cannot yet be after us," Agnes said. "He is just doing his job as a border guard. Leave the talking to me."

She waved, and the man shouted again, and began making his way through the snow towards them. "Maybe he'll fall and break his neck," Hector muttered.

The soldier approached, slowly, occasionally shouting. Agnes waited, her face calm. Hector stood behind her. "Where do you go?" the soldier inquired, coming up to them.

Agnes shrugged. "For a hike. We need the fresh air. Too much Christmas."

The soldier peered at her, and she unwrapped her scarf. "I am Agnes von Patten. My father is the Baron."

"You are a long way from home, Fräulein." The soldier was peering at Hector.

"A few miles. Do not worry, we are not lost."

"Then why are you making for the border?"

"We thought we'd go down to the stream, and then home again."

Still the soldier stared at Hector. Then he unslung his rifle. "You are the Englander who is staying at the *schloss*," he said. "You are trying to get to Switzerland."

He was still looking at Hector. Agnes acted without hesitation, throwing herself forward in a kind of rugby tackle, closing her arms round the soldier's thighs and bringing him down into the snow. Hector also reacted, stepping forward to seize the rifle and twist it from the soldier's grasp, swinging the butt as he did so to catch the man across the jaw and stretch him unconscious. Agnes rose to her knees, panting. "We must hurry."

"He's not going to be out for very long," Hector pointed out.

"He cannot harm us if we have his gun," Agnes said. "Come on." But as she got up there was a shot. She spun round and hit the snow with a squelching thud.

"Agnes!" Hector dropped to his knees beside her, a sudden movement which possibly saved his life, for there was another shot and a bullet sliced into the snow only inches away from him.

"Shit, shit, shit!" Agnes moaned, rolling into the shelter of the unconscious soldier, while another two shots smashed into the snow around them. She left a trail of blood on the white.

Hector rolled beside her, looking up the slope at the three men who stood there. Hastily he levelled the rifle and fired at them and they disappeared behind an outcrop of rock. "How bad is it?" he asked.

"I do not think it is very bad," Agnes said, with great composure. "But I will not make it. Give me the gun, and you run for the border."

"I can't leave you."

"You must. Listen, I will come to you, later. As soon as I can."

Hector bit his lip. He had used this girl shamelessly. Now he was being required to sacrifice her, utterly. "You'll be killed."

She grinned, her lips tight with pain. "They are not going to shoot at me again, because if they do they stand a chance of hitting their comrade. But I can shoot at them, and make them keep their heads down. And if he wakes up, I will hit him again. Go, Hector! Go. Hurry!" Hector hesitated a last

117

time. Her reasoning was fallacious in that they had already shot at her, taking the risk of hitting their comrade, who for all they knew might be already dead.

"But first tell me that you love me," she begged.

Chapter Six

The Price

The black Mercedes pulled into the courtyard of the Patten *schloss*; it was followed by a truck, with its canvas flaps down. Three men got out of the Mercedes, one, in uniform, standing to attention while the other two walked to the steps. One of the these men also wore uniform; he was Major Luttmann. The other wore a belted trenchcoat over a dark suit, and a slouch hat. He walked immediately behind the officer. The truck remained still; there was no movement from the people inside. Joachim von Patten stood at the top of the steps, bareheaded despite the January chill. "My daughter?" he asked.

"She is in hospital, Herr Colonel," Luttmann said.

"Will she be all right?"

"We think so, as regards her wound; they have managed to extract the bullet. She lost a lot of blood before our people managed to approach her, however, and she is also suffering from exposure. She held the border guards off for over an hour before she fainted." He allowed himself a thin smile. "Perhaps she should have been in the Army rather than a nurse." The smile faded. "However, there is no room in the *Wehrmacht* for traitors to the Third Reich."

"She is a foolish young girl who fell in love with an older man," Joachim said.

"Undoubtedly she is a foolish young girl," the major agreed. "May we go inside, Herr Colonel?"

Joachim looked past them at the waiting truck. Then he turned and went inside. Thelma stood on the stairs, hastily dressed. "Where is Agnes?"

Luttmann clicked his heels. "She is in hospital, Frau von Patten."

"I must go to her."

"That is not possible, at this time," the major said.

"She is going to be all right," Joachim said as reassuringly as he could.

"How many other members of your family are in residence, Herr Colonel?" asked the plainclothes Gestapo officer.

"My son, Lieutenant Rudolf von Patten. And my younger daughter, Charlotte."

The Gestapo officer looked at Thelma. "Will you ask your son and daughter to dress themselves and come downstairs, please, Frau von Patten."

Thelma looked at her husband. "I think there are questions that need to be answered, Thelma," Joachim said. Thelma hesitated, then turned and went back up the stairs.

"Who are you?" The Gestapo officer asked Johann, who had appeared in the pantry doorway.

"He is my butler," Joachim said.

"How many servants are there in the house?"

"Eight."

"You, Johann . . ." the Gestapo officer was taking control of the morning. "Assemble the domestic staff . . ." he peered past the butler, "In the dining room."

Like his mistress, Johann looked at the Baron for confirmation. Joachim nodded. "Do as the gentleman says, Johann."

"Do you have a study?" the Gestapo officer asked.

"Through there."

"Lead us."

Joachim went into his study, still redolent of cigar smoke from the previous night. "I understand that this is a shocking affair," he said, listening to the door close behind him.

"Yes," said the Gestapo officer. "You have a weapon?"

Joachim gestured to his belts, which hung behind the door. Luttmann took the Luger automatic from its holster. "Am I under arrest?" Joachim asked.

"That is up to you, Herr Colonel," the Gestapo officer said. "Your daughter has committed treason, in that she aided and abetted an enemy of the Reich to escape, in time of war, and that she fired upon and wounded a German soldier."

Joachim sat down. "She is a stupid, innocent young girl," he said. "She does not know what treason is."

"That is for the court to decide. But I can tell you what they will decide."

"Am I allowed to see her?"

"It would be better you did not see her. In any event, it is forbidden for one traitor to communicate with another."

Joachim's head came up. "You are accusing me of treason?"

"You are the traitor's father. You asked for permission to have the Englander here, as an act of gratitude. There were doubts, but permission was granted because of your distinguished war record. Now the Englander has escaped. The escape was made from your house, with you in residence, and in the company of your daughter. Can you really pretend you knew nothing of it?"

"Of course I knew nothing of it!" Joachim shouted. "It was Christmas night. We were all, well, drunk I suppose."

"Apparently your daughter was not drunk, Herr Colonel. Neither was the Englander. I suspect this 'drunkenness' was a little manufactured, eh?"

"Are you also accusing my wife and children?"

"Of course. They are clearly guilty. As are your servants. I have orders from Berlin that the entire Patten family, and their servants, are to be arrested, and closely questioned as to this affair. And then, most severely punished. As you should know, Herr Colonel, the Fuehrer does not like people who betray him. He treated you as a friend. He has spent the night in this house. And now . . . he was very angry when he heard the news."

Joachim got up and almost ran to the window. Neither man made any effort to stop him. Joachim stood at the window, which looked out onto the courtyard, at the twenty men who had disembarked from the truck and stood there, facing the house, rifles in their hands. "There is, however, a way for you," the Gestapo officer said.

Joachim turned, watched Luttmann place the Luger on his desk. "We will step outside for a moment," the Gestapo officer said. "If, when we return, you are dead, you will have accepted responsibility for what has happened, all charges against the remaining members of your family will be dropped, and the matter will be over."

"And if I refuse?" Joachim asked in a low voice.

The Gestapo officer shrugged. "Then your entire family and staff will be arrested and questioned, severely. And then either hanged or sent to a concentration camp. You understand what I am saying?"

Joachim licked his lips. "You give me your word that this will not happen if I kill myself?"

"I have just said so, Herr Colonel."

"And this amnesty will include Agnes?"

"Your daughter has already been arrested, Herr Colonel. As what she did was witnessed by several soldiers, she will have to stand trial. However, if it can be proved to the judge's satisfaction that she was acting on orders from you, it is entirely possible that she will get off with a light sentence."

"Possible?"

"Probable, I am sure, Herr Colonel. We will leave you, now. Please remember that if you attempt to use that pistol for any other purpose than to kill yourself, your family will suffer most dreadfully. A Merry Christmas to you, Herr Colonel."

He went to the door, and the major followed him.

"I am sure you mean '*auf Wiedersehen*'," Joachim muttered, as he picked up the pistol.

"Baron von Patten shot himself," the consul said. "I did not know he was involved in your escape."

"He wasn't," Hector said. "He was entirely innocent."

"Hm. Well, there it is. Pity. He seems to have been a good German."

"He was a good man," Hector said. "What has happened to his daughter."

"You mean the girl who actually got you out? She is in hospital, wounded. I understand that it is a military hospital. That is, she is under arrest, and the charge is treason."

"You mean they are going to shoot that lovely girl?"

The consul had never seen such a stricken face as that on the opposite side of the table. "I am very sorry to say that is extremely likely. Although . . ." he cleared his throat, "they are more likely to hang her." He watched Hector's fingers curl into the tightest of fists. "Colonel Brand," he said. "No blame whatsoever can be attached to you in this matter. You saw the opportunity to escape, and you took it. As a British officer, this was your duty."

"And doing my duty condemned at least two people to death," Hector muttered.

"They were Germans. Enemies of your country," the consul said, severely. "If you had possessed a weapon, and the Baron and his daughter had attempted to stop your escape, would you not have shot them down? You would have been justified in doing so."

"They were kind to me," Hector said. "They befriended me."

The consul sighed. He suspected the Colonel, however distinguished his record, was in need of psychiatric treatment. "It's done," he said. "Now for brighter news. You should be able to leave Switzerland in the next couple of months. Obviously the Swiss don't want to upset a near neighbour quite as powerful as Germany, but they are co-operating in every way. We are using compassion as our main weapon. With your wife unwell . . ."

"Jocelyn says she is perfectly fit again," Hector snapped. "That letter was dated only a fortnight ago."

"Of course. But I do not think any German has seen it. The fact is that your wife was very nearly killed, in her . . . accident." Another case for psychiatric treatment, in the consul's opinion. "She needs you, desperately. The Swiss understand this, and have virtually agreed that you should be repatriated. Naturally, there will be strings attached, such as your being forbidden to take any further active part in the war, but we are working on this. Now, isn't that an attractive prospect? England, Home and Beauty and all that?" He peered at Hector. "You really want to forget those Krauts. Colonel."

"Well, Fräulein!" Major Luttmann beamed at the girl in the hospital bed. "Dr Kramm tells me you are nearly as good as new. What's a scar between friends, especially as it is in such a private place, eh? Of course, I am told that, wounded

in such a place, you will never be able to have children, but
in some ways that might prove a blessing."

Agnes pulled the sheet to her neck. She knew exactly
where the bullet had penetrated – the operation on her womb
still hurt, mentally more than physically, now. And she did
not like Major Luttmann; he looked at her as though she were
a prize catch on the end of his fishing line. "What is going to
happen to me?" she asked.

"I am the bearer of glad tidings. You are not to be put on
trial." Agnes, having braced herself for that ordeal, could
not believe her ears. "Your father has arranged the matter
for you," Luttmann explained, beaming.

"Oh, Papa!" Agnes whispered. Oh, Papa! He had not failed
her. "Then I am to be allowed home?"

"Ah, no. You do understand that you committed treason
against the Reich? That offence carries the death penalty.
You are a very lucky girl to have escaped being shot. Or
hanged, which is worse. You do realize this?"

"Yes," Agnes said faintly. "I do realize this. You mean I
am being sent to prison, without trial?"

"You are considered to be an enemy of the Reich,"
Luttmann explained. "Therefore you are being sent to a
camp, where enemies of the Reich are confined."

"I am being sent to a concentration camp?" For a moment
she thought her heart had stopped beating.

"That is correct."

Agnes regained control of her breathing. She did not know
much about concentration camps, save that Mother and Papa
had always referred to them as rather jolly places, where the
inmates lived an open-air life, working for the Reich, to be
sure, but with lots of opportunities for socializing. "Why,"
Mother had said, "they even have their own orchestras and
music festivals. It is really a very civilized way of dealing
with dissidents." Of course, Mother had never supposed one

of her own daughters would be considered a dissident. But it had to be better than prison. Or death. "When will this happen?" she asked.

"As soon as you are fit to travel. In another few days, according to Dr Kramm."

"Will I be allowed to see my father and mother, and my brother and sister, before I go?"

"That will not be possible. You simply must understand that you are a convicted criminal."

I have not been convicted, Agnes thought, because I have not been tried. But she didn't want to antagonize the Major, who seemed determined to be pleasant. "I do understand that," she said. "You mean they will not even be able to visit me in the camp?"

"No." Luttmann sat on the bed beside her. "But I may be able to do so, from time to time. Would you like that, Agnes?"

Agnes stared at him. Oh, Lord, she thought. But in the camp he would hardly ever be allowed to be alone with her. And he would bring her news of the family. "Yes," she said. "I would like that."

"Then I shall look forward to it." Gently Luttmann extracted the sheet from between her fingers and pulled it down to her waist. He did not achieve much, as the bed gown was thick cotton, but to her consternation he rested his hand on her breast and gave a gentle squeeze. "I look forward to seeing a lot more of you."

Agnes licked her lips. But she was at least as angry as she was frightened. This lout . . . "Tell me, Herr Major," she said. "Did the Englander escape?"

Luttmann glared at her for a second, then grinned. "Yes. He is in Switzerland. We shall have to kill him, or capture him, all over again when we invade England. You see what a nuisance you have caused? One more Englander to kill, and probably several more bullets to be wasted." He gave her breast a last squeeze and stood up; now he was as angry as she. "*Auf Wiedersehen*, Fräulein," he said, and went to the door, where he turned. "Oh, I forgot to tell you, Fräulein. Your father saved your beautiful skin by shooting himself."

England, Home and Beauty! Hector was on deck as the ship out of Lisbon nosed its way up the Thames. As it was now late summer the country to either side looked warm and peaceful, but as they approached the capital he could see the damage, and fires were still burning in places. "Things have got a lot better for us since Hitler went East," Morton, the embassy man who was a fellow passenger, explained. "But they still come across from time to time."

"What exactly is the situation in Russia?" Hector asked. News had been hard to come by during his travels, or even when waiting for ongoing transport, through Vichy France, then Spain, and then Portugal.

"Pretty grim, I'm afraid. The Germans are running riot. If you believe a fraction of what they claim to have achieved in terms of Russians killed or captured, tanks and aircraft destroyed, it's hard to imagine there are any troops or materiel left in Russia to fight. Trouble is, the Russian denials of those astronomical figures are not entirely convincing. So when Hitler says he's going to celebrate Christmas in Moscow, well, we have to take him seriously."

"And there's nothing we can do about it?"

"What do you suggest? We're only just putting our army back together after last year's debacle. Oh, we're sending them what we can, stuff which really we could use ourselves, and the Yanks are doing their bit with Lend-Lease, but we have to face facts. It's been a hard year. Everything went wrong in Greece, and that had a domino effect on our campaign in North Africa . . . I suppose the old HMS *Hood* for the new *Bismarck* was a gain, but my God there was a flap on when that was happening!"

"You know," Hector remarked. "You sound very much like a man who thinks Hitler has won this war."

"I wouldn't bet my pension that he hasn't, in real terms, old man."

Hector was met on the dock by an officer from the War Office. "You're to get a gong. Did you know that?"

"Yes," Hector said. "When can I see my wife?"

"You'll have some leave as soon as you've been debriefed. There's a lot the brass want to talk about."

"Cheer me up," Hector groaned.

At least he was allowed to make a telephone call. "Hector?" Jocelyn's voice sounded different. "Oh, my God! Hector! Where are you?"

"London. You didn't know I was on my way home?"

"They said they were working on it."

"Well, I suppose the whole thing had to be fairly hush-hush. But are you all right?"

"Yes! Yes, I'm all right." Now she sounded breathless.

"And Alan?"

"He's fine."

"I can hardly wait to see him."

"Yes," she said. "You'll love him."

It was almost, he thought, as if she knew about Agnes. But there was no way she could. And he simply had to stop thinking about Agnes. But there was no way he could. It might have been better if she had been killed. Then it would be done. But before leaving Switzerland he had learned that she had been sent to a concentration camp. No one really knew what conditions were like in those camps. Some of the rumours propagated by Western journalists were horrifying. Others described them as no more than almost open prisons.

But either way, they were prisons. And Hector could not forget that when the British had first instituted concentration camps in South Africa during the Boer War for the confinement of the Boer women and children, although so far as he knew there had been no actual ill-treatment of the inmates, a high proportion had died from malnutrition and disease. The thought of Agnes's splendid body shrinking to a bag of bones was horrifying.

But he had an idea.

First though, there was the debriefing. Hector did not have much to offer them; in any event he had been debriefed by British agents in Switzerland before beginning his journey home, and he had no intention of telling these cold-faced officers anything of his relationship with Agnes other than that he had persuaded her to help him escape. His methods of doing that they would have to deduce for themselves. Then there was a visit to the War Office, where, to his great delight, he met his uncle, now Sir George Brand, a tall, heavy figure. George Brand and his Scottish cousin, William, had been the best of friends as young men, and George had perhaps felt the loss of William, killed in 1917, more severely than any other member of the family. Hector had been only three when his father had been killed, and he had no memory of him. His Uncle George had always seemed like a father to him.

"Hector!" George Brand shook hands. "Good to have you back. Fully fit?"

"Just about."

George gestured him to a chair. "That was some adventure."

"Briefly. I don't call kicking my heels in Switzerland an adventure. Will you tell me about Joss?"

George's face assumed a guarded expression. "Haven't you been kept up to date?"

"I want to see her."

"First things first. There'll be an investiture some time soon. Now, as to the future. You were released from internment in Switzerland on compassionate grounds, because of the illness of your wife. However, you have in effect given your parole to the Swiss Government that you will not again fight the Germans. The exact phrase used was 'bear arms' for the duration of this conflict."

"You can't be serious!" Hector protested.

"I'm afraid I am. His Majesty's Government feels obliged to act with complete honesty in your case, because if it does not it may be prejudicing the chances of other officers, or men, trying to get home. However, while we intend to honour the terms of your release, we also intend to interpret them literally. So, you cannot again bear arms into battle, i.e., against Germany."

"But I can go to North Africa and fight the Italians," Hector said eagerly.

"I'm afraid not. The Italians are included in the term enemy. In any event, there are now sizeable German forces in North Africa, stiffening the Italians. No, no, your future is on the staff, helping us plan the defeat of Germany."

"The staff!" Hector's face fell.

"As one of my assistants, Hector."

"Oh, well, Uncle George, that will be magnificent! But what I know about staff work wouldn't cover half the back of a postage stamp."

"Don't sell yourself short, Hector. Actual staff work, you'll learn. Usefulness you already possess. Things may be looking pretty grim at the present, but we intend to beat

130

Hitler, no matter how long it takes. And the only way we are going to beat the devil is by returning to Europe in force. It may not be practical for years, but it is going to be practical one day. I have been given the task of producing a format which will work. Of invading Europe."

Hector gave a low whistle. "That's a very tall order."

"Yes, it is. But it's the only way. And you, with your practical experience of fighting in France, are going to be very useful to our plans. Do you accept the job?"

"Well, of course I do."

George grinned. "As there's nothing better going, eh? Being on the staff is about the quickest way to make brigadier. Now, you'll spend the night with us, as you can't get up to Scotland before tomorrow."

"My God, where are my manners?" Hector cried. "What about Harry?"

"Harry is fit and well. He's back in service."

"In England?"

"In Malaya, as a matter of fact."

"Malaya?" Hector was incredulous.

"We're building up the garrison there, in view of Japanese threats. The best way to keep the little yellow men down is to make them understand that we intend to fight for what's ours, if we have to."

"Malaya," Hector said thoughtfully. "Do you think there'll be a scrap there, Uncle George?"

"Frankly, no. I have no doubt at all that the Japs want to grab as much of French Indo-China as they can, but with this ongoing war in China I don't see them wanting to get involved with us as well. You're better off here, Hector."

"Yes, sir. And Constance, and the boy?"

"Ah . . ." George Brand smoothed his thinning hair. "I'm afraid they've split up. Harry and Constance."

"Eh?"

131

"Well . . . I always had my doubts about that. Shotgun weddings are always on a hiding to nothing. The pity is, it being a shotgun wedding, there's the boy. We don't see much of him, now that she's gone home to mother."

"I'm quite shocked," Hector confessed. "I mean, Joss and I introduced them."

"And it was my idea that you do so," George Brand reminded him. "To get Harry's mind off his other problems. I had no idea things would progress quite so far and fast as to lead to a pregnancy. Modern youth!"

"But there must be some reason why they separated?"

"Neither one wanted to talk about it much, but I gather there was some woman Harry met in France, before he found out he had to marry Constance. Ah, well, water under the bridge." He looked at his watch. "Time we were leaving."

"Yes, sir." Hector's mind was still reeling at the news. But then he remembered his own problems. He'd never have a better chance than now. Some woman Harry had met in France, who had led to the break-up of his marriage! Some woman! But he would never forgive himself if he just abandoned Agnes. "By the way, have you seen Jim Davison recently?"

"Who?" George was tidying up his desk.

"That American correspondent."

"Jim Davison? I've never heard of him."

"But he said he was a friend of the family?"

"When did he say this?"

"He visited me in Germany. At the castle where I was being held. Claimed to be an old friend of the family."

"An American?" George Brand was incredulous.

"Yes. Well . . . I wonder what he was up to?"

"American," George said in disgust.

The house outside Bath was like stepping back through the

mirror into another world. There was some bomb damage in the vicinity, but all of that was more than a year old, and the house itself was undamaged. "We lost some panes of glass," Juliette Brand told him. "But that was soon put right." She also had not changed a bit and remained a tall, handsome, fair woman, although her once splendid yellow hair was now heavily tinged with grey. "It is so good to have you back," she said, hugging him again and again. "We were so worried. When are you going home?"

"Tomorrow, I hope."

"We've been so worried there too," Juliette said. "But with you home, everything will be all right, I'm sure."

Hector would have liked to find out if his aunt knew anything more about what had happened in Edinburgh than his uncle, but they were interrupted by George announcing, "Louise is home." He grinned. "I got her a pass, to meet you."

"Hector!" Louise screamed, throwing herself into his arms. "Oh, you darling man!"

They went through the rigmarole of how well he was looking and how pleased Jocelyn would be to have him back. "Lou was actually the last of us to see Joss before her accident," Juliette explained.

Hector looked at his cousin, who flushed. "She was fine then. But she was upset that you were wounded. I think it was preying on her mind."

"Lou!" her mother said severely, at the suggestion that Jocelyn might have jumped for any other reason than to escape her molesters.

"Well . . . I just thought Hector might like to know."

"Does the name Davison mean anything to either of you?" George asked at dinner.

"Davison?" Juliette inquired.

Louise dropped her glass, but caught it again before it

smashed, although wine spilled everywhere. "Oh, Lou!" Juliette admonished.

"I'll fix it." Louise ran to the kitchen for a cloth, hurried back, pink-cheeked. "Who's this Davison?"

"Over to you, Hector," George invited.

Hector explained about Davison's visit to the *schloss*, and the man's claim to be a friend of the family.

"Of all the cheek!" Louise declared.

"Oh, I agree," Hector said. "But I really would like to find him. There's something I think he might be able to do for me."

"An American?" George asked, as critical as ever.

It was after dinner, when George and Hector had smoked their cigars and they had all drunk coffee and brandy, that Louise went on the terrace. "It's a simply magnificent night," she called. "Come and see, Hector."

"Don't catch your death," Juliette admonished.

The late summer air was in fact distinctly cold. Hector closed the door and the black-out curtain behind him, joined Louise at the balustrade. "Why do you want to find Jim Davison?" she asked.

He frowned down at her. "Don't tell me you know him?"

"We're acquainted, yes. Oh, you may as well know, because Jocelyn will tell you. We had an affair."

"You . . . have had an affair?"

She tilted her head back. "Do you think I'm incapable?"

"Of course I don't. It's just that . . ."

"Nice girls don't do that sort of thing. Believe me, I know that now. Why exactly do you want to see Jimmy?"

"I told you, he came to see me in Germany . . ." he checked. "You sent him!"

"In a manner of speaking," Louise said.

"Well, anyway, he seems to be able to go wherever he likes in Germany, see who he wishes. I believe he may be able to find out something about the person who helped me to escape, and who I very much fear has been sent to a concentration camp. I'd like to find if she . . . if this person is all right."

Louise raised her eyebrows. "A German woman helped you to escape?"

"Yes. What's so alarming about that?"

"Alarming isn't the word I had in mind. You going to tell Joss about it?"

"Ah . . . I would say so. But I am gaining the impression that right now Joss has to be played minute by minute."

"Yes," Louise said thoughtfully. "Jimmy didn't mention anything about, well . . . anything, when you met him?"

"God save me from women who can't say what they mean. He didn't say anything about a relationship with you, if that's what's worrying you. I got the impression that he was a considerable gentleman, even if he is a Yank."

Louise licked her lips. "I'll give you the last address I have for him. It's an hotel in London. He may still be using it."

"That's great. Do I understand that you are no longer seeing him?"

"He," Louise said, "is no longer seeing me."

Hector went up to town the next day. He preferred not to think, and certainly not to pass judgement about his young cousin having had an affair. He did not feel he was in a position to pass judgements about anything. As for telling Jocelyn about Agnes, that would most certainly have to be played by ear.

His mind was obsessed with the thought of Jocelyn, so lovely, so innocent, so essentially *pure*, being attacked by a bunch of drunks. But his mind was also obsessed with the memory of Agnes. Did he love the girl? Had he loved her? He thought that was likely. But that could merely be guilt, that she had behaved with the utmost gallantry to save him, and was now suffering herself. He wondered if Jocelyn would be able to understand that?

From Paddington he telephoned the hotel where Louise had suggested James Davison might be found. "Why, yes, sir," said the clerk. "Mr Davison has a room booked with us permanently, for his use whenever he is in England. I'm afraid he's out right now."

"Do you expect him back?"

"Oh, indeed. He invariably returns just before lunch."

"It is most important that I contact him," Hector said. "I'd like to come along and wait for him, if that is all right with you."

"Of course, sir," the clerk said smoothly.

He was given a seat in the hotel lounge, where no doubt an eye could be kept on him, although the hotel staff were obviously very relieved to see that he wore the uniform of an officer. And promptly at twelve, Davison, having been alerted by the reception clerk, came in. "Well, glory be! I didn't expect to see you again, Colonel. So you did get out, after all." His tone, and his look, were watchful.

"I made my own arrangements," Hector said.

"Well, congratulations." Davison shook hands, sat down, and called for two gins. "When did you get back?"

"Yesterday. I was interned in Switzerland for several months until my people could get me out."

"Yeah. Seen your wife?"

"I'm going up to Edinburgh tonight. You know she had an accident?"

"I heard something," Davison said. "Well, I'm sure she'll be glad to see you. Nice of you to look me up, Colonel, and

I'm really sorry I didn't see my way to help you in Germany. I guess one of those little girls gave you a hand, eh?"

"Yes," Hector said.

"Must've been fun. Well, like I said, it's great to see you again, Colonel, and best congratulations on getting out. But I have a luncheon date, so . . ." he finished his drink.

"I need your help," Hector said.

Davison had got up. Now he sat down again. "You are asking for *my* help?"

Hector grinned. "So I asked for it once before, and didn't get it. Now I'm asking again."

"What kind of help?"

"As you surmised, one of the Patten girls, the eldest, Agnes, helped me get out. But she didn't make it."

Davison gave a low whistle. "Now there's a real shame. She was a class act."

"Yes," Hector said.

Davison did not look the least embarrassed. "So she told you I made a pass. Well, it's a weakness of mine, I guess. But maybe I was just making sure her feelings for you were genuine."

"Maybe you were," Hector agreed. "But I'm sure you'll be interested in what happened to her. She wasn't killed. She was wounded and captured. I know it sounds like mock melodrama, but real life is so often like that. I did want to stay and shoot it out beside her. She persuaded me that would be a waste of my life. So . . . here I am."

"Carrying a heavy stone around your neck. I can see that. The Germans have a habit of executing traitors, pretty quick."

"I'm told she hasn't been executed, but has been sent to a concentration camp."

"I'm not sure she's better off. Poor kid."

"I would really like to know if she's alive, how she's

faring, and if possible to let her know I haven't forgotten her."

Davison frowned. "Me?"

"You seem able to get in and out of Germany at will, and go where you like when you're in."

Davison stroked his chin. "I'd need an angle."

"It's there. An article, on concentration camps."

"No dice. The Germans wouldn't play with that one. But, maybe, an article on what makes a nice, wholesome, loyal Nazi girl help a swinehound of an Englander to escape . . ." he grinned. "Right?"

"Anything you can think up," Hector said. "Just get to her." He finished his own drink. "I'm quite prepared to pay for your services."

"Nope, that won't be necessary."

"That's very generous of you."

"Not at all. I figure I owe you one."

"You'll have to explain that."

"Well, I didn't help you last time, eh? This'll makes us even." He stood up again. "But there is one thing I'd like from you."

Hector stood up also. "Name it."

"I'd like you to promise that you'll remember what I'm doing to help you. No matter what may crop up in the future."

"My dear fellow, I shall certainly do that."

"No matter what," Davison repeated. "That's crucial."

"No matter what," Hector agreed, and watched the American leave the lounge.

What a strange fellow, he said to himself.

Chapter Seven

The Quest

The truck rolled to a stop before high wooden gates, set in an equally high barbed-wire fence, which stretched out of sight in either direction. The women moved, restlessly; over the gate there was a large sign, Strength Through Joy. They looked at each other, but no one spoke; there were four guards in the back of the truck with them, and the prisoners had early on learned that to speak meant a blow on the buttocks or in the kidneys from the rubber truncheon each guard carried. Sometimes they were beaten for just looking too hard. Actually, speech was not necessary. The twelve women had become intensely intimate over the past week, without ever exchanging a word. They had shared too much to remain strangers.

The truck was moving again, as the gates swung in. Then it stopped on the edge of a large courtyard, surrounded by low buildings. "Out, out!" bawled the guards.

The women jumped down. One of them, whose name was Christina, was middle-aged and overweight; she stumbled to her knees and was immediately hit three times by the guards. She screamed in pain and Agnes hastily helped her up, to receive a stinging blow herself across the buttocks which brought tears to her eyes, but they were tears of anger and humiliation as much as pain. She could still feel anger and humiliation.

"Line up!" a guard was shouting, and Agnes realized this was a woman. The male guards had got back into the truck and the truck was turning. They had entered an entirely female world. They stood in a line, to attention, as they were surrounded by these new guards; their faces were cold, and like their male counterparts, they carried rubber truncheons to supplement the pistols hanging from their belts.

The prisoners waited, standing to attention, for the arrival of the camp commandant. They stood for perhaps half an hour, then the door of the nearest and largest building opened and the commandant came down the steps and towards them. Even staring straight head, Agnes was terribly aware of the woman, who was tall and strongly built, in contrast to her adjutant, who was short and plump. Equally, the commandant was yellow-haired, where her assistant was a brunette. She was also an extremely handsome woman, if one made allowance for the somewhat severe expression. Her features were strong, with a good bone structure, her eyes were blue, her mouth a flat line. She wore uniform and a sidecap, and like all her people, a holster hung from her belt.

She walked slowly down the line of prisoners, staring at each one, not speaking. When she reached Agnes, she remained staring at her for several seconds, while her gaze slowly drifted down from Agnes's face to her ankles, and then back up again. At last she spoke, "Number Six," she said. Six was the number stencilled to Agnes's prison blouse.

The adjutant made a note. Oh, lord, Agnes thought; was she going to be singled out for special treatment?

The commandant continued down the line. "Number Ten," she said, and the adjutant wrote it down. Helga was the second best-looking girl in the group. Agnes knew *she* was by far the best looking.

The commandant turned away, and the guards began

shouting. "To the baths. Quickly. To the baths. On the double."

They had learned what that meant in prison, and obediently broke into a trot, across the courtyard to the bathroom. At the door they were stopped, and then made to enter, one by one. "Strip," commanded the guard inside the door. They obeyed without hesitation; they had learned to obey. "In there," said the guard.

They stepped into the showers. There was no soap, but several powerful jets of water, which scored their flesh as they struck them, had them staggering, breathless. The water was also very cold, and it was a cool autumnal day. That also took their breath away, had them gasping. Agnes shuddered, less from the cold and the force of the water than because when she looked through the open door of the shower room she saw the commandant standing there, watching her – and only her.

Then the water was switched off, and they were herded through into another room. They were not given towels, but were left there shivering while the first of them was led forward and made to sit on a table, while two women, armed with electric shears, scissors and a razor, proceeded to remove all her hair. For a moment the woman did not understand what was happening as her hair was gathered on the top of her head and there cut off close to the scalp in a vast tuft. She stared at it as it was thrown past her face to the floor, and then began to weep as the electric sheers were driven up the nape of her neck and began surging through the rest of her hair. Agnes instinctively put her hand up to her own splendid, thick tresses, and felt the girl Helga against her. Unlike Agnes's dark Bavarian colouring, Helga was a brilliant blonde, but her hair was just as thick. "Oh, God," Helga whispered. "Oh, God!"

For the first woman was now entirely bald, and was being

stretched on her back, her legs pulled apart, so that the women could attend to her groin, which they did with much physical probing accompanied by laughter. "I'm going to faint," Helga said.

"Fall down and they'll beat you," Agnes warned.

Her heart was pounding now, as the first woman was dragged off the table and thrust through another door into what seemed to be the open air. The thought of having to go outside, completely hairless, was nauseating. And she and Helga were only three away from the front, as the next woman was marched forward. "Halt there!"

Everyone froze as the adjutant strode into their midst. "Numbers Six and Ten," the adjutant said. "Outside."

For a moment no one moved; without their prison uniforms they had forgotten whose numbers those were. Then Agnes remembered. "That's you and me," she said, and grasped Helga's arm. Whatever fate was in store for them had to be better than to be cropped and shaved.

"Outside," the adjutant repeated, indicating that they should return through the shower room. They stumbled past her, hesitated where their prison clothes remained piled on the floor. "Out," the adjutant said behind them.

They looked at each other, then emerged into the sunlight and the chill breeze. There were several guards about, but at least no men.

"Over there," the adjutant commanded, pointing at the largest of the houses. The one from which the commandant had emerged to inspect them. "On the double."

They ran across the stony ground, hurting their feet, but not daring to hesitate. "Go in," the adjutant commanded, as they checked at the closed door. Panting, they opened it and stumbled inside, into warmth, and a room filled with several desks and several trim-looking female secretaries, writing or typing away, all of whom stopped work to gaze at the two naked, shivering, panting girls. "Go in," the adjutant said again, indicating the next door.

Agnes opened it and they stepped into another large office, but this contained only a single desk, behind which was a chair, in which sat the commandant. There were also several filing cabinets, and in the far corner another door. The commandant leaned back in her chair, surveying the girls. Behind them the door closed, as the adjutant took her place. The commandant continued to gaze at them for several seconds, while their breathing slowly settled down. Then she flicked open one of the files on her desk. "Helga Mueller," she remarked. "Guilty of disseminating anti-Nazi literature. Your sentence is severe imprisonment, for life. Do you know that what means, Helga Mueller?" Helga's lips were puckering. She could not speak, so she shook her head, her still-wet hair flopping to and fro. "It means that you should be flogged, once a week, before the assembled inmates, for the rest of your life," the commandant said.

Tears dribbled down Helga's cheeks. "But I can save you from that," the commandant said. "A pretty girl like you should not have her backside marked, except by men. Do you not agree? I am sending you to a military brothel in Berlin. There you will be well cared for. All you have to do is lie on your back, or on your front, and let men play with you."

Helga inhaled, slowly. It was easy to see, from the state of her hands and her hair and her general demeanour, not to mention the clothes she had been wearing when she had arrived at the prison, that she belonged to at least a middle-class family. Thus despite the excesses of the regime, she had no doubt retained a middle-class morality. Which she was now being required to discard along with her clothes. "You could say thank you," the commandant recommended.

"Thank you, Frau Commandant." Helga's voice was faint.

The commandant nodded. "Take her outside and have her dress," she told her adjutant. The adjutant looked at Agnes, and licked her lips. It was a gesture Agnes did not much care for. Then the adjutant touched Helga on the shoulder. She too looked at Agnes, as if wondering why she was not coming. Then she left the room, the adjutant behind her. The door was closed.

Agnes remained at attention before her desk. But she could not stop herself shivering from time to time. The commandant opened a second file. "Now you, Fräulein von Patten," she said, "have been convicted of treason. I really do not see how you escaped the death penalty, even if your father did accept the blame for what you did." She looked up. "Or perhaps I do. I imagine it would be an entrancing sight, to watch you wriggling your life away at the end of a length of piano wire. But it would only be available once. Someone as good-looking as you can surely be put to better use."

She got up and came round the desk. Agnes tensed her muscles and forced herself to stand still, as the commandant stroked her wet hair, then her neck, then her breasts, then her buttocks and pubes, and then, suddenly and violently, grasped her neck again and brought her face forward to kiss her on the lips. "Oh, indeed," the commandant said. "They would be very happy to have you in a military brothel. Does that thought excite you, Fräulein von Patten?"

"I . . ." Agnes licked her lips. "If that is what you wish, Frau Commandant."

The commandant returned behind her desk and sat down. "It is something to be considered. Would you not rather stay here?"

Agnes stared at her. "As an inmate, Frau Commandant? I think I would rather be a whore."

"Suppose you stayed here as a servant," the commandant suggested. "As my personal servant. Think of it, Agnes. Good food, a glass of wine if you behave yourself, no labour and no beatings. And a soft bed to sleep in."

"What would my duties be, Frau Commandant?" Agnes asked, as ingenuously as she could.

"They would be to keep my apartment . . ." the commandant gestured at the door behind her, "clean and tidy. And . . . to amuse me."

They gazed at each other. She supposes I am as innocent as I look, Agnes thought. But survival was her business, until Hector could come back for her. That would happen one day, and she needed to preserve her health and her beauty until that day. That would hardly be a practical proposition in a military brothel. "Does that prospect please you, Agnes?" the commandant asked.

Agnes drew a deep breath. "It pleases me very much, Frau Commandant."

Hector had not been able to tell Jocelyn which train he would be arriving on, thus there was no one on the platform at Edinburgh Central to meet him when the overnight train from King's Cross arrived just after dawn. He had only a valise, so did not bother with a taxi as he walked to the platform for the Glasgow stopper. It was nine when he got off at Drumbooee, and walked down the road to his house. With the black-out curtains still drawn, the house looked deserted. But the gate creaked as he swung it open, and a moment later the front door opened as well, and Jocelyn came outside.

He went up to her, put down the valise, took her into

his arms. He had forgotten how good she felt, how she seemed to fit against him, hilltop and valley, how gently moist were her lips and tongue. "God!" she whispered. "To have you back!"

"To be back. Is . . . ?"

"Waiting for you, inside."

Alan was eighteen months old, struggling to get on to his sturdy feet. Mary Macartney stood by, proudly, while her son-in-law lifted the boy into his arms.

"I'm your daddy," Hector said.

"Daddy? Hallo!"

Hector looked at Jocelyn. "He's growing up very fast," she said. Hector kissed the boy again.

"It's time for his bath," Jocelyn said.

"May I help?"

"Oh, please!"

Mary Macartney hugged him and kissed him and poured him a cup of coffee before he followed Jocelyn upstairs.

Mary could recognise that there was so much to be said, between the two of them. "I'll do the clearing up," she volunteered after he had finished his breakfast. "I'll bring some coffee into the lounge."

Hector and Jocelyn held hands as they sat together on the settee, Alan crawling around their feet, chattering happily. "Would you like a whisky?" Jocelyn asked.

"At ten in the morning?" But he did feel like a drink. "If you'll join me."

"I will." She poured two glasses, sat beside him again, brushed her glass against his. "I never thought I was going to see you again."

"Is that why . . ." he bit his lip.

"I didn't jump, Hector. Not into the sea, intentionally

There were some men," Jocelyn explained. "Sailors, returning from shore leave. They were drunk, and I was alone in the dock area, and I suppose they thought I was a tart. I . . . I was a bit confused, I suppose. So when they surrounded me, I just wanted to get away, and I jumped over that wall. Only . . ." she forced a smile. "There was nothing there. Save water."

"Bastards!" Hector said. "But you didn't report this."

"What good would it have done? I couldn't have identified any of them. And it would have meant, well, going public, I suppose. Appearing in court."

"And explaining why you were there at all," he said softly. She shot him a quick glance, drank some whisky. "Don't you think I'm entitled to know about that?" he asked.

"There are so many things that we are both entitled to know about," she said, softly.

"Coffee!" Mary Macartney bustled into the room behind her voice and her coffee tray, paused for only a moment at the recognition of a crisis, then sat down with them, with great determination. She had a lot of questions to ask, about the state of the war, about London, about the other Brands, and, inevitably, about the state of play between Harry Brand and his wife.

"I feel so guilty about that," Jocelyn said.

"I think Uncle George and Aunt Juliette accept it as almost inevitable," Hector said. "In all the circumstances."

"Apparently Harry had some affair with a Frenchwoman, before he even knew that, well . . . he would have to marry Constance," Jocelyn said, delicately. But she was staring at her husband as she spoke.

"Yes," her mother said, sadly. "So possibly there was no love involved at all. Just lust. Terrible thing, lust. But in the long run, it's what makes the world go round. More than love." She gazed at daughter and son-in-law from beneath

147

arched eyebrows. "Why don't I take Alan for a walk? Then, ah . . . you could lie down if you wished, Hector. You must be very tired, after travelling all night."

"I am, as a matter of fact," Hector said, and stood up, holding out his hand.

"This is awfully kind of you, Mummy." Jocelyn said.

"It's time he had a proper walk," Mary declared. "Come along, Alan, my boy. Let's get your coat."

"I'm glad you're home, Daddy," Alan said, and Hector gave him another hug.

Mary Macartney kissed them both, and they stood in the doorway to watch her push the pram through the gate. Then they held hands as they went up the stairs. They didn't look at each other. "Are you pleased with your son?" Jocelyn asked.

"I could never tell you how pleased. Did I ever tell you how proud I am of you?" Hector asked.

"Not since you got back." She opened the bedroom door, switched on the light, leaving the curtains drawn to shut them out from the day.

"And there were no complications?"

She glanced at him. "At the birth? Not one. Dr Smithies said I was born for childbearing."

"Then maybe we should try again."

"I'd like that. I feel like a virgin again," she confessed.

"Then let's pretend you are." He took her in his arms, this time for a real kiss, seeking her tongue, allowing his hands to roam up and down her back. She made no protest, kissed him back, but there was a stiffness about her body which did not indicate total acceptance of the situation. He released her, went to the wardrobe, looked inside at his civilian clothes hanging there. "I wonder if I can still get into these," he said.

"I would say with ease. You've lost weight."

"I lost more. But I put it back on in Switzerland." He began to undress, while Jocelyn wandered about the room. Carefully he removed his uniform, hanging it in the wardrobe, and then his underclothes.

"My God," she muttered. She was standing behind him.

"I don't get to see them very often, actually by choice," Hector said. "I should have warned you."

She came closer, touched his back with one finger. "Do they still hurt?"

"Only when it rains." He turned, suddenly, before she could step away, held her against his naked body. "I feel quite virginal too."

She could feel him rising between them, licked her lips. "We'll have to hurry slowly."

"I don't recall us doing that on our wedding night." He released her and got into bed, but remained on top of the covers, watching her. She sat down to take off her shoes, lifted her skirt to release and roll down her stockings.

"I'd forgotten what splendid legs you have," he remarked.

She flushed, stood up to lift her jumper over her head. "Do you want to talk about your escape?" she asked, her face for a moment hidden.

"Yes," he said. "But not right now."

She laid the jumper on a chair, turned her back on him to loosen her skirt and let it slide round her ankles. "I suppose you're very grateful to the people who helped you," Jocelyn remarked, still with her back to him as she lifted her vest over her head.

"I am. They took an enormous risk." He gazed at her breasts, only half visible, but so large and comforting.

"They were Germans?"

"I was in Germany, darling." He could not prevent a slight touch of acerbity entering his tone, because now he could have no doubt that she knew more about his escape than

149

she was supposed to, and was afraid to come right out and say it.

Still with her back to him, she slipped down her knickers. If she had large breasts, her buttocks were even more splendid. Agnes had had such slim buttocks. "I know. I'm sorry." She reached for her nightdress.

"No," he said. "I'd only have to take it off. I want to look at you, Joss. It's been eighteen months." Slowly she turned, her hair moving gently on her shoulders. "A man can only dream, so much," he said.

She came across the room towards him, stood by the bed. His put his arm round her hips and brought her down to sit beside him, facing him. Gently he stroked round her nipple with his finger. He was retaking possession of his wife, as surely he was entitled to do. But as he was an officer and a gentleman, he was only entitled if she wished it. Jocelyn never moved, for some seconds. Then she leaned forward and kissed him on the lips, allowed her body to stretch out on top of him. "I have dreamed, too."

Passion, overlaid by tension, produced exhaustion. The passion was there, again and again and again. They had never made love, never had sex on such a scale before. Then Hector slept heavily, but then there were more dreams. Of Agnes, lying in the snow, the rifle laid across the wounded border guard's body. And then of Agnes, standing naked beside his bed as Jocelyn had done a few hours earlier. Agnes had had none of Jocelyn's voluptuousness. But Agnes had been utterly beautiful. What was happening to that beauty, now? He looked at his watch; twelve, and there was noise downstairs where Mary was entertaining Alan. He got up to go to the bathroom, heard the light switched on behind him. Jocelyn joined him, and they went back to bed together.

"I suppose we should get dressed and rescue Mother," he suggested.

She lay with her head on his shoulder. "Would you like to tell me?"

"How much do you know?"

"I know about a girl named Agnes."

His head turned, and she rolled away from him, to lie on her back. "Davison," he said. "By Christ, Davison! When did you meet him? I know he's had an affair with Lou. She told me."

"Had?"

"She says it's over."

"Thank God for that. Yes, I . . . we asked him to see if he could find out how you were, where you were. We only knew that you had been wounded and captured . . . I was so worried, Hector." She was still staring at the ceiling.

"So he found me, and came back, and told you about Agnes." Hector lay on his back himself. "What did he tell you?"

"That you seemed to have struck up quite a relationship. And that she was very beautiful."

"Both perfectly true. Would you believe me if I told you I struck up that relationship to get her to help me escape?"

"If you tell me that is the truth, I will believe you, Hector."

How simple to end the problem here and now. Hector thought. A simple lie, which would in any event only be half a lie. But he had never been able to lie. "It was the truth," he said. "In the beginning. I conceived it my duty to escape if I could, and I knew I would never have a better opportunity than while I was in a private home rather than a prison camp. It was simply a matter of regaining my strength . . . and seducing one of the sisters. Did Davison mention the other sister?"

"Yes," Jocelyn said. "He said you had a relationship with her, too."

"I considered it," Hector said. "Agnes was clearly the better bet, as she was older and more experienced. I mean, she was more capable of handling the situation." Shit, what was he saying?

"So you seduced her."

He sighed. "Yes, I did. In cold blood. And she helped me escape. And here I am. I did what I had to do, Joss."

"I know," Jocelyn said. "But there was more, wasn't there?"

He rolled on his side, to face her. "I'm a human being, not a monster. I've never seduced anyone before. You know I wasn't a virgin when we got married. But any sex I had had was either paid for or a matter of mutual, irrational passion. To set out to win the heart and mind of a girl a dozen years younger than myself, knowing that I was going to discard her at the end of it. I would have been a hundred times a cad if I'd been able to do that in cold blood."

"So you fell in love with her."

"Not as I love you, Joss."

"But you yearn after her."

"No," he said, not sure he was telling the truth. "I fear for her. She would have crossed the border with me, but she was wounded and demanded to be left behind. So I left her behind. Now I do not know if I acted the coward or not. What I do know is that she was captured, and has been sent to a concentration camp. For God's sake, Joss, whatever she suffers is because of the help she gave me, an enemy of her country."

"Do you think she fell in love with you?" Jocaleyn asked.

"I am bound to think that."

"Well, one would have to say that she is fortunate, in being sent to prison instead of being executed."

"She was sent to prison instead of being executed because her father blew his brains out when he realized what she had done. Can you imagine the effect that must have had on the girl?"

"It would have destroyed me," Jocelyn said.

"Then perhaps you can understand the burden of guilt I am carrying. As for these camps . . . nobody really knows what goes on in them."

At last she turned over to face him. "Why are you telling me all this?"

"Because you asked," he reminded her. "And because . . . well, I have asked this chap Davison to see if he can find out exactly where she is, and how she is. After all, he's involved. He met her when he came looking for me."

Jocelyn sat up. "You've seen Davison?"

"Yes. I saw him in London, yesterday." Hector sat up as well, frowning. "Do you know something about him I don't? Come to think of it, he made a rather enigmatic remark just before we parted. Can't say I really took to the fellow, but he's the only chance I have of finding out what happened to Agnes."

Jocelyn turned away from him and lay on her face. He leaned over her. "Tell me you forgive me. I wanted to get home, by hook or by crook. I suppose I overestimated my emotional strength."

Jocelyn rolled over again to face him. "Did James . . . did Davison tell you that he knew me?"

"Well, he claimed that when he visited me in Germany. I didn't press the matter."

She licked her lips. "But you knew it was I who sent him to find you." She gave a half smile. "Just as you have sent him to find this young lady of yours."

"I don't think he minds. Getting involved in personal

153

stories is his life's blood. He's probably going to write about it in some American tabloid."

"That wouldn't bother you?"

"He can write what he likes, as far as I'm concerned. As long as it doesn't harm us. Or Agnes. You haven't said you forgive me, yet."

"There is nothing to forgive," Jocelyn said, almost fiercely. "You did what you had to do. That is all one can ever do, what one has to, at the time."

He kissed her. "That's a profound statement. You have no idea how glad I am to have it off my chest. Let's go and see how Mother is getting on." She got out of bed, began filling a bath. He stood behind her, stroked her shoulders. He meant what he had said, felt that a huge burden had been lifted from his mind. And from hers? He couldn't be sure. She trembled as he touched her.

James Davison thought that the Patten *schloss* was one of the most beautiful places in the world. Not the building, which was a conventional enough German castle, or the grounds, which were no less conventional, but because of the backdrop of the mountains. When he had first visited here, just over a year ago now, those mountains had been covered in snow. Now, at the beginning of December 1941, they were again covered in snow. An entire year, just like that, and it seemed like yesterday.

It had been a long year, dominated by Hitler's determination to settle with Russia before finishing England. Assuming that the Fuehrer did not regard his non-aggression pact with Russia as worth the paper on which it was printed, and further assuming that he supposed the Russians felt the same, there was sound strategical reasoning behind his move. James had felt at the time that he might be making a mistake, remembering the disasters that had overtaken so many other famous generals and leaders when they had invaded Russia. But he had to admit that he had been proved wrong: it certainly looked as if the Germans would achieve their aim of occupying Moscow and bringing down the Stalinist regime by the end of the year. That might be interesting; James had never been to Moscow. But he was well satisfied with what he had achieved. Save for that young woman's obvious distress. And then to attempt suicide, because he had no doubt that was what had happened . . . although he thoroughly enjoyed the challenge of women, he wished he knew more about what made the darlings tick.

And here was an entirely new set, an entirely new challenge. He stepped out of his car, and the guard on the door of the *schloss* looked at him, inquiringly. "I have come to see Baroness von Patten," he explained. His German was excellent.

"Frau Patten no longer lives here," the guard informed him.

"Ah. Well . . . any member of the family will do."

"None of the family lives here now," the guard said.

"Somebody must," James said, equably.

"I do," said another voice, and he looked at an officer wearing the black uniform and insignia of a colonel in the SS. "My name is Luttmann," the colonel said. "And you are . . . ?"

"James Davison, accredited US war correspondent," James said. "My card."

Luttmann came down the steps, looked at it. "We have met, Herr Davison. Here, on the occasion of Charlotte von Patten's sixteenth birthday party. I was a major then. Do you not remember?"

"Ah . . . yes," Davison said, not sure that he did.

"And what brings you back to Schloss Patten?"

"I happened to be in the vicinity, and I thought I'd look the family up."

"Of course, you are old friends." Luttmann gave a brief smile. "Come in, Herr Davison." He led the way into the castle, and then into Joachim von Patten's study. Servants stood to attention as he passed. "Have a chair. Schnapps?"

"Thank you." James took a chair, accepted the small glass of clear liquid.

"Heil Hitler!" Luttmann said, tossing his down.

"Oh, absolutely." James also drank his at a gulp.

Luttmann refilled their glasses, then sat behind his desk. "You know what has happened to the family?"

"Actually, no. I had heard there was some scandal."

"You will recall that when you visited here for Charlotte's birthday, there was an English officer in residence," Luttmann said.

"Yes, indeed. I remember thinking that it was a bit irregular."

"It was very irregular. But Baron von Patten had friends in high places," Luttmann said, disparagingly. "And it seems that his family owed the family of this British officer some favour. Naturally it was a set-up, as I had deduced all along. So they attempted to get him over the border into Switzerland. It didn't work out, of course. I was too smart for them. Unfortunately, as you may know, the Englander did make his escape."

"I had heard. So what happened to the family?"

"Well, the Baron committed suicide. He blew out his brains, right where you are sitting, Herr Davison."

"I see you've had the covers cleaned," James said, as equably as ever. "What happened to the rest of the family?"

"They were deprived of their nobility, of course. Frau Patten is in a military brothel in Berlin. The son was reduced to the ranks and is serving in Russia."

"There were also two daughters," James ventured.

"Oh, indeed! The young one was also sent to a military brothel." Luttmann grinned. "Would you like to interview her, Herr Davison? I can probably get you a pass. She is a pretty little thing. Or perhaps you prefer the mother?"

"Charlotte was not so pretty as her older sister. Is she also in a military brothel?"

"Ah, no. Agnes Patten is in prison. She was the one deputed to escort the Englander to the border, thus she did actively aid and abet an enemy soldier. She is very fortunate to be alive."

"I'm sure. When you say she is in prison, do you mean prison, or a concentration camp?"

Luttmann sipped his second glass of schnapps. "It is a word invented by the British, widely used in the West. We prefer to regard them as open prisons."

"I would like to see her."

Luttmann raised his eyebrows, then chuckled. "Of course. I remember now. You were very taken with her."

"Was I?"

"Oh, yes, it was very obvious. Do you know, I even formed the impression that you had a . . . relationship?"

"Well, you were mistaken."

"But you have come all this way to find out about her? Do not pretend to me, Herr Davison. You are not the least interested in the rest of the family. You showed no emotion when I told you that your old 'friend' Joachim had shot himself. Or that your other old friend should now be lying on her back with a different man every five minutes, eh? It is Agnes you are after. Why not admit it?"

"I think she would make an interesting subject for an interview," Davison said. "You know, well-born German girl falls for enemy soldier . . . why?"

Luttmann refilled their glasses. "Can it be that you are jealous?"

"My information is that the officer in question is married and has a family," Davison remarked.

"Then he must be a regular Casanova. I did not really take to him, I must admit."

"Perhaps Agnes fell in love with him and sacrificed herself to help him escape," Davison said. "I think the whole business is very romantic."

"I see. And now you would like to denigrate our regime by showing how a German girl can fall for an Englander."

"My dear fellow, if you read any of my articles you would understand that I have never done anything but praise your regime."

Luttmann studied him. "I might be able to arrange a visit to the camp where Agnes Patten is being held."

"I would be very grateful."

"I would like to see her again myself," Luttmann said. "But I have not yet found a reason to do so. An article, yes . . . you would have to show me the text before it was published."

"Willingly, my dear fellow," Davison said,

The December air was crisp and cold, but Luttmann insisted upon being driven in an open tourer. Davison assumed this was to prove his German indifference to climate, as it took them all the next day to reach Berlin. He was at least well insulated, as Luttmann, having made a few telephone calls, insisted upon entertaining him to dinner, at which they had consumed a good deal of wine, and had then given him a bed for the night. He was a detestable fellow, especially as the more he drank the more often he returned to the theme that Davison was only interested in Agnes because they had had an affair. Chance would be a fine thing, Davison thought, as he wrapped his scarf round his face and wore goggles, pulled his cap flap down over his ears, while looking forward to the next comfort stop on the road north.

They stopped at Gestapo Headquarters in Berlin, for Luttmann to go in and collect the permission he had obtained. Davison remained in the car, slapping his hands together, and accepting a glass of schnapps from the driver. The camp was situated quite close to Berlin, but it was dark before they reached it, approaching through a pretty little village, the houses well-to-do and the gardens well kept. There was no evidence of a black-out. "One would hardly think there was a war on," Davison remarked, as the car neared the gates and he could unwrap the scarf and wonder if he still had a nose.

"It is not the Fuehrer's intention to inflict hardship on his people," Luttmann explained, "only to increase their standing in the world. Their power."

"Absolutely," Davison agreed, and looked at the sign above the gate, Strength Through Joy.

Female guards inspected Luttmann's credentials in the light of powerful overhead lamps, then the gate was opened, and they drove through. Davison was interested to see that while the guards were, quite reasonably, armed with pistols in holsters hanging from their belts, they also each carried, also hanging from their belts, thick rubber truncheons. He looked at the buildings, neat and orderly, and at the compounds beyond an inner row of fences, also surrounded by buildings, all illuminated by the glaring lights. "The inmates are locked up for the night, now," Luttman explained. "But during the day they have to work."

"What do they work at?"

"They work in the potato fields, mostly. It is good for them, and it is good for the economy, eh?"

"Oh, quite." Davison tried to envisage Agnes von Patten, so tall and slim and elegant, hair always sweet-smelling, harvesting potatoes. "Do they never escape?"

"Perhaps, sometimes. It is not a good thing to do. You must remember that the people in here are anti-socials. That is, they can expect no help from anyone outside the camp. And when they are brought back, they are subject to punishment. Depending on how often they try to escape, and what damage they may do, either to guards or property in the attempt, such punishment can be quite severe."

"You mean they are beaten?"

Luttmann grinned. "All women need to be beaten from time to time, Herr Davison. They need it, they certainly deserve it, and do you know, my friend, they actually enjoy it!"

"Now is that a fact?" Davison said. "One learns something new every day."

"Bah!" Luttmann said. "You Americans are too soft in your dealing with your women. That is why your country will never be great."

"As I said," Davison commented. "One learns something new every day. In your company, Herr Colonel, it is every minute."

Luttmann, apparently impervious to sarcasm, led the way to the command building. "I telephoned," he told the woman on duty. "I have an appointment with Commandant Hauser."

"Of course, Herr Colonel." She went up the steps and opened the door for them. They entered the immense warmth of the office and were greeted by the adjutant.

"Commandant Hauser is expecting you, Herr Colonel." She glanced at Davison, but made no comment, although his clothes were obviously not made in Germany. She knocked on the inner door, and then opened it. "Herr Colonel Luttman, Frau Commandant."

Gerda Hauser stood up. "Colonel! What brings you to Ravensbruck?"

"This is a friend of mine," Luttmann explained. "A Herr James Davison. Herr Davison is an American journalist."

Commandant Hauser had been smiling; now the smile faded. "What does a journalist want in my camp?" she asked. "No articles are permitted."

"Herr Davison understands that, Frau Commandant. He actually wishes to interview one of your inmates."

"That too is forbidden," Frau Hauser said stiffly.

"I have written permission, from General Heydrich." Luttmann held out the paper.

Hauser took it, opened it, read it, frowned. "You have been granted an interview with Patten? This is very irregular. This woman is a convicted traitor."

"Herr Davison is a confirmed supporter of the regime, Frau Commandant," Luttmann said. "And his article will be approved before it is published."

Once again Hauser glared at Davison. "How do you know of this girl, anyway?"

"I knew her family," Davison explained. "I knew her, when she still had a family."

Hauser snorted, and looked him up and down. Then suddenly she smiled, the harsh features dissolving to become quite attractive. "Very well, Herr American. As you have come all this way to see an old friend. You understand I cannot let you see her alone."

"Of course." Davison was his invariable equable self.

"Then come." To the surprise of both men, when she got up from behind her desk, she went to the inner doorway and opened it, waited. Luttmann raised his eyebrows, then followed her, Davison behind him. They entered a hallway with a polished wooden floor and some quite pleasant pictures on the wall. "This is my home," Hauser explained.

She opened the door at the end of the corridor and showed them into a kitchen/diner, to the right of which there was a lounge. Here again the floor was polished, the paintwork was bright, the pictures artistic and interesting, and the kitchen equipment modern, the warmth intense. But neither man really took their surroundings in as they gazed at the girl who had been standing before the stove, and who turned at their entry, to give a little shriek of alarm. Agnes von Patten wore only a pair of knickers, without discomfort as the house was well heated. Hastily she folded her arms across her breasts, but with her flowing dark hair, her long, slender legs, and flat belly she made a quite entrancing sight. "These gentlemen have come to see you, Agnes," Hauser said. She stood beside the girl, ran her hand up the naked back and into the hair. "But I do think you should put something on." Agnes scuttled from the room. "Such a dear," Hauser said, looking from face to face. "Come into the lounge, and sit down. Will you gentlemen take schnapps?"

Davison and Luttmann gazed at each other. Then they sat together on the settee, rather like two errant schoolboys, Davison thought. Hauser poured four glasses of schnapps. Before she had finished, Agnes returned, having added a loose shirt, but nothing else. Hauser gave them each a glass, including Agnes. "Heil Hitler!" The drinks were tossed off. "You may sit down, Agnes," Hauser said. Agnes sat in a straight chair, knees pressed together. "Herr Davison says he knows you," Hauser said. "Is this true?"

Agnes licked her lips. "He visited my family at the *schloss*, for my sister's birthday." Her voice was low and controlled, but as she spoke she looked at the commandant, not at the two men.

"Ah! Now I think he wishes to know if you are well. Are you well, Agnes?"

"I am very well, Frau Commandant."

"Have you been beaten recently, Agnes?"

"No, Frau Commandant."

"In fact, have you been beaten since coming to Ravensbruck?"

"No, Frau Commandant."

"Show the gentlemen, Agnes. Get up and turn around." Agnes obeyed. "Bend over," Hauser commanded. Agnes bent over. The flesh on the backs of her thighs was silky smooth and unmarked. "Slip down the knickers, Agnes."

Agnes obeyed. Once again the two men gazed at softly rounded, unmarked flesh. They also caught a glimpse of the scar on her lower back where the bullet had entered.

"Pull them up and sit down, Agnes." Agnes obeyed. "Are you well fed, Agnes?"

"Very well fed, thank you, Frau Commandant."

"And you enjoy your drink, don't you? Refill our glasses, Agnes." Agnes got up and refilled all of their glasses; still she did not look at the men. Hauser did, her eyebrows arched. "Is there anything else, gentlemen?"

"Ah . . ." Luttmann looked at Davison who stood up. "No, Frau Commandant. Thank you for your time."

He bowed to Agnes. "And yours, Fräulein."

Hauser stood at the window to watch the car drive out of the compound. "Was that man involved in the escape of the Englander?" she asked.

"I do not think so, Frau Commandant," Agnes said. "Colonel Brand told me he did not really know him, did not know what his purpose was in visiting the *schloss*."

"He was not, by any chance, your lover?"

"Oh, good heavens, no, Frau Commandant."

"Only the Englander, eh?"

Agnes bit her lip.

"I think you are a naughty girl, Agnes," Hauser said. "I have never punished you, have I?" Agnes began to breathe heavily. "Thus those men had to do nothing but admire your bottom," Hauser said. "You have a superb bottom, Agnes. And today I feel like marking it." She went to the cupboard, opened it, and took out a thin cane.

"Please, Frau Commandant," Agnes said, her voice trembling. "I have done nothing wrong. I swear it!"

"I know that you have done nothing wrong since coming here," Hauser said. "But that is not relevant. I feel like caning you. Take off those knickers and bend over that chair." She smiled. "I do not think anyone else will be along to examine your bottom for some time."

"What an experience," Luttmann remarked as he drove back to Berlin. "Women at play! Do you know, I had intended to get between the sheets with that girl the moment the opportunity presented itself."

"She seems to have got between the sheets with Hector Brand," Davison remarked.

"And not with you?"

"No," Davison said. "Not with me, more's the pity."

"You did not know she was a lesbian?"

"I think she was only doing what she was told to by that outsize harpy. Anyone could see that she was terrified."

"I do not think it would be a good idea for you to write that," Luttmann suggested. "Not if you intend to return to Germany. Now, what is happening?" For the street was suddenly crowded with people, shouting and cheering.

"Something, certainly," Davison agreed.

Luttmann pulled in to the side of the street, where a policeman was watching the excited crowds. "You there!"

The policeman clicked to attention. "Herr Colonel!"

"What has happened?"

"Have you not heard, Herr Colonel? This morning at dawn the Japanese air force attacked the American naval base at Pearl Harbor. The entire American Pacific Fleet has been sunk."

Chapter Eight

The Plot

Luttmann looked at Davison, enjoying the expression of total consternation on the American's face. "Did you say the entire fleet?" the colonel asked.

"That is what is being said, Herr Colonel."

"I wonder if you could drop me at our embassy?" Davison said, all thoughts of Agnes forgotten.

"I'm afraid there does seem to have been serious damage," the under-secretary confirmed. "Several battleships have gone down, for certain. We're still waiting for the full facts." He grinned; the two men had known each other for several years. "You going to hurry home for a reposting, Jim?"

"If we're at war with Japan, it kind of makes what's happening in Europe into a side show," Davison said.

"Well, I don't suppose you'd say that if you were a Brit, or a Kraut, or an Ivan," the under-secretary pointed out. "Now, how about lunch? I know a neat little . . ." his phone rang. He listened. "Yes, he's sitting here." He put his hand over the mouthpiece. "I don't know how he knows you're here, James, but there's a fellow called Luttmann on the phone, wants to speak with you."

"He dropped me," Davison explained, and took the phone. "Davison."

"Herr Davison, I am glad I caught you. Is it possible for you to come down to Gestapo Headquarters?"

Davison raised his eyebrows. "Am I under arrest?"

"Oh, good heavens, no, my dear fellow! But there is someone here who is most anxious to meet you. I think there could be considerable profit in it for you. You can lunch here, if you wish."

Davison considered, very briefly. Then he said, "I'll be right down." He replaced the phone, waggled his eyebrows at the under-secretary. "Could be a story. I'll be in touch."

Luttmann was waiting for him in the lobby of the huge building, while black-uniformed sentries stood to attention. Davison had never been inside this building before; he was impressed, and oppressed, by the immense stealthy rustle that seemed to be going on all around him. "Have you ever met General Heydrich?" Luttmann asked.

"As a matter of fact, yes. I did an interview with him when I was over here last year."

"Ah! So that is why he was immediately interested when I mentioned your name." He was leading the way up a wide flight of stairs.

"May I ask *why* you mentioned my name?" They had reached a broad gallery, where more black-uniformed sentries clicked to attention.

"I am sure General Heydrich will tell you, Herr Davison."

Doors opened before them, secretaries also came to attention, and then inner doors opened and Davison was shown into the office of the Deputy Chief of the Gestapo. The office itself was wide and deep and high-ceilinged. It glittered, with red and gold drapes, and behind the desk there was a huge portrait of the Fuehrer, looking nobly into the distance. But the man behind the desk, as Davison well remembered, was no less striking than his surroundings, with his placid, handsome face and his crisp golden hair, and above all, his expression of total contempt, presumably for all mankind. "Mr Davison," he said. "Welcome back to Berlin. Heil Hitler!"

"Heil Hitler," Davison agreed.

"Sit." Reinhard Heydrich indicated the chair before his desk. "Thank you, Luttmann." The doors closed behind Davison. Heydrich sat down himself. "Cigarette?" Davison took one. "What an odd world it is, to be sure, Herr Davison." Heydrich drew smoke into his lungs and leaned back in his chair. "Did you know that it was I who gave you permission to interview the Patten girl?"

"No, I didn't," Davison said. "But thanks, anyway, General."

"Did you have a successful interview?"

"I would say not."

Heydrich raised his eyebrows.

"The girl has been, shall I say, seduced, General. She belongs to the commandant, from tit to toe, if you will pardon the expression, and all the hills and valleys in between."

"I see." Heydrich flicked ash. "Would you like to make that official? Homosexuality, as I am sure you know, is a serious crime in Nazi Germany."

"What would happen if I did make it official?"

"The commandant might well find herself an inmate of her own camp. I would say she would have a rough time."

"And the girl?"

"Would become an ordinary prisoner. Unless the outstanding charge against her were resurrected, in which case she would be hanged."

How casually, Davison thought, these people spoke of life

and death. "Then I won't make an official accusation, if you don't mind, General."

Heydrich regarded him for some moments. Then he said. "I think you would like to have this girl for yourself. I do not blame you. I have seen her photograph. She is very attractive."

Davison stubbed out his cigarette. "Did you summon me here to offer me a woman, General?"

Heydrich's smile was as cold as his face. "Perhaps. Your country finds itself at war. How does this affect you?"

"I've cabled my paper to find out. I'm a little old to be drafted, unless things go very badly indeed. So I imagine I will continue as before, European War Correspondent. After all, what has happened in the Pacific does not really affect what is happening here."

"I'm afraid it does, Herr Davison. I will make you a confession. No one in the Reich Government had any idea what our little yellow friends were planning. We are as surprised as your people by the attack on Pearl Harbor, and now on Malaya and the Philippines."

Davison sat up. "Is that true?"

"Oh, indeed! Pearl Harbor was no hit-and-run raid. It was the start of a carefully planned and very extensive campaign to give Japan control of the Pacific and South-East Asia."

"And do you believe they can do that?"

"They would appear to *be* doing that, Herr Davison. And I have no doubt that they will succeed. Because, you see, while they have behaved in a most unpredictable manner, they are still our friends, and the Fuehrer stands by his friends. Even friends who are really liabilities, such as the Italians." The expression of contempt grew.

Davison was frowning. "You trying to tell me something, General?"

Heydrich placed his elbows on his desk, rested the tips of

his fingers together. "I am telling you that it is the Fuehrer's intention to declare war on the United States. The necessary document is being prepared now."

"You'd be committing suicide, General. Why take on the States as well as Britain and Russia, until and unless you have to?"

"You lack a strategical brain, Herr Davison. Taking on the States, as you put it, has been much in our mind for some time. Your country, while repeatedly declaring its neutrality, has ever since the war began been giving the most open assistance to Great Britain. That assistance, this so-called Lend-Lease, has now been extended to Soviet Russia. This is intolerable. However, as you have suggested, it would not have been in our best interests to go to war with America until Britain and Russia had been eliminated as enemies. This requirement has in fact just about been achieved. Russia is shattered; she can never recover from the defeats the *Wehrmacht* has inflicted upon her. Britain struggles on, but she too is shattered, and can hardly be regarded as a worthwhile enemy. And now the situation has changed, dramatically, in our favour. We have obtained a most formidable ally."

"Do you seriously suppose Japan can defeat America?" Davison asked.

"If you mean do we believe that Japan can invade and conquer America, of course that is unrealistic. But they have already won their war against them. The Americans, as I am sure you know, Herr Davison, are more interested in making money and driving their automobiles and watching their movies than in fighting and getting killed, certainly when they are not getting themselves killed actually for the defence of their homes and loved ones, but merely because their politicians tell them to. I will tell you what will happen, Herr Davison. For the sake of their face the Americans will attempt to defend the Philippines and possibly even Hawaii. But without a fleet they will lose these and all their Pacific possessions, at which time the Japanese, having established their hegemony over all South-East Asia and the Pacific – I can assure you that India is a teeming hotbed of incipient revolt against the British and will collapse the day, not very far in the future, that one Japanese soldier sets foot in the sub-continent – will invite Washington to stop rattling its sword and come to a reasonable agreement, and Washington will accept, because otherwise they would have a war on their hands that could drag on for the rest of this century."

"And you want to be in on the act," Davison muttered.

"By no means. We have no interest in Asia or the Pacific. We have no interest in America, per se. I wish you to understand this, Herr Davison. What we do want is to force the United States to stop supplying Britain and Russia with material, because once that supply ceases, so will their ability to fight. This may happen without any action on our part; America will be forced to turn all its attention, and all its military capability, to containing the Japanese. But we intend to make sure that happens."

"America has the potential to produce enough guns and bullets, and ships and aircraft, to defeat Japan *and* continue to supply Britain and Russia," Davison said.

"You think so? Now, that is interesting. That is why you are here, Herr Davison. You have indicated, by your writings over the past few years, that you understand what the Third Reich is all about, and that you believe in our ideas. Well, you are a sensible, thinking man. You understand that International Communism is the greatest threat the world has to face, or perhaps has ever faced, certainly since the hordes led by Genghis Khan were watering their horses in the Danube. Our dedicated duty is to defeat this fresh Asiatic tide and throw it back, hopefully forever.

The Anglo-Saxons, through entirely misguided prejudices against us, are opposing us in this. But you know better, do you not?"

Davison studied him. "Are you asking me to work for you? To *spy* for you?"

Heydrich smiled. "How brutally you put things, Herr Davison! I would like to think that we might be of profit to each other. Over the past few years you have revealed a good deal of sympathy and understanding of the Nazi movement. We appreciate this. We are also aware that you are of Irish Republican extraction, and that therefore you bear no love for the British. Equally, I am certain, you have no sympathy with Communism. However, of course, you are a loyal American subject. Now I will repeat that we wish America no harm. Perhaps we even wish her well in her war with Japan, providing she does not obtain any startling success too soon. All we want to do is keep her out of Europe, as completely as possible. Now, it seems to us that with your reputation, articles by you to the effect that America has no business meddling in Europe, that her true business is confronting Japan, would be of great use to us."

"General, once you have declared war on my people, they will regard you as just as much an enemy as Japan."

"Quite so. But they cannot harm us, any more than we can harm them. Except at sea. At sea we are going to prosecute this war most aggressively. We are going to sink American ships until there are none left. We are going to prevent any Lend-Lease supplies from reaching either England or Russia. This is going to be sea warfare on a scale your people can never have envisaged. It is up to you to make them realize that there is no necessity for them to suffer these grievous blows; that they would not were they to withdraw their entire merchant marine and fleet into the Pacific to fight their real enemy, Japan."

Davison scratched his head. "I don't think I can promise you that will happen, General."

"But you can try. You can also, through perhaps a series of interviews and talks with leading American statemen and leaders, keep us informed of just how American thought is shaping up, what are their intentions, their true feelings towards us. This would be very useful for us."

"You haven't yet told me why I should do all this. Apart from my sympathy and understanding, of course."

"You are a mercenary, Herr Davison. Be sure we understand that. Shall we say, a retainer of ten thousand American dollars, paid into a numbered Swiss bank account?" He studied Davison's face. "And perhaps, the girl Patten?"

"Just like that?"

Heydrich smiled. "It is my privilege to be able to make things happen, just like that, Herr Davison."

"Suppose I told you that the girl has never been my mistress? Luttmann is mistaken."

"I would say there is no necessity for you to tell me the truth. But if she has never been your mistress, and you have the opportunity to make her so, I think it would be a grave mistake of you not to take advantage of such a situation."

"You mean I could take the girl out of Germany?"

"If that is what you wish to do, certainly."

"And what makes you think she would remain with me for a moment, out of Germany?"

"I do not think there would be a problem with that. We would make it perfectly clear to her that should you ever complain to us about her behaviour, her mother, sister and brother would all be executed. I think you would find in those circumstances she will be very pliant."

"You reckon everyone is utterly venal – corruptible – is that it, General?"

"In my experience, Herr Davison, everyone is."

"OK, so let me ask you two more questions, if I may."

"Of course."

"First, what is to stop me taking the girl, and the money, and returning to the States, and then writing a series of articles telling the world just how corrupt this regime of yours is?"

"There would be nothing to stop you doing that, Herr Davison. There would, however, be a negative side to your action. I am sure you have heard of ying and yeng. Were you to betray us, we should of course launch a campaign of vilification against you, and I think you would find that we could effectively end your career by letting slip aspects of your visits to Germany. We should also, of course, execute Agnes von Patten's family, as traitors. In case you are not aware of it, execution for treason here in Germany can take a peculiarly unpleasant form. Have you ever seen anyone strangled with piano wire? Sometimes it can take up to a minute." Davison swallowed. But he was not going to show fear of this smiling, handsome monster. "You had another question, I believe," Heydrich said.

"It was what would happen if I simply refused to go along with you? Would you then strangle *me* with piano wire?"

Heydrich laughed. "My dear Herr Davison, we are not barbarians. You are an accredited foreign journalist. I am afraid, should you refuse to co-operate with us, I would have to lock you up for a day or two, until war is declared. You would be in possession of information, what you call a scoop, is it not, which we could not possibly allow you to use. Once war has been declared, you would be expelled from Germany along with all other Americans. However, nothing else would have changed. We would still discredit you as a journalist, and we would still execute the Pattens. In this instance this would include Agnes herself, of course."

Davison licked his lips. "Am I allowed to consider your offer?"

"You have twenty-four hours."

"During which I will be kept in confinement."

"No, no, Herr Davison. You are free to do what you please, in that time. We should prefer it, however, that you should not visit the American Embassy. You will be watched. And I should point out that the telephone lines to the embassy have been tapped. Nor would I advise sending any telegrams or making any telephone calls from your hotel, elsewhere. The twenty-four hours have been granted for your sober reflection, nothing else."

"I do not have an hotel in Berlin, General."

"But of course you do. I have arranged one for you. My car will take you to it. Think carefully and well, Herr Davison." Heydrich stood up to indicate that the interview was at an end.

Davison stood also. "You are confident that I will accept your offer."

Heydrich smiled. "It is the only logical course for you to take."

Heydrich left his office by his private elevator, which took him down to the basement garage, where his car and chauffeur were waiting for him. "Ravensbruck," he said.

The gates of Ravensbruck were opened and the camp sprang to attention at the arrival of the tourer with the swastika flag on its bonnet. The commandant had been telephoned from the gate, and Frau Hauser hurried down the steps to stand to attention before the Deputy Commander of the Gestapo. Heydrich acknowledged her salute by touching the brim of his cap with his swagger stick. "I wish to see the girl Patten," he said.

Hauser swallowed. "The girl . . ."

"I am a very busy man, Hauser," Heydrich said.

Hauser almost ran in front of him. The women in the office stood to attention, staring at their ultimate master with terrified eyes; they also knew that homosexuality was a very serious crime in the Third Reich. Hauser opened the door to her apartment. "Patten!" she bawled. "Patten, present yourself." If she was hoping that Agnes might have the wit to dress herself first, she was disappointed. The girl wore her habitual house garb of a pair of knickers, and she moved hesitantly. "She is an insolent slut," Hauser declared hotly. "I will have her whipped for this, Herr General."

Heydrich had recognized the limp. "Again, Frau Hauser?" he inquired. Hauser bit her lip. "Leave us," Heydrich commanded.

Hauser drew a deep breath. "The girl is an habitual liar, Herr General. She does not know what the truth is."

"It is a common complaint," Heydrich agreed. "Out."

Hauser hesitated a last time, then left the room, giving Agnes a warning glance as she did so. Heydrich waited for the door to the office to close, then he took off his hat and laid it on the table, together with his stick; to these he added his gloves. "Come here," he said. Agnes approached him, slowly, trembling; even her breasts were shaking. "Bend over the table," he commanded.

There was a sudden sharp intake of breath, and her eyes brightened with the tears which filled them. "I am not going to whip you again, silly girl," he said. "I wish to see what has been done to you." Agnes placed her hands on the table, and lowered her torso to touch the wood. Heydrich stood behind her and gently eased the knickers down her thighs; he could see the red weals on the white skin, in such strong contrast to the deep purple scar a few inches higher. "Who did this to you?"

176

Agnes inhaled, and her trembling grew as he stroked her buttocks. "I have no doubt at all that it was Commandant Hauser," he said. "But I shall be very angry if you do not confirm that." Agnes's head moved up and down, her chin bumping the table top. "Do you like being beaten by Commandant Hauser? Do you like Commandant Hauser, for that matter?" Agnes rested her cheek on the wood; he was still stroking the bruised flesh, parting the buttocks to slip his hand between. She was breathing heavily. "I am going to take you away from here, today, anyway," he said. "So you can tell me the truth."

Agnes took a deep breath. "She is a fiend," she muttered.

"Does she make you sleep with her?"

"Yes," Agnes said.

"Does she do this to you?" His fingers were busy, sending delicious sensations racing through the groin despite herself.

"Yes," she gasped. When Heydrich suddenly moved his hand, she slid off the table and knelt, her body a vast shudder.

Heydrich sat down. "There is paper and ink on that desk over there," he said. "Go and sit down and write a statement about your relations with Commandant Hauser. Begin it, 'This is my statement', write it, and sign it, then print your name under your signature. Oh, and date it."

Agnes glanced at him, then stood up, pulled up her knickers, and went to the desk. There she hesitated. "Go on," Heydrich commanded. Agnes sat down, carefully. Once again she hesitated for several seconds, then she began to write.

Heydrich watched her for a few moments, then got up and moved around the room, picking up various ornaments to examine them, replacing them, looking out of the windows.

When he reached Hauser's bar, he looked at each bottle in turn, before filling two small glasses with schnapps. Then he moved to stand behind Agnes as she finished her deposition, signed and dated it. "And print your name," he reminded her.

Agnes obeyed. Heydrich picked up the sheet of paper and read it. "This is very good," he commented. "You are an educated girl, Agnes. Have a drink."

He put the glass in her hands, and after another of her hesitations she drank it. He did the same. Some colour reached her cheeks, and her breathing was now normal. "Are you going to arrest Frau Hauser, Herr General?" she asked.

Heydrich returned to the settee and sat down. "You never told me if you liked being her lover." Agnes shuddered. "Did you find it distasteful, or her distasteful."

Agnes licked her lips. "Her."

"Ah! So you could love a woman, if she was appealing to you. And why not? I have loved men who have appealed to me. But that is not something you should repeat, little Agnes. Pretty Agnes. Desirable Agnes." Agnes finished her schnapps. "Refill your glass," Heydrich invited.

She obeyed, with trembling hands, turned towards him. "I will not, at the moment," he said. "Come and sit here." Cautiously she lowered herself onto the settee beside him. "Tell me about the Englander," he said.

"I fell in love."

"With an enemy of the Reich?"

"I . . . I know it was very foolish of me."

"But a young girl cannot control her heart. I quite understand."

Agnes gazed at him with enormous eyes. Could she trust him? She so wanted to trust somebody. But Reinhard Heydrich? "And the American? Did you fall in love with him as well?"

178

"The American?" For a moment she had no idea of whom he was speaking, as he could tell. Then she remembered. "Good lord, no!"

"Did he not make advances to you?"

She flushed. "He tried."

"But you did not care for him."

"I was in love with Hec . . . with the Englander."

"Such faithfulness," Heydrich said. "Suppose I told you that the American is deeply in love with you."

"I do not see how that can be, Herr General. We have only met once. Oh . . . !"

"You mean twice," Heydrich reminded her. "He came here to visit you, did he not? Only yesterday." Agnes bit her lip. "He was disturbed to observe the relationship between yourself and Frau Hauser. But of course, we are going to end that, aren't we?" Agnes raised her head; her eyes were watchful. "Would you like to leave this place, Agnes?" Agnes drew a deep breath.

"Well, I am going to release you, on certain terms." Agnes stared at him. "I am going to give you to the American." He held up a finger as she would have spoken. "He is about to leave the country, and he will not be returning, for a while. But he will be working for us. You will be his mistress, travel with him, be with him always. Obviously you cannot do this as a German citizen, as a good deal of his work takes him to England. You will therefore be provided with a Swiss passport and identity. As a northern Swiss, German will be your mother tongue, but you are anyway fluent in both English and French, are you not?" Agnes's head moved slowly up and down. "There," Heydrich said. "You are made for the job."

"Just to be this man's mistress?"

"That is not quite all. Of course I wish you to please him, sexually. But you will also be his watchdog. His brief is to support us in his writings, and to supply us with information. Should he do anything which might be construed as a betrayal of that brief, I wish you to kill him." Agnes mouth sagged open. "We will of course make the decision when this should happen, should it become necessary," Heydrich went on. "You have but to obey the command. The word will be Disposition. Remember this." He smiled at her expression. "But I hope, and actually do not think, it will ever come to that."

"But I have never killed a man."

"Is that so? You showed a great inclination to kill at least one of our border guards, last Christmas."

"I . . . I did not mean to hit them. I was shooting to give Hector the time to escape."

"And you succeeded. Just as you will succeed in everything you will do for me. Because you see, if you do not, I am going to hang your mother, and your sister, and your brother, slowly, and before each other's eyes. I do wish you to remember this, Agnes. On the other hand, if the flow of news and support from Davison are satisfactory, and continue to be so, it may well be possible for me to alleviate the conditions in which your family are existing." Agnes panted.

"I am glad we understand each other. Did I ever tell you how beautiful you are, when you are agitated? I think, before you commence your new duties, that I would like you to give me something of what you gave the Englander. That way I will know what the American is enjoying." Agnes got her breathing under control, and looked left and right. "We do not need a bed," Heydrich said, unbuckling his belt. "Just your lips." She stared at him in consternation. "Did you never do that for the Englander? Dear me, but you have a lot to learn about pleasing men, my little Agnes. However, I shall be happy to teach you."

Part Three

The Return

'If thou wilt ease thine heart
Of love and all its smart,
Then sleep, dear, sleep.

But wilt thou cure thine heart
Of love and all its smart,
Then die, dear, die.'
            Thomas Lovell Beddoes, *Death's Jest Book*

Chapter Nine

The Trap

James Davison lay on his hotel bed and stared at the ceiling. In some ways he supposed he should be amused by the errors the Nazis could commit because of their warped sense of values, their inability to understand that not everyone in this world was on their level. Equally because of their temptation to rush to judgement. To suppose that he would betray his country for 10,000 dollars a year was an insult. It would have been an insult for double or triple that. To suppose the deal could be crowned by the offer of a girl's body . . . of course, they supposed he loved the girl. That was clearly based on Luttmann's information. Someone he had only seen twice in his life.

Of course he had made an advance . . . it was in his nature to do so to any pretty woman. Luttmann had no idea that he had been turned down without hesitation. On the other hand, he owed it to his real employers to go along with Heydrich, because that way he might pick up the entire German courier system in North America. And the girl? She could be nothing more than a nuisance, however beautiful she might be. A well-brought-up young Fräulein could not possibly be any great value in the sack; he had no doubt at all that Hector Brand had seduced her merely to make his escape.

The double-dealing bastard! Who was now suffering from

an outsize dose of guilty conscience! The phone rang. "Good morning, Herr Davison. Luttmann here. I hope you slept well?"

"On and off."

"We need your decision this morning, Herr Davison. The declaration is tomorrow, when you, and all other Americans, will be required to leave Germany."

"I might be tempted. For double the money."

There was a brief silence. Then Luttmann said, "You value yourself very highly, Herr Davison."

"Doesn't everyone?"

"I will have to refer back to my superior. But if he agrees, you definitely accept our offer?"

"I reckon so. Tell you what, though, forget the girl."

Another brief silence. "You do not wish Fraulein von Patten?" Luttmann asked at last. "She will not interfere with your peccadilloes, Herr Davison. She will just be there when you come home, eh?"

"I said, forget the girl, Luttmann."

"This too I will have to refer to my superior. Do not go out. I will contact you."

"Make it brief, old son."

He showered, and Luttmann was back on the phone before he had finished breakfast. "General Heydrich feels that you and he should have a meeting Herr Davison, in order to clarify one or two points."

"But he accepts my terms?"

"In outline, yes. My car will call for you in half-an-hour."

To Davison's surprise, he was not driven to the Gestapo Headquarters, but to another building, unmistakeably a prison, on the outskirts of Berlin. Here Luttmann was waiting for him. "Am I under arrest?" he asked, jocularly.

"You are a tourist, eh?" Luttmann was equally jocular.

They were admitted through a heavily barred and guarded doorway into a corridor, at the end of which was a flight of steps leading down. "Medieval," Davison commented. The place even smelt medieval, the odour of ancient walls and floors being overlaid by the atmosphere of brooding terror.

At the foot of the steps there was an empty lobby, and then a door, leading to a brightly lit, warm, and well-furnished room, the far end of which was curtained off. "Herr Davison! So glad you could come." Heydrich might have been welcoming him to a cocktail party. "Luttmann tells me you drive a hard bargain."

"You are asking me to betray my country, General."

"Quite so. Well, I think we can rise to twenty thousand dollars a year. But the girl . . . I really would like you to have her. I have gone to so much trouble to procure her a Swiss identity. It would be a great shame not to carry it through."

"I'm afraid she would be more trouble than she is worth, General. It would, for example, mean that I could never return to England."

"I don't see why not, as she will be a Swiss."

"And supposing I ran into Colonel Brand, with Fräulein von Patten in my company?"

Heydrich studied him for several seconds, then grinned. "I should think that would be quite amusing, as Brand would be very pleased to see that his lady-love had escaped. However, I take your point; he would certainly realize that she was travelling under a false identity. I think you should stay away from Colonel Brand. But that does not mean you can no longer visit England. You are hardly likely to run into him unless you do so deliberately." He eyes flickered. "You were not planning to do this, were you, Herr Davison?"

"Of course not. But I still feel it is taking an unnecessary risk. I don't *need* the girl."

"That is a pity. But . . . Luttmann told me this might be your final decision. That is why I invited you here. There is a little ceremony I would like you to watch. Luttmann." Luttman dragged on a cord, and the curtain was pulled aside to reveal a sheet of glass. "This is one-way glass, of course," Heydrich said. "We can see what is happening, but no one in that room can see us. We can also hear, if we wish. Not right now, Luttmann," he said, as the Gestapo colonel reached for the speaker switch. "I wish Herr Davison to take in the scene, as a journalist, perhaps."

Davison stood beside him at the window, looking into the room beyond, and took a sharp breath as he realized it was an execution chamber, and yet, like no execution chamber he had ever seen before – and he had visited more than one. The room was bare, with no trap and no platform. But from the central beam there was suspended a length of rope, at the end of which was a noose of wire. There were four men in the room, and a large tripod camera. "We photograph them as they hang," Heydrich explained. "It amuses the Fuehrer." He flicked a switch and spoke into a small microphone. "It is time, Feldman."

The men in the chamber clicked to attention, and one of them went to a door in the far wall. This he opened, to allow two more men to enter, and once again Davison caught his breath, for between them they marched Agnes von Patten. She was naked, and her wrists were bound behind her back. There were no marks on that exquisite body, but she was breathing heavily; her hair hung in black profusion about her ears and past her shoulders, half obscuring her face. "You cannot mean this," Davison muttered.

"Well, you see, she is guilty of treason," Heydrich explained. "And has been sentenced to death. The sentence was never commuted, only held in abeyance, as it were. Now, as you have no use for her, and neither do we, the sentence will be carried out, and then, of course, on her mother and her sister, and her brother."

Davison stared at Agnes in consternation, as she was made to stand on the floor immediately beneath the wire noose. When it brushed her face her knees gave way, and she would have fallen but for the two men holding her arms. "There are two ways of carrying out this execution," Heydrich said, "depending upon the seriousness of the crime. One is merely to place the noose around her neck and hoist her from the floor. That way death will be fairly quick, perhaps a minute, as the wire eats into her neck and she chokes. The other way is less merciful. We release her hands, you see, and *then* hoist her from the floor. Naturally she attempts to prolong her life; that is instinctive. So she tries to get her fingers between the wire and her throat. If she fails, she is left clawing at her neck. She may even claw right through the flesh and draw blood. All this time she is kicking and writhing at the end of the rope. If she succeeds, well, that is even better, because she lives as long as her fingers can take the strain. I saw an execution once, admittedly it was that of a man, who sustained himself until the wire had eaten right through his fingers. He lasted fifteen minutes. I shall never forget it. But I doubt that delicate flesh like Agnes could last that long. However, as she *is* guilty of betraying the Fuehrer, we shall release her hands. Do you not agree?"

He glanced at Davison, who stood quite rigid. "Why, Herr Davison," he commented, "you have grown quite pale. I assure you, you are about to see a sight you will never forget." He bent over his microphone. "Commence. Release her hands."

One of the men placed the wire noose over Agnes's head, settled it around her neck. Now she was breathing so hard it seemed likely her heart would burst out of her chest. "Wait," Davison said, his voice thick with saliva.

"Wait," Heydrich said into his microphone. "Was there something?"

"I will take the girl," Davison said.

"You see," Luttmann said, as the Mercedes tourer drove south-west from Berlin. "General Heydrich is really a very civilized man."

Davison glanced at Agnes. She had not spoken since she had been presented to him, fully dressed in her own clothes, and indeed in the height of fashion, with a fur hat and coat and kid gloves. He suspected that her mind as well as her face was closed. He did not yet know if she knew he had watched her mock execution. He did not know so many things. Was he guilty of an act of supreme weakness, of submitting to blackmail? Could Heydrich really have so barbarously executed a beautiful young girl? He did not know that either. But he felt that it could have happened.

But he, of course, had been the ultimate victim. Why? It made no sense for Heydrich to have insisted he take Agnes von Patten out of Germany, save for some ulterior and unknown motive. And having got her out, what then? It would certainly make the gossip columns: Famous columnist escapes Nazi Germany with beautiful Swiss miss. And all it needed was one photograph to appear in a British daily and Hector Brand would know this was no Swiss miss. Heydrich had to realize that. But for two very good reasons Hector Brand would never betray Agnes von Patten. The first was that it might well break up his marriage. The second was that Davison had no doubt at all that Hector *had* fallen in love with the girl, however inadvertently – hence his desperate wish to find out what had happened to her. Had Heydrich known *that* as well? "Where are you taking us?" he asked.

"General Heydrich thought you might like to spend your

last night in Germany at Schloss Patten." Davison heard the sharp intake of breath from beside him. It was the first reaction she had shown. "He thought that would be romantic," Luttmann went on. "He also felt that it would not be a good idea for you and your mistress to be embroiled in the general exodus of American diplomats and journalists that will take place tomorrow morning. Once the declaration of war has been made, you will be escorted across the Swiss frontier quietly and without fuss by my people. You will have made it just about a year late, eh Fräulein?"

Agnes made no reply. "Spending the night at Schloss Patten will also enable the Fräulein to pick up some more of her clothing," Luttmann said. "Hers is all still there, stowed in the attic. You see, we are being very civilized about this. I'm afraid it is a long journey, but if you wish to start honeymooning now, please go ahead. We shall not object. Eh, Hans?" He grinned at the driver.

Davison looked at Agnes, and she looked back. Her emotions were back under control, and her features were composed. "I am sorry about this," he said, in English.

She raised her eyebrows. "You have saved my life. And those of my family." She also spoke English.

"I meant, well, being forced together like this."

She gave a half smile. "No doubt there are worse people than you in the world, Mr Davison. In fact, I am sure of it." Which was about the most severe put-down he had ever experienced. From a nineteen-year-old girl! But no doubt he had had it coming.

They travelled as fast as they could over the snow-covered roads, but after a stop for lunch it was just on midnight when they reached the *schloss*, having covered well over 300 miles. They had made two other stops, in each case to change their driver. Luttmann talked a great deal from time to time, but also dosed occasionally. Davison and Agnes also dozed much more of the time, sometimes even with her head on his shoulder; he was very tempted to put his arm round her, but decided against it. Presumably, he thought, during one of Luttmann's somnolent periods, he could risk seizing control of the car. But to what purpose? The odds on his succeeding without a smash were poor and, even if he did, what could he accomplish more than what was being done for him – leaving Germany with Agnes? For the time being, everything was running his way, and it made no sense to upset things.

Luttmann's talk varied between the boisterously obscene, tinged with jealousy – Davison knew he had hoped to get Agnes to bed himself – and the triumphalist, as he spoke of Germany's huge victories, and the even greater victories that would follow in the new year. The trouble was, Davison had an awful feeling that he might be right. But at last they were stopping in the snow-covered courtyard, and the dogs were barking.

"The dogs!" Agnes shouted, suddenly waking up, and hurrying across the snow to the enclosure, there to kneel and stroke their heads, before looking over her shoulder. "I had never expected to see them again. I thought you had put them down."

"What, magnificent creatures like these?" Luttmann had followed her. "I would no more have dreamed of it, Fräulein, than I would have dreamed of putting down a gorgeous creature like yourself."

Agnes slowly straightened, brushing snow from her gloves. Davison wondered if she was reflecting that Luttmann's superiors *had* been about to put her down like an unwanted dog, or that she was classed, in Luttman's mind, only with the animals. He held her hand, and she glanced at him, and then looked away again.

Sentries clicked to attention, and they entered the warmth of the baronial hall. "A midnight snack, I think, after our journey," Luttmann decided. "Johann! Here is one of your mistresses back again."

Johann goggled at Agnes as if she were a ghost – and a possibly antagonistic one. She had to wonder what he had done, or confessed, to retain his position under the Gestapo. "It is good to see you again, Johann," she said.

The butler bowed in relief, and took their hats and coats and gloves. "Sandwiches," Luttmann instructed him. "And you know what, Johann? A bottle of that Krug from the Baron's cellars. No, two bottles. We are celebrating, eh?"

Johann hurried off, and Luttman ushered Agnes and Davidson into the drawing room. "I really think we need our beds," Davison suggested. "I assume we are making an early start tomorrow?"

"And you are anxious to spread the Fräulein's legs, eh?" Luttmann guffawed, and Davison glanced at Agnes. Her cheeks were pink, but that might have been the sudden warmth. She ignored both men as she went to the fire and held out her hands to the heat. "But you have time, Herr Davison," Luttmann said. "We will not leave the *schloss* until tomorrow afternoon. You see, war will be declared tomorrow morning, the moment the necessary notes can be delivered, both in Berlin and in Washington. In Washington, this really cannot be done in a civilized manner before dawn, or anyway, six o'clock. That is one o'clock in the afternoon here. So we cannot start expelling Americans from Germany until after one o'clock. Least of all you, Herr Davison. We do not want anyone to suspect that you knew of the declaration before it was made, eh?" He laughed. "So you and the Fräulein have my permission to stay in bed until noon, if you wish."

Again Davison looked at Agnes, who still would not look at him, sitting down instead in one of the chairs close to the hearth and staring at the flames. Johann brought a plate of sandwiches and the two bottles of champagne. Davison and Agnes only sipped theirs, but Luttmann clearly intended to drink both bottles himself. "Now I think we *will* retire," Davison said. He stood up, and Agnes followed his lead.

Luttmann waved his bottle and splashed champagne on the carpet. "Then I will wish you a joyous night."

"Thank you," Davison said, and held the door for Agnes. Now at last she allowed him a glance as she walked through, and up the stairs. Johann was waiting in the hall, to bow to them. Agnes lip curled, but she made no comment. One of the maidservants was on the gallery, indicating that they should use the master bedroom. Again Agnes ignored her as she entered the room. Davison followed and closed the door. Here again there was a roaring fire, and their cases were arranged in a neat group against the far wall. Just as if we were honeymooning, he thought. Because that is what we are doing.

Additionally, a pile of clothing lay on the table, with another suitcase, empty. Agnes riffled through them. "Are they yours?" Davison asked.

"Yes." Agnes stood at her mother's dressing table, which remained much as she remembered it, save that anything of value, such as the silver-backed brushes, had been removed. Almost absently she took off her earrings, then unpinned her hair, allowing it to flow past her shoulders.

Davison remained standing by the door, watching her. "Would you like me to leave?" he asked.

She raised her eyebrows in the mirrow. "Why should you do that?"

"So that you can undress in private."

"A gentleman," she remarked, as contemptuously as she had regarded the butler. "But I have no secrets from you, Herr Davison. You have seen them all."

"In slightly different circumstances."

She shrugged, and reached behind herself to unbutton her dress. "I do not wish you to leave."

He sat down to watch her. "And you do have a secret, you know, Agnes. Why are you doing this?"

This time her glance was surprised, as she carefully folded the dress over a hanger and placed it in the wardrobe. "I am instructed by General Heydrich."

"I understand this. I understand that your family is being held hostage for your good behaviour. But did Heydrich give you no reason for having you accompany me?" This time she did not look at him as she stepped out of her shoes. Nor did she reply. "Suppose I was to tell you that once I carry you across the frontier you are as free as air."

She had been lifting her slip over her head, uncovering her truly splendid legs and thighs, and the no less magnificent breasts, outlined beneath her camiknickers. Now she held the silk in front of her almost like a shield. "You cannot do that."

"You do not wish to be free?"

"I am not free. I can never be free." She regained her composure, folded the slip across the back of a chair, slipped the straps from her shoulders and allowed her camiknickers to slide down to her ankles. He watched her in total absorption. Her every movement was as perfect as what she was uncovering.

"No one would know," he said, his voice thick. "It would be our secret, Agnes."

She released her suspender belt, sat on the bed to roll down her stockings. "I am to be your mistress. General Heydrich has said this."

"Do you wish to be my mistress?"

"What I wish has nothing to do with it." Naked, she stood before him.

"You are trying to force me to be the ultimate heel."

"I do not understand."

"A heel is someone who takes advantage of women."

"You cannot take advantage of me, Herr Davison. I am yours without reservation."

She made to turn away and he caught her wrist. "Trouble is, I *am* a heel." For the first time in his life he was ashamed of that. But the adrenalin was not going to stop flowing now, as he pulled her back towards him. She made no effort to resist, sat on his lap and allowed him to stroke where he chose. But he was quite unable to respond. "Get into bed," he said.

She obeyed. It was warm in the room and she did not pull up the covers, but lay on top of them, so that he could look at her as he undressed. But now she was looking at him. Another first: she actually made him embarrassed. She was the strangest mixture of sophisticated innocence, and utter worldliness, as if her personality was split, between what she was, and what she had been forced to become. Naked, he sat on the bed beside her. "I assume you had sex with Brand? Did you love him?"

"I do love him."

"So, no regrets."

"Yes, I regret." For the first time her voice was animated. "I regret my father's suicide. I regret my mother and sister being made into whores. I regret my brother likely to freeze to death in Russia."

"But for yourself, nothing."

She turned her head. "No."

He leaned over and kissed her mouth, stroking down from her breast to her pubes as he did so. There was the faintest movement beneath his hand, but no attempt at resistance. Nor did she refuse him her tongue. She tasted sweet, as her body felt sweet. But there was still no erection. When he took his mouth away she gazed at him with enormous eyes; his hand still rested on her pubes, and when his fingers again moved between her legs she licked her lips.

He wanted her quite desperately. It was as if every woman he had ever known had come together in this one slender body. But to take her would be rape, no matter how willingly she accepted him. James Davison had never raped a woman in his life. He had never had to. Odd failures such as Jocelyn Brand were to be expected, from time to time. He had never let them upset his self-confidence. But this girl, who had already suffered so much . . . still she stared at him. Then she moved, slightly. She was spreading her legs. Anger bubbled through his system. Self-hatred, mostly, but equally hatred of the regime that had created this, that had created so much destruction of humanity, body and soul. But not to touch her . . . it was impossible, anyway, while he was impaled upon those eyes. He held her shoulder, rolled her on her face. Once again, no resistance, but now she brought her legs back together. He drove his hands up and down the curve of her back, as if he were a masseur, moving up to her neck to throw her hair over her head, moving down to the superb curve of her buttocks. He kissed her there, and recoiled as he made out the now faint lines of a caning.

Still she had not moved. Her face was turned away from him, and she was breathing, slowly and evenly. Had her eyes not been open, he might have supposed she was asleep. Certainly she might have been alone, his attentions nothing more than a whisper of summer breeze playing across her body. He lowered his head again and sank his teeth into the soft flesh. "Oh!" At last her head came up.

"I thought perhaps you had fallen asleep," he said.

"Do you like my taste?" she asked.

He had actually drawn blood, which he now licked from his lips. "Yes. I am sorry. Shall I fetch something?"

"No," she said. "Whatever you wish to do, do it. Now. Please."

Her sudden vehemence took him by surprise, and as if to encourage him more, she rose slightly onto her knees. He panted with desire, got between her legs, thrust himself at her . . . and knew it was not going to happen. He rubbed himself against her, put his hands under her thighs to bring her ever more firmly against himself, then threw her away from him. She lay absolutely still, while he lay on her for several seconds, before rolling off on to his back. Again she waited for several seconds, before she got up and went to the bathroom. He stared at the ceiling, then turned his head, to see her standing in the doorway, looking at him. He had never seen such an expression before in his life, and for the first time in his life he was suddenly afraid. Then to his consternation she returned to the bed, straddled him and took him in her mouth. "I am to make you happy," she explained.

At last! Hector tore at the letter which he had plucked out of the morning's mail the moment he had spotted the American stamp. He had just about given the bastard up for lost. *Dear Brand*, Davison had written, *I must apologise for not having been in touch before, but you will understand that I got rather caught up in the events of last December. Didn't we all? Sadly, I have no good news for you. I did manage to trace something of the Pattens, but it appears the assistance they gave you had them all classified as traitors, and the Reich, as I am sure you know, takes a dim view of this. Both Thelma and Charlotte are now serving their time in military brothels, Rudolph is with the army in Russia, and Agnes, most sadly, was after all executed. I know how deeply you were in love with her, and I also know the plans you had for after the war. Thus I know how deeply my news will grieve you. What more can I say, save that I am at least happy that we are now all on the same side. Please give my regards to your wife. Sincerely, James Davison.*

Hector slowly crumpled the paper into a ball in his fist; Davison's absurd assumptions were meaningless beside the plain fact that Agnes was dead, dead, dead. And it was his senseless patriotism that had killed her as surely as if he had placed a loaded revolver to her ear and pulled the trigger. Jocelyn stared at him across the table, while Alan kept up a steady drumming with his porridge spoon. Now that Hector was on the staff they had found themselves a small flat in London, and none of them was enjoying it much. There was a gulf between them which could not be bridged by a few frantic sexual moments from time to time. "Bad news?" Jocelyn asked.

"Is there such a thing as good news, nowadays," Hector said, his voice almsot savage. "I must go." He bent over her to kiss her forehead, did the same to Alan, and left the room, throwing the crumpled paper into the grate as he did so.

He had lit the fire immediately on getting up, an hour before, and it was now blazing merrily. But the moment the door had closed behind her husband Jocelyn seized the tongs and got the letter out. It too was burning well, and she had to stamp on it to put out the flames. Then she slowly opened it out to read what she could. "Ma," Alan remarked. "That's Daddy's letter!" He was watching her with some interest.

"It's all right, darling," Jocelyn said. "It's all right."

But was it ever going to be all right again?

"As I am sure you all understand," General Frederick Morgan said, looking around the staff officers seated before him, "The entry of the United States into the war has created, as the Americans would say, a whole new ball game. Now I have some tremendous news for you. At the recent meeting of the American Chiefs of Staff with our own, it was decided that the war against Nazi Germany should take priority over all else, and that specifically means the Pacific." He paused to allow that to sink in; certainly his audience was astounded.

"I know the situation is pretty grim over there and, frankly, the way we were tossed out of Malaya and what happened at Singapore hasn't given us too much clout. All we can hope to do is hang on to India for the time being. The Yanks are certain that they can defend Australia and Hawaii, and in effect contain the Japs, until there is a US Pacific fleet in being, and ready to counter-attack. In the meantime, as I have said, they plan to co-operate with us in knocking Hitler out of the war. We therefore have a more immediate objective than long-term planning. Now we can go for it." He grinned at them. "Let's hear some preferences."

"Pas de Calais," someone said.

"That's too obvious," objected someone else.

"We need to be realistic," the first speaker argued. "We must assume the Germans have sufficient agents in the UK to have some idea of what's going on. Once there is a massive build-up of US troops here, as I assume there will be, they will know we are planning an invasion. That being so, we have to chose the best option, knowing that we will be opposed in strength. Our best option is the shortest possible line of communication across the Channel. Ergo: Pas de Calais."

"Pas de Calais also happens to be the most heavily defended part of the French coast," George Brand remarked, quietly. "And, incidentally, when we're talking about the French coast, it is at the end of the Germans' shortest line of communication as well."

"Sir George is right," Morgan said. "We have to take into consideration that this war is being fought in the eyes of the media, as it were, and that means the eyes of the man in the street. Casualties are going to be high, no matter where we go. To launch a frontal attack on what is probably the strongest fortified front in Europe will involve astronomical casualties. If we were to suffer those, and not succeed in the invasion, well, . . ."

"Holland," someone said.

"Same objections," George Brand said. "And, historically, Holland hasn't been a happy hunting ground for British invasions of the Continent. Remember the Grand Old Duke of York."

"Norway," someone suggested. "Short lines of communications, and we have people who know the ground. You, George."

"We know it would please the boss," said someone else. "He was all for getting at Germany through Norway in the last lot."

"Norway is not a place I have any desire to revisit, at least as part of an invading force," George said.

"In any event," Morgan put in, "it's not really on, because of the weather."

"With respect, sir," said a junior staff officer, "we are proposing to cross the English Channel, where most of the year there is the worst weather in Europe."

"I was thinking of the shortness of the summer, Graves," Morgan said. "What about farther afield? I know it would mean long lines of communication, but that also applies to the enemy. And if we could put a large number of men ashore without too much opposition . . ."

"You mean Biscay?" someone asked.

"It's a possibility."

"Well, what about the Med? We could build-up the forces we already have there, and get at the Germans through the Aegean and Greece. Sort of flank attack on their armies in Russia. Uncle Joe would love that."

"So would the boss. That's another of his pet projects."

"So would the Afrika Corps," George pointed out. "I think we need to smash Rommel before we can consider attacking out of Africa."

"I agree," Morgan said. "But hopefully Auchinleck is about to do that thing. Well, gentlemen, we seem to have exhausted all our options, to no great effect."

"What about you, Hector?" George Brand asked. He had observed that his nephew had been in a brown study all morning.

"Yes, come on, Hector," Morgan invited. "You must have an idea."

Hector pulled his thoughts together. Agnes, dead! Hanged! The thought made him feel quite sick.

"I can only think of a compromise," he said. "Pas de Calais is too heavily fortified, Biscay is too far away, the Med is not on at the moment, so what about the Bay of the Seine? And the Cotentin Peninsula, of course. If we could take Cherbourg and Le Havre we'd have two seaports ready to use. Why, we could even liberate the Channel Islands at the same time. That would be popular."

The two generals exchanged glances. "Compromises are always the worst options," George said. "The Bay of the Seine is almost as strongly defended as the Pas de Calais, it would entail crossing the widest part of the Channel, the Germans would certainly defend Le Havre and Cherbourg to the last man, and destroy the port facilities if they felt they were going to lose them, and the bay also has some of the highest, and therefore lowest, tides in the world. That would complicate matters beyond belief."

"Well, gentlemen," Morgan said. "I think we'll have to adjourn and do some more thinking. Good day to you."

Chapter Ten

Cousins

"Hector!" Louise had opened the front door. "How splendid to see you!" Then she frowned. "You don't look too good. Baby's not ill, is he?"

Hector hadn't expected to encounter his cousin. "What are you doing here?" he demanded.

Louise raised her eyebrows. "I have a weekend pass. I have one most weekends. What is the use in having a general for a father if you don't get preferential treatment?"

"Did anyone ever tell you that you are a totally amoral female?"

She grinned, and kissed him. "Nobody's perfect. Now tell me what's troubling you: Auntie Lou will solve it for you."

"I might, if you'd let me in." She stood aside and he entered the hall. "Your dad home?"

"Yes, he is."

Hector went into the drawing room, where George and Helen were enjoying Saturday afternoon tea, while the spring sunshine warmed the conservatory. "Hector!" Helen said, getting up to greet him. "How nice to see you! Didn't you bring Jocelyn and Alan?"

"No," Hector said.

"Well, sit down and have a cuppa," George invited. "I'm

sorry I had to shoot you down yesterday morning, Hector. You know, I've been thinking about your idea, and it does have one enormous redeeming feature: total surprise. I would estimate it's the one place the Nazis would never expect us to go. If it could be possible to find a date when the tides were just right . . . but there it is. The powers-that-be feel that Biscay is the best option, and are even planning a trial run."

Helen had been studying her nephew-in-law while she handed him his cup. "I don't think Hector has come here to discuss the invasion of Europe," she said.

George raised his eyebrows, and Louise sat beside Hector on the settee. "Jocelyn has left," Hector said. "Together with Alan." For a moment the family was speechless. "I assume she's gone back to her mother," Hector said. "There was no note. I spent most of last night trying to telephone Drumbooee, but there was no reply. Uncle George, I know times are fraught, but I need a furlough. I have to go up there and see her."

"But . . . you say she didn't leave a note? There has to be a reason," Helen said.

"That business in the Firth," George said darkly. "I don't think she ever did recover."

"That's not true," Louise snapped, so sharply her father looked at her in surprise.

"She left this." Hector placed the half-burned sheet of paper on the coffee table. "I threw it in the fire before leaving the flat yesterday morning, but she must have got it out."

Helen picked up the paper and studied it, then she passed it to her husband without a word. "Is this something to do with the German family who helped you escape?" George asked, handing it in turn to Louise.

"Yes. I think you had better hear the whole story."

"You mean it wasn't an Anglophile and anti-Nazi family

who helped you? That's how it was reported in the papers," Helen said.

"It wasn't the family. They may have been Anglophile, but they were ardent Nazis. I knew I would never have a better chance of escaping than from the *schloss*, but I also knew I would need help. So . . . I seduced one of the daughters. This girl Agnes."

"You seduced her?" Helen asked cautiously.

George was again lost for words. Louise clapped her hands. "Bravo! And I always thought you were an old fuddy-duddy."

"I seduced her," Hector repeated. "To do that, I had to make her fall in love with me. I'm sorry, but there it is; I felt it was my duty to escape if humanly possible."

"Absolutely," George murmured, with a guilty glance at his wife.

"And you . . ." Helen picked up the letter again.

"I'm not made of stone, Aunt Helen. Agnes von Patten was a very lovely young woman."

"You fell in love with her!" Louise was not accusing; her face was a romantic glow.

Hector sighed. "I'm not going to lie to you. It is not possible, well . . ."

"To have sex with someone on a continuing basis and not fall in love with her," Louise suggested.

"Louise!" her mother cried, shocked.

"Or him," Louise added, sotto voce.

"Anyway," Hector went on. "She was very much on my conscience, as you can imagine. So I asked Davison, as being the only person I knew with access to Germany, to find out what he could. And . . ." his shoulders sagged as he picked up the letter.

"That's exactly what happened with Harry and Connie," Louise said.

"Except that Harry's lady love was a Frenchwoman, not a German," Helen pointed out, coldly, as if that made all the difference in the world. "And," she added for good measure, "he wasn't married when it happened."

"But he wasn't trying to escape, either," Louise argued. "Anyway, Constance seems to have forgiven him, as she went chasing off to Malaya after him."

"And a lot of good that did her," Helen said. "She got herself killed, or locked up in a Japanese prison camp."

"You're not serious!" Hector protested, realizing that his troubles might not be as severe as he had supposed.

"Oh, yes," Helen said. "They got out of Singapore, just, and Harry was then taken into the Burma Corps. Constance was supposed to come home, but the plane flying her out of Rangoon was shot down, and nothing has been heard of her since."

"My God!" Hector said. "I am most terribly sorry."

"What's done is done," Louise said. "It's you we have to worry about. Listen . . ."

"That fellow Davison has turned out to be a real bad hat," George remarked, having been ruminating while the discussion had flowed about him.

Hector frowned. "What do you mean?"

"Well, since America entered the war, he's been writing a series of articles about how absurd it is for Germany and America to be enemies, how the Yanks really are on a hiding to nothing, how their shipping is going to be blasted off the seas, and the damnable thing is that he seems to be being proved right. The U-boats are creating havoc in the Caribbean and off the East Coast."

"Shit!" Hector said. "I do beg your pardon, Aunt Helen."

Helen looked as if it was a word she might have used herself, if she had known what it meant.

"I'm sure Mr Davison is only expressing a point of view," Louise said. "As he is quite entitled to do."

"That point of view is treason," her father insisted. "He should be locked up. I can tell you that if he was in England he'd be locked up."

"We're drifting off the point," Louise said. "Can Hector have a furlough to go and see Jocelyn."

"Well . . . I suppose so," George said grudgingly. "As it's a domestic crisis."

"Can I have a furlough to go with him?" Louise asked.

"You?" George asked.

"You?" her mother inquired.

"You?" Hector was astonished.

"Me," Louise said. "I think there is going to have to be a bit of arm twisting, and I'm the person to do it. I'm probably closer to Jocelyn than anyone."

"It really is most awfully decent of you to pitch in like this," Hector said, as he sat opposite his cousin in the train hurrying north. It was a sleeper, but there were no berths left, so they had to sit up all night.

"I think it's important. What did old Oscar Wilde say about losing parents? One may be a misfortune, two sounds like carelessness? That applies even more to marriages in the family. Anyway, I wanted to get away. It's all been a bit traumatic."

"I assume you're talking about Davison rather than Jocelyn."

"Well . . ." she flushed. "It's a bit much to discover that the man to whom you have given your all is hardly better than a traitor."

"Oh, come now! As you said, he's expressing an opinion, nothing more."

"As Daddy says, if he was an Englishman he'd be locked up. Have you any idea what would happen if the Yanks were to pull out?"

"I think that is the remotest of all possibilities," Hector said. "And they are certainly not going to drop out because of a few articles or speeches by Jim Davison."

Louise hugged herself. "Anyway, the man's a rat, sporting this new woman of his."

"Ah!" Hector said. "Do I hear the green-eyed monster? Next thing you'll be telling me she's ugly as sin and has a squint."

"Ha!" Louise said. "I wish I could say that. But actually, she's rather gorgeous."

"Don't tell me you've seen her?"

"Her photograph was in one of the American papers Daddy brought home. Standing next to James, arms round him, hair streaming in the wind, looking as happy as a dog with two tails. I think I should have said, bitch. He picked her up in Switzerland, or some place like that."

"I think," Hector said pontifically, "that you should put Mr Davison right out of your mind, Lou."

"Don't you think I'm trying? But I did fall for him, Hector. Hook, line and sinker. I'm that sort of person. Washing him out of my hair isn't just a matter of using a strong brand of shampoo."

Hector knew just how she felt. She was a Brand, as was he. He hadn't succeeded in washing Agnes out of *his* hair, and she was dead! "Edinburgh," he said, with some relief.

They reached Edinburgh at dawn, as usual, and as they had to change trains for the slow stopper to Drumbooee, and that involved a lengthy wait, there being fewer trains than before the war, they had a wash and brush up then breakfast in a cafe.

"Do you think we should telephone?" Louise asked, drinking her tea.

"No. I don't want to give her time to erect any barriers before we get there."

"Suppose she's out?"

"Then we wait for her to come back in. Anyway, what would she be doing out?"

"Just a thought," Louise said.

It was ten o'clock before they finally walked up the path to the cottage. Louise rang the bell, and after a moment the door was opened, by Mary Macartney. "Louise!" she said. "What a pleasant surprise. And . . ." she looked past Louise. "Don't you think you should have let us know you were coming?" Her tone was cold.

"Don't you think you should have expected me?" Hector inquired.

"Well . . . come in." Mary allowed them into the house, closed the door. "Jocelyn is upstairs with Alan."

"Right." Hector went to the stairs.

"Wait!" Mary said. "Don't you think you should wait for her to come down?"

"Mary," Hector said, with great patience. "I think you are forgetting that this is my house, and that I am entitled to go wherever I choose in it."

He had not spoken loudly, but his voice carried. "I would really like to be left alone for a little while, Hector," Jocelyn said from the upper landing. "I need to think."

"I would like to say hello to my son," Hector said, beginning to lose his temper.

"Well," Jocelyn said. "I suppose . . . you come up too, Lou."

Hector and Louise looked at each other, and Louise waggled her eyebrows. Then she led him up the stairs. There was obviously good reason for Jocelyn not to be alone with a man she perhaps doubted was still her husband: she had not yet dressed, was wearing a nightdress and dressing gown. She kissed Louise, and looked at Hector over her shoulder. "I do think it would have been proper for you to let us know you were coming."

"Would you have been here?" Hector asked.

She flushed, stepped aside, and Hector went into the nursery. "Daddy!" Alan said, waving a building block at him. "Look what I got!" It was a new set. Bribery? Hector leaned over to kiss him.

"He's very tired," Jocelyn said pointedly. "We only arrived yesterday, It's a very long journey."

"Which we have just made," Hector pointed out. He kissed Alan again. "See you in a little while." He stepped outside, and Jocelyn closed the door. "Is there somewhere we can talk?" Hector asked. "Privately."

"You mean, without Mother."

"That's what I mean, yes."

"There's our bedroom. But I want Lou to be present." Again Hector and Louise exchanged glances. "Lou and I have no secrets from each other," Jocelyn said.

"Then come along, Lou." Hector went into the bedroom, waited for Louise to close the door. She remained standing against it, like a sentry, her cheeks pink.

"I was a bit upset," Hector said, "by the way you just took off, without even a note or a message, and with my son."

"Our son," Jocelyn said. "Perhaps I felt the same way you do, that to start telling you what I was going to do would lead to endless argument."

"And you feel no conscience that you read a letter which was not addressed to you."

"It certainly concerned me, Hector."

"Listen, Joss . . ." he reached for her hands, but she retreated across the room. "All right, so I used the girl to get out of Germany. I told you all of that."

"*Used!*"

"Put whatever connotation you like on it. I had to take my chances while they were there. She helped me, and has suffered most dreadfully for it. I didn't know just how badly. I asked Davison to find out. I told you all that, too. And, well . . . there it is."

"You didn't tell me she was going to escape with you?"

"That was the plan. But she got wounded and couldn't continue."

"And when you got to Switzerland, what were you going to do with her?"

"Well . . . I thought I'd bring her to England. I mean, I felt responsible for her. God knows, I still do."

"And we were going to set up a *ménage à trois*, I suppose?"

"Of course not. I am sure we'd have sorted things out. Agnes was a very sensible girl, and . . ."

"Agnes?" Louise asked. "Heavens! I knew that name rang a bell."

Harry glanced at her. "You read the note?"

"I'd forgotten," Louise said. "Shit!"

"What is it?" Jocelyn asked.

"Oh!" Louise said, cheeks now pink. "It's just a coincidence, I suppose, that James's new lady friend is called Agnes as well."

"What did you say?" Hector asked.

"But not Agnes von Patten," Louise explained. "Agnes

Emmerich. She's Swiss. Or . . . that's what it said in the paper."

"My God!" Hector slowly sank onto the bed. "She's alive! That bastard!"

"Do you really think . . . ?" Louise began.

"Of course it's the same girl," Jocelyn said. "Who your friend Davison has taken for himself. He couldn't keep his hands of anything in a skirt." She bit her lip at her inadvertent slip, but Hector was too dumbfounded to notice, and she hastened to regain the high ground. "So what are you going to do now?" she demanded. "Now that you know your lady love is alive and well? And no doubt kicking."

"Oh, shut up!" Hector snapped. Jocelyn and Louise both stared at him in consternation; he was normally such a mild-mannered man.

"Well," Jocelyn said. "It seems to me that you have a great deal of deciding to do, Hector."

"There is no deciding whatsoever to do," Hector said. "I will admit that I seduced the girl. I had no very clear idea as to what I was going to do when we got out of Germany. I only knew that I had to get out of it. I was distressed beyond belief when Agnes was hit and so gallantly sacrificed herself that I could escape."

Jocelyn snorted, and Louise squeezed her hand.

"I was even more distressed when I knew she had been sent to a concentration camp," Hector went on. "And quite frankly, when I received Davison's letter saying she had been executed, I, well, I was distraught. That girl sacrificed her all to help me, Jocelyn. And then I was told she had died for it, in a peculiarly horrible and degrading manner. Now I know that she is alive, and that somehow Davison got her out of Germany. I am intensely happy about that. I'm man enough to be jealous of him, but that cannot alter the course of my life. I am your husband. Agnes von Patten was an episode, a vital episode in my life. However, it is now ended, happily, I would hope."

He paused. There was a moment's silence, then Jocelyn said, "But you are still in love with her."

"For God's sake," he shouted. "You are my wife!"

"You have not answered my question," Jocelyn said. "Are you, my husband, in love with another woman?"

"Oh . . ." he looked at Louise.

"I think we're all a bit fraught," Louise said. "Why don't we sleep on it, and tomorrow . . ."

"Sleep where?" Jocelyn demanded.

"Well . . ." Now it was Louise's turn to look at Hector.

"If you find my presence distasteful," Hector said, "I shall leave. Get in touch when you have come to your senses, and hope that I have retained mine."

He left the room and went down the stairs.

Louise licked her lips. "I'd better go with him," she said. "Or he may do something stupid." Jocelyn's face remained cold. Louise hurried down the stairs, where Hector was just collecting his valise. Mary Macartney gazed at him from the lounge doorway. "We'll say goodbye, Mrs Macartney," Louise said. "Maybe we could call, perhaps tomorrow."

"I'm sure that you will do whatever you think best, Louise," Mary said, as coldly as her daughter.

Louise hurried down the path behind Hector, carrying her own valise. They had reached the station before Hector said, "Damnation! I never said goodbye to the boy!"

"Do you want to go back?"

He hesitated, and a train pulled in. "Not right now. Let's go."

"Ah . . ." But Louise changed her mind about what she would have said and got in beside him. "You really are in a mood," she remarked.

211

"Wouldn't you be? Weren't you, when Davison stood you up?"

"I suppose I was. So, tell me your plan."

"Back to London, I suppose. Back to work. Joss wants time. She can have time."

"Hm," Louise remarked. "How exactly were you meaning to get back to London?"

"Oh, for God's sake, Louise."

"I meant, we need to go back to Edinburgh. This is the Dundee train."

"The what?" He gazed out of the window at the Firth racing by on their right. "Oh, shit!"

The conductor arrived at that moment. "I'm afraid we haven't any tickets," Louise said. "It was all a bit of a rush. What do we owe you?"

"We actually wish to go to Edinburgh," Hector said.

The conductor looked from one to the other. He could identify Hector's insignia as being that of a colonel, and his expression indicated that if this was the quality of the country's military leaders the prospects were grim. "Ye passed the Edinburgh bifurcation five minutes ago," he pointed out. "Ye should've been on the next train."

"We realize that now," Louise said.

"Aye, well, ye can change at Dundee and go back," the conductor said. "That'll be three pound, the pair of ye."

Hector paid. "Not my day," he said.

"I don't know," Louise said. "We're not due back in London until Tuesday, so there's nothing to worry about. We can take a day off. I know, we'll get off at Dysart, have a pub lunch – I'm ravenous – and catch the next train back to Edinburgh this afternoon."

"Lou," Hector said, "this is Scotland. On a Sunday!"

"I'm sure we'll find somewhere," she said.

*   *   *

They didn't, especially as they did not get out of the station at Dysart until past two. "Were you born in this blasted country?" Louise inquired, at their fourth firmly closed restaurant.

"I'm afraid so."

"Well, we'll have to try an hotel," she decided. "In addition to feeling like eating a living ox, I am slowly beginning to freeze."

The wind off the Firth was like a solid sheet of ice. But most of the hotels were shut as it was not yet summer. They finally obtained some response from a small establishment a couple of streets from the front. "We're closed," said the man who opened the door.

"Listen," Louise said. "All we want is a sandwich and a glass of beer."

"Beer!" the man commented. "On a Sunday? D'ye not know the law? Ye're not residents."

"Surely with a meal . . . ?"

"Not residents," he repeated, making to shut the door.

But Louise had her foot in it, and she was a sturdy young woman. "Then we'll become residents," she said. "Rent us a room."

The man goggled at her, and she pushed past him. Hector gave him an apologetic smile and followed. "Lou . . ." he ventured.

"I'm sorry," Louise said. "I am not going anywhere until I have had something to eat, and something to drink."

"What's the trouble, Ian?" A woman emerged from the end of the hall, drying her hands on an apron.

"These people . . ." Ian began.

"Are you the lady of the house?" Louise inquired.

"I am that. And as me husband says . . ."

"*My* husband and I," Louise announced, "came to your fair country to honeymoon, only to find that our

213

reservations have been cancelled. No one has been able to tell us why. Now we are cold, starving, thirsty and, at the moment, disappointed. You simply cannot turn us away."

The landlady looked from uniform to uniform. "Married, are ye?"

"Yesterday," Lou told her.

"We could gi'e ye a room," she suggested, glancing defiantly at her husband.

"And something to eat."

"Well, the kitchen's nae open, ye ken."

"All we want is a glass of beer and a sandwich." Louise said.

"Cold beef do ye?"

"That sounds terrific," Louise said. "And a beer?"

"Serve the guests, Ian," the landlady said. "The room," she continued, showing them into a small and gloomy dining room. "How long would ye want it for?"

"Well . . . just tonight, if possible."

"Aye, well, we've a room. But 'tis only a single bed."

"Oh, we don't mind that," Louise said.

"Aye, well. I'll make the sandwiches, shall I?" She retreated to her kitchen.

Her husband appeared with two foaming tankards of beer. "I think we'll have two more of those, landlord," Louise said, "Then you can get back to whatever you were doing." The landlord retreated, and Louise chose a table in the far corner of the room.

"Just what the hell are you playing at?" Hector demanded.

"Keep your voice down," she recommended. "I'm trying to get us somewhere to rest our weary bones, and reflect. In addition to being hungry, I am very tired. Aren't you?"

She looked up with a bright smile as the landlord placed

the two new mugs of beer before them. "But we can't share a bedroom, Lou. Much less a single bed."

Louise took a deep drink of beer. "Why, are you intending to make mad, passionate love to me?"

"This is a serious matter."

"I'd like that," she said dreamily. "I've always wanted to commit incest. And with my favourite cousin." She took another gulp. "Come to think of it, my only cousin."

"I think you are drunk."

"Getting there," she said, and flashed another dazzling smile as the landlady returned with a plate of sandwiches.

"When ye've eaten I'll show ye the room," she offered, and added, "There's nae hurry, if ye're residents. Ye can have another drink."

"We might just do that," Louise agreed. "Isn't she sweet," she commented, as the landlady disappeared again. "So understanding."

"She'll be less understanding when you take off your gloves," Hector pointed out.

"I need only take off one," Louise pointed out, removing her right glove to pick up a sandwich. "I have cold hands. And if she spots anything tomorrow morning, well, we'll be leaving anyway. Yummie! These are awfully good. Come on, Hector, have one."

He couldn't resist the smell of the food, and they ate in silence for some seconds. Then he said, "This is only going to make a fucking awful mess a whole lot worse."

"You keep seeing ghosts and spectres in every corner," she said. "You, a man who has screwed his way across half Europe."

"That is entirely untrue."

She grinned. "But you would have done, Hector, if you had had to, to escape. Wouldn't you?"

"When Jocelyn finds out that we have slept together, that will be absolutely it."

Louise started on her second sandwich. "That feels a whole lot better. Look, Hector . . ." she paused to smile at the landlord, who had pushed his head round the corner to look at them. "Has it ever occurred to your male chauvinist mind that it is possible to share a bedroom with a woman and not have sex with her? I mean, Jocelyn . . . oops!"

"What about Jocelyn?"

"Nothing, really."

"Lou," Hector said, "if you don't tell me what you were going to say, I am going to take you upstairs and ram you until I'm coming out of your ears."

"What a magnificent prospect! I shan't say another word."

"But before I do that, I am going to put you across my knee and whale the tar out of you. I imagine in this neck of the woods they have nothing against wife-beating. It's probably a Saturday night pastime."

"Oh . . . phooey!" Louise hunched her shoulders and drank beer. "I told you I had a thing going with Jimmy Davison. We wanted to have a few nights together, so we came up to Edinburgh. I persuaded Jocelyn to stand in as chaperone, but the hotel couldn't find her a room, so she slept in a cot in ours."

"Jocelyn slept in the same room as Davison?"

"Yes, she did. But he was in bed with me."

"And never left it?"

"Well . . ." Louise drank some more beer. "He did get up in the middle of the night, and went out onto the balcony. With Jocelyn."

"For how long?"

"Oh . . . ten minutes, maybe."

"What were they wearing?"

"Well, she was in her nightie, and Jimmy was in his

pyjama bottoms. But really, Hector, they couldn't have done anything, on the balcony. There just isn't room. Although I suppose . . .''

"What?"

"Have you ever done it standing up?"

"No I have not. But I am sure it's possible." Joss! Davison had called her Joss. He could feel the already simmering anger beginning to race through his arteries. "Did you get the impression that he was fond of her?"

"As a matter of fact, yes."

"And when did he stop seeing you?"

"Well . . . he was leaving for Germany the next week. He was away for several weeks, but he had given me a date for his return. So I telephoned his hotel, the one where he always stays, and was told he was out. I left a message that I would call back, gave a time, but when I did he was still out. The third time too. Well, I know I'm a dumb bunny, but even dumb bunnies can get the message. The bastard had had his fun and was moving on."

"And this date was?"

"Ah . . . December 18, last year."

"And on December 20 last year Jocelyn fell, jumped, or was pushed, into the Firth of Forth," Hector said.

Louise stared at him with her mouth open.

"You folks want anything else to drink?" The landlord stood above them. "I'll be closing the bar, now."

Louise and Hector looked at each other. "Why not?" Hector asked. "Do you have any drinkable port?"

"I drink it meself."

"Two schooners."

The landlord raised his eyebrows, then fetched the drinks. "Help yourself if ye wish some more," he invited. "Just write it on the tab."

"Decent fellow," Hector said.

"So what's your plan?" Louise asked. "To get gloriously drunk?"

"My plan," Hector said, drinking the port. "Is one day to catch up with Jimmy Davison and break every bone in his body. He's had my cousin, and dumped her, he's had my wife, and dumped her, in the sea, and now he has my mistress, and will presumably dump *her* as soon as he is ready. In addition, he is a Nazi sympathiser and a complete bastard."

"You don't know he had Jocelyn," Louise said, trying to undo some of the damage she had caused.

"Wouldn't you say it looks like that? Another port?"

"Um." She drained her glass. "Do you prefer me drunk or unconscious?"

She held his hand as they climbed the stairs, not entirely for balance.

The landlady was waiting at the top. "Here ye are," she said, opening a door for them. "I've made the bed. And there's the bathroom, right opposite."

"Couldn't be better," Louise said. Hector eyed the washstand, with its china ewer and bain and slop bucket, with distaste.

"Well, then, I'll leave ye to it. Will ye be having supper?"

"Is there any alternative?" Hector asked.

"What my husband means," Louise said, "is that we wouldn't want to trouble you, but there doesn't seem to be too much open."

"There isn't," the landlady said. "We eat at seven. Ye'll be going to evening service?"

"Ah . . ." Louise said. "We really are very tired."

The landlady nodded, as if she had expected nothing better.

"Seven o'clock," she said, and closed the door.

"I don't think she likes me," Hector remarked.

"We're adventuring," Louise said. "I do love adventuring."

Harry's sister, Hector thought, watching her take off her tunic and hang it in the cupboard. But then she dropped her khaki skirt.

"Just what are you doing?"

She took off her shirt and tie. "I am going to bed. That port really hit the spot. And I assume you are doing the same."

Hector surveyed the one straight chair. And there was no carpet on the floor.

"Oh, don't be a chump!" she said. "There really is room for two."

Chapter Eleven

The Return

"Gentlemen!" General Morgan looked over the assembled faces before him. "I've considered all of your proposals. My decision is – the Bay of the Seine." A rustle ran round the officers. What a difference twelve months can make, Hector thought. When the idea had first been suggested, a year ago, everything had been nebulous. Now, suddenly, it was definite. Just like that. Some had doubted it would ever happen, after the failure at St Nazaire. But they had learned a lot from that disaster.

"And as everything that is said in this room is classified," Morgan went on. "I can also tell you the name of your new commander-in-chief. It is Dwight D Eisenhower." There was another rustle. None of the English officers had met Eisenhower, a year ago, most had not even heard of him. "General Eisenhower," General Morgan continued, "is at present, as you know, commanding the Allied forces in the invasion of Sicily, as he commanded the invasion of French North Africa. He will be taking up his position here as soon as the Italian business has been sorted out."

Of course everyone now knew that Eisenhower had commanded Torch, the invasion of French North Africa. But down to that time he had been a totally obscure staff officer, and while his men had been wading ashore at Casablanca and

Oran, and later receiving several bloody noses as they tried to fight their way into German-dominated Tunisia, Bernard Montgomery had been defeating the Germans and Italians at Alamein. Montgomery was far too junior to command a force the size of that proposed for the invasion of Europe, but most of the British would have chosen his superior, Harold Alexander. Sadly, that had never been a practical proposition. The Americans had assumed the position of senior partner in the Allies, and they would have the overall command. The best the British could hope for was naval seniority, in accordance with tradition. But the Yanks had many more famous generals that Dwight D Eisenhower. If President Roosevelt seemed to need General MacArthur in the Pacific, what about General Marshall? But President Roosevelt seemed to need General Marshall in Washington.

"What we are aiming for," General Morgan continued, "is the spring of next year. This apparent delay will make Uncle Joe scream and shout, especially as some of our people have estimated we could launch such an attack this coming summer, but we simply cannot afford to start something we cannot finish. I can tell you that we are not going to be idle in that time. There is every prospect that the Italian business will have been cleaned up by then, and indeed that Italy will be out of the war. And meanwhile, we have a great deal to do. The Bay of the Seine . . ." he looked over their faces, "has been chosen for a variety of reasons. The first and foremost is because of the surprise factor. It is the last place the Germans will expect us, according to our best information. I do not want you to get the idea that it is less defended than most other places. It is adequately defended. But it is still the least obvious place, from a German point of view. The main difficulties are weather and logistics. We must assume that the weather in the Channel will be normal

– that is, abominable. Attacking in the Bay of the Seine will only be practicable at certain states of the tide. When the decision to go is taken, and," he added drily, "it will have to be taken by General Eisenhower, who I understand comes from the State of Missouri, which is a very long way from any sea, it will have to go ahead. We must pray that weather and tide will coincide, just once.

"As for logistics, well, these are immense. It has been determined that, if the invasion is to be a success, we must secure a firm lodgement in the first twenty-four hours. Attacking in the Bay of the Seine gives us the best chance of this, as it is estimated that the Panzer Army which constitutes the German mobile reserve is mainly concentrated in the area between Calais and Paris. So it will take at least twenty-four hours to launch a counter-attack against any forces on the Normandy beaches. Obviously it is up to our counter-intelligence, and to the ability of the RAF and the USAAF to knock out sufficient bridges to make movement difficult, to ensure this Panzer force moves as late and as slowly as possible. But the twenty-four hour lodgement is still essential. It has therefore been decided that we shall not make a direct assault upon either the ports of Le Havre or Cherbourg. I know they sound enticing. Capturing either one reasonably intact would give us an entrée port through which we could pour all the mass of materiel that we shall require. But we need to be realistic, gentlemen. In the first place, both ports are very heavily defended, and the capturing of them may be beyond our ability in that crucial first twenty-four hours; the assaults on both Dieppe and St Nazaire showed just how difficult it is to attack a defended town from the sea. In the second, we must assume that should the Germans realize that either port is likely to fall, they will immediately destroy the entire facilities, thus rendering them useless to us. We are therefore going for the open beaches inside the Bay of the Seine."

Another pause, another look around the faces before him, most of them now anxious. "This means that we shall be required to improvise. The boffins are already hard at work. Their business is to create some artificial harbours, which can be maintained off the beaches, and also some means of constantly supplying our vehicles, tanks and trucks, with petrol. They are confident they can do these things. Our task is to make that lodgement and get our people ashore. Once we do that in sufficient force, and are able to fan out from the bridgeheads, Le Havre and Cherbourg will fall of their own accord, but by then it should not matter whether or not we take them with their dock facilities intact. Thank you, gentlemen."

"All very simple," George Brand remarked as they left the room. "Give or take a few thousand lives."

"You think it'll be expensive?" Hector asked his uncle.

"It will be expensive. But it won't be as expensive as any offensive on the Western Front in 1914–18, or in Russia over the past two years. For which we should all offer a prayer of thanks."

"But still no chance of a job for yours truly."

"I'm afraid not, Hector, if by a job you mean leading a battalion onto the beach. But you'll be there, with the staff. I would have said you've done, and are doing, a pretty good job over the past year. Nothing to be ashamed of there. And you've your DSO to prove you have done your bit."

"I gather Harry has got a bar to his MC," Hector remarked.

"He got them both together, if for different events."

"And he's OK?"

"When last we heard. He's working with that oddball

Wingate at some hush-hush scheme for carrying the war to the Japs."

"And Constance?"

George sighed. "She is in a Jap prison camp. That came through the Red Cross. Seems she's all right, but . . ."

"What a hellish existence!"

"Yes," George said. "We just have to keep our fingers crossed. Meanwhile, Helen's a bit disappointed you haven't been down for the past few months." He grinned. "I suppose she wants to know about things on the Jocelyn front."

Hector shrugged. "Things haven't changed. She writes me now and then, to tell me how Alan is getting on . . ."

"So there's no definite split?"

"There's no talk of a divorce, if that's what you mean, Uncle George. On the other hand, she hasn't actually ever asked me to come back."

"And you're determined to wait on that?"

Hector understood the implied censure. "Let's say I feel it should all wait on this war business. The end is in sight, isn't it?"

"I believe so, Hector. But it could be a long time yet. And meantime, you're living a fancy-free life. Can't say I blame you. But, remember we'd love to see you, if you can spare us the time."

"I will come down, Uncle George. Seriously."

Whenever he could be sure Lou wouldn't be there, he thought. They had wound up in each other's arms that night in Dysart. Nothing had happened beyond mutual embarrassment, and they had both been wearing sufficient clothing to prevent catastrophe – but it had threatened, and they had kissed as lovers. The trouble with Lou was she was a woman who cared nothing for yesterday, and even less for tomorrow. Only today mattered.

But in the middle of a war, wasn't that the only way to live?

Conway gestured James Davison to a seat. Conway was heavy set and overweight; he smoked too much. Maybe, Davison often thought, it was the job, sitting behind a desk like a huge spider, moving people about like pawns in a gigantic chess game. Or maybe it was because he didn't have an Agnes von Patten to go home to; James had met Mrs Conway. But he sensed crisis. It was unusual for him to be called to the State Department, which preferred to maintain the facade that it heartily disapproved of him and his writing. "Great news about Italy, eh?" Conway asked.

"Will the Germans try to hold it?"

"For sure. There's going to be a right old mayhem in the south of the boot. But that's good for us. It ties up a big German force."

"While we get ready for the invasion."

"That's right." Conway flicked ash. "James ... you realize this is going to be one big do? The biggest do there has ever been on the face of this earth. I've seen the logistics involved. Christ!"

"Well, we sure don't want to make a mess of it," Davison said.

"That's it. We can't *afford* to make a mess of it. Nothing about this caper can be allowed to leak. Nothing! I can tell you that the whole of the south of England is being turned into an armed camp and that nothing, and virtually nobody, is being allowed out. Now, we can't turn the whole of North America into a sealed camp, but we can reduce the odds as much as possible. So, we're taking certain steps. One of those is to collect all the known German agents who have not yet been put behind bars. I know," he hurried on, as Davison would have spoken, "that your contacts are in many cases merely Nazi sympathisers, and that knowing who the real agents are has done us a lot of good as regards interception of messages. But that can no longer do us any good commensurate with the harm that would ensure if Berlin were to get the faintest whiff of what we are actually about. They must know we're planning to invade, but they don't know where, or when, or how, or with how much. Those are things they simply cannot find out. You with me?"

"Yes," James said.

"But you don't like the idea?"

"If you arrest all my contacts, Berlin will surely know who put you on to them."

"So? If they're all in gaol there won't be anyone left to get at you. But you can have protection, if you feel like it." He grinned. "You can also stop writing that puerile rubbish and come out on our side."

"It's not quite as easy as that," James said.

Conway grinned. "You're not going to tell me Agnes will object. Isn't she one hundred per cent anti-Nazi? And if you're worried that some busybody FBI agent is going to try to pick her up, forget it."

"I never told you the whole story about Agnes, Conway."

Conway frowned. "What didn't you tell me? You managed to get her out of her concentration camp, and across the border into Switzerland. You fixed her up with a Swiss persona, and brought her to the States. Real heroics. What don't I have right?"

"You never asked me how I got her out of Ravensbruck."

"Ah . . . cloak and dagger? Bribery? I don't believe in prying too deeply into how my people manage things."

"Well, I can tell you that one does not spring people from concentration camps, either by force or bribery, except at the top. Nor did I fix her up with her false identity. I did a deal with Reinhard Heydrich. At that time he was deputy head of the Gestapo."

Conway frowned. "What kind of deal? We know about the money."

James nodded. "Heydrich had got hold of the idea that I was in love with Agnes. So he said that in addition to the money, I could have her, as long as I kept on writing my articles, and feeding back those items of information I picked up from talking to the high and the mighty in Washington."

"And were you in love with the girl? Everyone here supposes that you are. She's a class act."

"Let's say I have grown very fond of her," James said.

"So what's the problem? OK, maybe it's not quite ethical to accept a dame in payment for services rendered, but so long as she didn't object . . ."

"She didn't object, Conway, because she was informed by Heydrich, personally, that if she didn't go along with the idea, her mother and sister would be hanged, and her brother would be shot for treason."

Conway gazed at him for several seconds. "Christ!" he commented. "And you think that if the Krauts work out you have changed sides, that's what they'll do? Well, I'd say the best thing you can do is keep it from little Agnes. We're not going to make a front page story out of arresting some German sympathisers and agents. And anyway, with Heydrich dead, assassinated in Prague, the deal is dead too. How many other people knew of it?"

"Some. One in particular." James regarded Luttmann as someone lower in the human scale than even Heydrich. "Conway, I am thinking of the Pattens, not of Agnes."

"Yeah. Well, maybe you should start thinking of the extra few thousand of our boys who are going to die if the Germans are waiting for us, when we land in . . . wherever we're going to land. Sure, it's tough. But they wished this kind of world on us. Make it easy on yourself, James. You don't have to tell Agnes anything. The Nazis aren't likely to blow their end of the deal. So she won't find out what's happened to her family until after the war. With the best will in the world, that's likely to be a year or two away. Time for you to smoothe the path, eh?"

Davison stood up. "Did anyone ever tell you that you're a bastard, Conway?"

Conway grinned. "War makes us all into bastards, James. All that matters is the guy who's on his feet when it ends."

Agnes von Patten walked down to the newsagents on the corner every day, and invariably bought a few newspapers, Swiss and American. But there was little to interest her in the American papers. There was little to interest her in America. Not now.

She had attracted a good deal of attention in the beginning. James was a well-known, if controversial figure. She did not think he had many friends, but she had quickly realized that in New York one did not have to have friends to be a social success; all one needed was notoriety. Returning home from Europe, still well known as a Naziphile, and with a beautiful Swiss miss in tow, had provided all the notoriety necessary. For a little while they had been lionized.

She had been overwhelmed by it all. Everyone had found her entrancing. That had been caused by a combination of her beauty, the air of mystery that surrounded her, and her unchanging air of unhappiness, which but increased the mystery – what could cause such unhappiness when associated with such a dashing figure as James Davison? She wondered what they would have said had they known her misery was caused entirely by her reflections on the fate of her mother, sister and brother?

But social acceptance, based on notoriety, requires continual notoriety, and this had not been forthcoming. To her great relief, the invitations had gradually dried up. She had then been able to concentrate upon keeping James happy. Which, after all, was her prime reason for existence. She felt she had succeeded fairly well at that. James was a very sexually experienced man, but as he had always sought his conquests from among ladies who were better born or better socially situated than himself, he was always in the position of trying to get them to do things that were either repellent or incomprehensible. To have in his possession a woman who was not only better born and brought up than any of his previous mistresses, and who was not only beautiful but willing to accommodate his every whim, sexual or otherwise, had been all that a man could ask.

"I would like you to marry me," he had said one night.

"Now you know I cannot do that," she had said. "Not without Heydrich's permission."

"Well, then, have a child by me. Heydrich would never know."

"I would like to wait until the war is over," she had said. "It cannot last very long, and I am only nineteen."

"You mean you don't love me." He had sounded almost like a petulant schoolboy told he could not have another slice of toast and jam.

"Give me time, James," she had begged. "Give me time."

He had returned to the theme when the news reached them of Heydrich's assassination. "You'll forgive me for saying that it couldn't have happened to a nicer guy," James had said.

"I agree with you."

"Well, then . . . He set this deal up. Surely now . . ."

"There will be records. There is also Luttmann."

"Luttmann," James had said, sitting on the side of the bed. Never had she heard a tone so redolent of anger and outrage.

"I cannot do anything to change my situation until I know what *their* situation is," she had said. "Can you not find out?"

"Yeah," he said. "Yeah. I'll find out."

But Heydrich had been dead more than a year now, killed by a grenade on 27 May 1942, thrown by the Czechs he had tyrannized, and James had not been able to find out. She didn't know whether to be glad or sorry about that. Just what was happening in the war, how long it would last, was really a matter of opinion. American opinion considered that, since the surrender of 60,000 Germans outside Stalingrad followed by the catastrophe for the Afrika Corps in North Africa and the collapse of Italy, the war was won; the dead man just would not lie down. But Fortress Germany remained intact, her borders protected by buffer states. Even the Americans accepted that she could not be beaten until the Allies could land in France, and there was no sign of that happening. It was still possible for both sides to run out of steam, and for there to be a negotiated peace.

How Agnes hoped and prayed there could be a negotiated peace, which would surely carry with it the removal of the Nazis from power, and save her beloved Germany from total destruction. The important thing, from her point of view, was that there was no immediate end in sight. Therefore she had to continue with her allotted task. She did not want to contemplate a change. Were James to come to her and say that he had learned her family had all been executed, she knew she would hate him, unreasonably and illogically, but he was the only thing she would have left to hate. Were he to tell her that Mother, Charlotte and Rudolf were alive and well, that would simply mean she would *have* to continue as before.

As for their relationship, it did not seem to have occurred to him that she might still be in love with Hector, still dreamed of one day regaining those protecting arms. James was too much the male egotist to accept that. Oh, Hector, she thought. Alive and well and back in the arms of his wife. She wondered if he ever thought of her? She bought all these newspapers in the hopes of seeing his name. She had to, one day. She turned back for the apartment, the sheaf of papers under her arm.

"Miss Patten?" Agnes half-turned her head, raised her eyebrows. This was not someone she had ever seen before. "Please continue walking," the man in the slouch hat said. "We are acquaintances, passing the time of day."

"Are we?" Agnes was not alarmed by the approach; they were on a crowded street, and she had learned, since coming to America, that one need not necessarily be afraid of men in slouch hats, certainly in public.

"Of course, because we have a mutual acquaintance, General Luttmann."

Agnes stopped walking, and he held her elbow to urge her onwards. "I am doing what is required of me," she said, suddenly breathless.

"Of course! You have performed admirably. And I am to assure you that your family is well, and in good health. Unfortunately," the man went on, "Your paramour has betrayed us."

Agnes frowned. "James?"

"I am afraid so. Therefore it is necessary for you to carry out Operation Disposition. You understand this word?"

Agnes had some difficulty breathing. "But . . . ?"

"There can be no buts, Agnes. However, I wish you

to know that the Reich looks after its own. When you have carried out the execution, you will not be sacificed to American justice. Instead you will be taken back to Germany, and there you will be a heroine, receiving the maximum publicity. You will also be a warning, to such other of our people who may be considering changing sides. And I am authorized to tell you that all charges against your mother, your sister and your brother, as well as yourself, of course, will be dropped."

Agnes licked her lips. "When is this to be done?"

"Tonight."

"Tonight? But . . . I have no weapon."

"You have knives in your kitchen. Use one. Do it some time between eight and midnight. Then wash yourself clean of blood, dress yourself warmly, go down to the street, turn left, and walk for two blocks. There is no necessity to take any clothes, these will be provided for you. And in very short order you will be back in Germany. As a heroine. Will that not be nice?"

"Having committed murder," she muttered. "Of someone who has never been other than kind to me."

"That is the sad thing about war, Agnes. One kills, because one is directed to do so. That is all the motive one requires. But that also absolves the individual of guilt. Now, there is one last thing; we shall of course require proof of your having carried out your assignment."

"You told me to wash away the blood."

"Of course. To walk around with blood-stained hands or clothes would be a serious mistake. But you are a keen photographer. We have observed this. We wish you to take several photographs of the dead man, photographs that will leave us in no doubt that he is dead. Bring the film with you, and we will have it developed. Do you understand me?"

"You are a monster," Agnes muttered.

"I am making it possible for you to go home, Agnes. To be reunited with your family. I will say goodbye, or rather, *auf Wiedersehen*, Fräulein."

Agnes went up to the apartment, threw the papers on the table, looked around her. She had been happy here, or as happy as it was possible for her to be since her life had turned to catastrophe, and had come to regard the place as home. Now she was required to destroy it. To keep her family alive. There was no element of choice.

But it also meant ending forever her dream that one day she and Hector Brand might again be able to get together. Hector owed her his life. But that debt would be negated if she took the life of his friend. But, again, there was no element of choice.

She was certainly not in the mood for reading the papers. She left them on the table, prepared a meal, waited for him to come in. She dared not consider her feelings towards James. As she had told that man in the street, he had never been other than kind to her. But she had been given to him, like some medieval slave, as payment for his loyalty. He had enjoyed her, had even suggested that he might be in love with her. And now . . . she opened her wardrobe, took the camera from one of the shelves. To kill him was bad enough. To photograph him afterwards was unholy. But there was no choice.

She undressed, put on a dressing gown, made herself a cup of coffee. She desperately needed a drink, but that would be too risky; she had to have a cool head. She sat down, flicked through the newspapers as she watched the clock. He was usually home by seven, but tonight he was late. Supposing he did not come in at all? Or supposing he brought someone home with him? But he never did that.

Eight o'clock! She realized she was trembling, and then she heard his key in the latch. She stood up, sat down again, and stood up again as the door opened. "Christ, what a day!" he remarked, going straight to the bar to mix a martini. "You?"

"No, thanks." For the first time he noticed she was wearing a dressing gown, and looked twice to make sure it was only a dressing gown. "I feel romantic," she said. "Would you like sex before, or after dinner?"

"Certainly not before a drink and a shower." He drank half the martini in a gulp, went into the bedroom carrying the cocktail shaker. "How was your day?"

"The same as any other day." It had to be now, now, now. She had less than two hours, and there would be a lot to be done. She went into the kitchen, selected the large chopping knife. It had a point as well as a very sharp edge. She felt sick, sure was not going to be able to do it. But she did not have a choice. "Your day must have been pretty busy," she remarked, going into the bedroom, the knife held behind her back.

He had stripped, was drinking the second half of his martini. His back was turned to her. It had to be now, now, now. She grasped the handle tightly, watched him pour his second drink. "This really hits the spot," he said. "You know what, sweetheart? Maybe we will put dinner back half an hour."

If he spoke again it would not be practical. Agnes stepped against him and drove the knife into his back. For a moment he did not move, and already blood was spurting over her hand and soaking the dressing gown. Then he gave a choking gasp, and began to turn. She stepped away from him, watched blood bubbling from his mouth, choking back what he was trying to say. His eyes were enormous. His knees hit the floor and then his body. It was less of a crash than she had anticipated. Nothing to alarm those on the floor below.

She ran to the dressing table, snatched up the camera. He was lying on his face, and she photographed his back, twice, with the knife sticking out of it, surrounded by the welling blood. Then she held his shoulders and rolled him half over, panting, tears streaming down her cheeks. She photographed him again, showing his face, but at the same time still the knife in his back. She took two of those. Then she closed the camera, took out the film, placed it in its little box. The dressing gown slid from her shoulders, and she let it lie on the floor, half across the man, and ran into the bathroom and turned on the hot shower.

"Hi!" Louise said. No sooner had she entered the tiny room than she was making herself at home, taking off her cap and tunic, loosening her tie, putting the kettle on the small gas ring. "How're things?" she asked.

"Better for seeing you." He meant that. Louise, he felt, was reality. Because Louise was the here and now. They both lived in the middle of a totally unreal world, in company with several million other people. They were surrounded by unending noise. Nothing dramatic, just the constant growl of engines, and of people too, living shoulder to shoulder, each man, and each woman, aware that they each had a covenant with death, waiting to be fulfilled. Each taking part in an enormous secret, which could only be shared by others in the same deadly society, but about which no one really wanted to talk.

The entire south-east of England had been turned into an armed camp. There was no access, save for those required to join the secret; there was no exit, for anyone, except the highest brass. And now it rained, ceaselessly and it seemed endlessly. From his window on this Southampton waterfront, Hector could not at this moment even make out the Isle of Wight across the Solent, so unceasing was the rain. And with the downpour, the wind, which drove the rain almost horizontally over the ground. Spring, in England What had Brooke written, in another war, at another place People forget.

But for those engaged upon this greatest of all military operations there was an insidious relaxation. Rain and wind meant high seas outside the Solent, meant there was little prospect of going in such conditions. And as Hector, one of the original planners, knew, once this next week was past, moon and tide would not again be right for another three weeks.

Meanwhile, the isolation continued. "No mail?" she asked.

"The usual."

Jocelyn wrote every month. Jocelyn was sufficiently an army wife to appreciate that he could not reply, and therefore her letters were not either querulous or complaining. But she was in Drumbooee and he was in Southampton, a very long way away. And although she filled her letters with news about Alan, and how much Alan missed his daddy, there was never a suggestion that Alan's mother missed her husband never a hope that they might soon be reunited.

Pure pride? Perhaps even guilt, about Davison. But most likely pride. She had not forgiven him for Agnes. But had he forgiven her for Davison?

"I have news of your little friend," Louise said.

Hector frowned. "What news? Don't tell me the Yanks have at last found out who she really is?"

"Oh, they've found out something," Louise said. "She' stuck a knife into James." Hector sat up, violently. "It's fact," she said. "It was in one of the US papers Daddy gets.

"Agnes killed James Davison?"

"The report just said she'd stuck a knife into him."

"Agnes?" But she had been prepared to kill the German border guards. He really knew very little about what went on behind that beautiful mask. "She's been arrested?"

"She's disappeared."

"Then how do they know it was her?"

"She left the knife in the body, and the prints on the haft match most of the other prints in the apartment, which are clearly hers." He turned his head to look at her. "Oh, sure," Louise said. "Maybe James had it coming. He was a bastard. But he was my bastard." She grinned. "One of them. I hope they catch that little bitch, and they strap her to a chair, and they burn her into a cinder. They still do that in the States, don't they?"

"It varies from state to state." Hector spoke absently. Agnes had survived so much, to kill Davison? Whatever had possessed her to do such a thing? Only unbearable mistreatment, surely.

"They will catch her, you know," Louise said. "They always do. Unless it really was a lovers' quarrel, and she's thrown herself under a subway train or something."

"Is that what they think happened?"

"There's a suggestion."

"Lou . . ." the phone rang. Hector picked it up. "Yes?"

"Report immediately, Colonel Brand. It's on."

"On?" Hector looked at the rain lashing his windowpane. "When?"

"Tonight. Move it!"

"But . . . in this weather?"

"The Met office says there is going to be a moderation for forty-eight hours, starting tomorrow morning. So Eisenhower made the decision. See you down there, Colonel."

237

Hector slowly replaced the phone.

Louise was already pulling on her tunic. "Did I hear what I just thought I heard?"

"I never thought he'd have the guts to make a decision like that." Hector was also dressing as fast as he could.

"You *are* still with Daddy?" Louise asked. Hector nodded. "Great! So am I. Maybe we'll get together, in France."

"Maybe we should ask the Germans about that," Hector said.

"Munich," said the embassy official. "You are home, Fräulein Patten."

Agnes could not believe her eyes. It was all so familiar. She must have used this station a hundred times in her life. Yet it all belonged to another world. A world in which she was apparently supposed to take her place as if she had never left it.

She had, in fact, had this sense of unreality ever since the moment she had plunged the knife in James's back. Then she had taken the definitive step, outside of reality. It could not have happened, be happening. Even as she had been showering, watching blood wash from her breast, where it had soaked through the dressing gown, and from her thighs and then her hands, she had known this could not be happening. She had thought that about many things since that dreadful day she had felt the bullet smashing into her body in the snow on the Swiss border. She had thought, then, this cannot be happening. But she had gone on living, then consumed with a mixture of passion and anger, seizing the guard's discarded rifle to fire at his companions, shouting at Hector to get away, knowing that this simply could not be happening to her, that she could not be dying. Not her. And she had been right. Dying is reality, and she had entered the world of the unreal.

She had known it again when she had realized what Commandant Hauser wanted of her. She was no stranger to lust; she was a beautiful woman. She had seen lust in the eyes of James Davison, when he had first come to Patten *schloss*, and in the eyes of Fritz Luttmann. Even in the eyes of Reinhard Heydrich. And even in the eyes of Hector Brand.

That was her due, as a woman. But if in her girlhood naturism with others when camping in the woods she had known, and shared, brief episodes of sexual passion, it had never occurred to her that there could be a total commitment of feeling towards someone of her own sex. Her emotions then had been mainly bewilderment, again overlaid by the conviction that this could not be happening. Of course Hauser had never loved *her*. Hauser had loved her body and in the course of time, and nature, she would have grown tired of even that body, and no doubt sent her to the barracks to join the beaten and the shaven heads. She had had a lucky escape.

And then, James and New York. A world she had not known to exist, outside of the cinema, but which was apparently real enough for millions of people. Not for her. Again, bewilderment, that she should be so fortunate where so many people, her own family, could be so unfortunate. Of course dream worlds always end, and more often than not with a very rude awakening. But her awakening had been the most unreal thing of all. Every time she looked in a mirror, stared at that solemn, innocent, beautiful face, she thought, "I have stabbed a man, a man with whom I have had sex, time and again, a man who wanted nothing more than to make me happy. I have *stabbed* a man!"

That second escape, the drive south to the Mexican border,

the crossing, with forged papers, the ship bound for Portugal, the journey through France and then into Switzerland, had been the most unreal aspect of the whole thing. She was being shepherded by a succession of agents. To what fate? She no longer had any faith in promises. But there, on the station to meet her, was Luttmann.

General Luttmann, she realized he was now, as she was helped down to the platform. "Fräulein! Agnes! How good to have you home!" She was embraced, tightly. Then he held her hand to lead her to the side, away from the other people detraining, all looking at her curiously. "These gentlemen wish to take your photograph." Agnes blinked at the cameras. "Look confident, happy," Luttman told her. "Not afraid! What have you got to be afraid of? Smile!"

Agnes smiled, and the shutters winked at her. There was, she realized, even a newsreel camera being cranked, and it was to this she was now led. A man held a microphone before her. "Are you pleased to be home, Fräulein von Patten?"

Luttmann squeezed her elbow. "I am very pleased to be home," Agnes said.

"Is it true that you had to kill a man, Fräulein von Patten?" Agnes stared at him with her mouth open.

"Fräulein von Patten did what she had to do for the good of the Reich," Luttmann said. "Gentlemen, you have had your photographs and your film. Now you must excuse Fräulein von Patten. She has had a tiring journey, and is anxious to get back to her home and her family."

He held Agnes's arm to escort her down the steps and assist her into his Mercedes saloon. "Did you say family?" Agnes asked.

"Your mother and sister are waiting for you at the *schloss*. We are people of our word, Agnes."

"But . . ." right this minute she wasn't sure she wanted

to see Mother and Charlotte: "Did . . . do they know, about
. . . well . . ."

"The story has been widely circulated, yes. Of course, the
newsreel will make it even more widely known." Agnes bit
her lip. "You were working for the Reich," Luttmann pointed
out. "You have nothing to be ashamed of. Rather you should
be proud. I can assure you that the Fuehrer is proud of you.
When you have spent a few days recuperating, he wishes
me to take you to Berlin, to meet him again."

Agnes didn't know what to say to that. The Fuehrer, as
she remembered, had been the man who had condemned
her to be strangled with piano wire. But this was reality,
at last. She was home, and she had burned every boat she
had. She was a Nazi, in the eyes of the world. She had to
become one in her own eyes, as well.

The *schloss* had not changed. That at least should have been
reassuring. How she wished it could have changed! Because
her last memory of it had been with James, when she virtually
had had to seduce him, because he had been so determined
to act the gentleman, and she had been so determined to
begin her allotted role. She could remember that night as if
it were yesterday, that memory accentuated by her beloved
dogs, waiting to be hugged and kissed.

And then Mother and Charlotte. Mother as thin as a rake,
her hair entirely white, her features tight. Charlotte still
inclined to be plump, but with a world of experience in her
frightened eyes, her sudden movements. They stared at her
as if she were a stranger, and she stared at them, because
they *were* strangers.

"Aren't you going to give your mother a hug?" Luttmann
asked. Agnes went forward hesitantly and embraced Thelma,
but the older woman's body remained stiff. For what am I

being condemned? Agnes wondered. For causing the death of Father? Or for my more recent crimes? Or merely for looking strong and healthy, when she no longer is?

"It is good to be home," she said, and kissed Thelma's forehead, then turned to Charlotte. Charlotte at least was not stiff, but she was trembling.

"Oh, Agnes!" she said. "Oh, Agnes!"

"We will all have a good talk later," Luttmann said. The *schloss* was very much his headquarters, not their home. "Come upstairs, Agnes."

He let her go before him. "The master bedroom," he said.

Agnes turned to him with a frown. "That is Mother's room."

"No, no." Luttmann said. "It is my room." He opened the door for her. "But I would like you to share it with me. I have waited a very long time for that pleasure."

Agnes stepped past him. Definitely, she was back in the real world.

Chapter Twelve

The Long Road Back

Even the battleship moved up and down and occasionally rolled, so rough was the sea. The cluster of army officers on the bridge grasped stanchions while the naval officers went about their duties with complete nonchalance. Presumably they never felt seasick. Hector couldn't be sure whether his own churning stomach was a result of the motion, or of the coming head-on clash with the Germans. Or simply of being part of such a vast enterprise.

It was all around him, and above him. There were more than 1,200 warships at sea, including seven battleships. They were escorting over 1,500 merchantmen and auxiliaries, and over 4,000 landing ships and crafts; even had there been no wind at all, the Channel would still have been churned into a maelstrom by their wakes. Above his head there droned, either on their way or returning from their missions, over 3,000 heavy bombers, over 1,500 medium bombers, over 5,000 fighters, over 2,000 transports – the 800-odd gliders had been towed in some time before to land their men behind the German front line.

This vast armada was conveying over 75,000 British and Canadian soldiers, nearly 60,000 American, along with their 900 armoured vehicles and their 600 guns. The airborne troops, just under 8,000 British and over 15,000 American, were already in France and engaged. And this enormous accumulation of men, ships and aircraft was just intended to gain a lodgement. The big stuff was still to come.

George Brand appeared beside him. "We'll be opening fire in about five minutes. It'll be some show. I imagine you're happy to be going back. We'll be landing not that far south of St Valery."

A few miles, Hector thought. From the event which changed my life forever. But this kindly old uncle did not know that, and never could know that. "I'm glad to be going back," he agreed. "I just wish I could be in the first wave."

George grinned. "I'm just as happy you're not."

"I never did ask you," Hector said. "We *are* going ashore, some time, I suppose?"

"Of course. We're Monty's headquarters staff. We'll be there as soon as the lodgement is secured."

"Right. Now, Uncle George, I'm on parole not to engage in armed conflict with any Germans. What happens if I'm poking around, say, Caen, and I am confronted by a German sniper who forgot to leave or surrender, or get himself killed?"

"I would shoot him, if I were you."

"And that wouldn't be breaking my parole?"

"That would be self-defence, Hector. Of course, if the conditions were right, you *should* request him to surrender, first. But, then, the conditions for that sort of thing are so very seldom right, are they?" He grinned at his nephew. "Now you tell me, where is Lou? I haven't seen her since we left the Solent?"

"I think she's been seasick ever since then," Hector said.

Then they couldn't speak any more, as the guns opened fire.

*   *   *

It came as something of a shock to Hector to realize that he had never walked over a battlefield before. That was because he had never actually been on the winning side in a battle. In June 1940 he and his battalion had been on an endless retreat; they had not even had the time to bury their dead. He had no idea what the village of Hornoy had looked like to the Germans who had occupied it after he had led his men south to the Bresle. Well, he saw as he splashed ashore through the still-high surf on the beach outside Ouistreham, they were only just starting to bury their dead here, too. But these were the victorious dead. There were far too many of them, but he could tell from the shattered remnants of the concrete bunkers protruding from the sand dunes behind the beach that the Germans had probably suffered at least as much.

In fact, he later learned that the Allies had suffered twice as many casualties as the Germans on the first day, not so much among the British and Canadians, who had lost approximately 4,000 men, but among the Americans farther to the west, where over 6,000 had fallen; but the Americans had had the more difficult objectives in that their beaches were in many places backed by cliffs. The total German casualties were just over 6,000. But the difference lay in morale. The Allies were ashore, and they were staying. As he stood on the beach, watching the stretcher-bearers solemnly collecting the dead, Hector was passed by an unending stream of men and vehicles, disembarking from an equally endless stream of transports. Despite the dead, the knowledge that hard fighting lay ahead of them, men were grinning and cracking jokes, some were even singing as they formed up before marching off into the interior. Hector wondered if there were any, like him, who had laid down their arms outside St Valery in June 1940; he doubted that. Now the wheel had gone full circle. The aircraft circling overhead, and swooping down to bomb and machine-gun any enemy movement on the ground, belonged to the RAF and the USAAF. The hospital ships loading the wounded were protected by both aircraft and destroyers.

And to top it all he could watch a column of German prisoners, dishevelled and despondent, marching down on to the beach for embarkation to England. Had his men looked like that, four years ago? But there had not been a soul in his command who had not truly believed that the wheel would spin, no matter how long it might take. There was no prospect of a reversal of fortune for those Germans.

A captain stood beside him. "Piece of cake, really, isn't it, sir?" Hector glanced at him, and walked away.

Piece of cake, Hector thought. It took some five weeks for the British to capture Caen. Now they were faced with the strongest opposition, tank battles which were slogged out track to track, enemy strongpoints that had to be taken at the point of the bayonet, then Caen itself, reduced to rubble by the constant bombardment, and even after the British had entered still a maze of snipers and hidden enemy units. Hector, staying as close as he could to the front line, prayed for someone to take a shot at him so that he could carry out George's admonition, but no one did. Yet the casualties, on both sides, were frightful enough.

The Americans had rather better going on the Cotentin Peninsula, even capturing Cherbourg before the end of June. The war was won, so everyone said. Yet nobody had told the Germans, and those who believed it and tried to topple Hitler were made to suffer most dreadfully, hanged slowly on piano wire, while their pants slipped down to their ankles and the newsreel cameras whirred. But Caen was secured eventually, and the British could storm north along the coast, as the Americans were doing farther inland. Hector even found the time to visit St Valery, stand on the hills above the town, to look down and remember. So very much.

The next day he received a letter from Jocelyn. *I am so proud of you,* she wrote. *Alan sends you his best love.*

Which was as close as she would come to sending her own. He sat and stared at the letter for several minutes. The end *was* in sight, no matter how many more months it might take, and he could contemplate going home. After so very long. And so very much.

There remained only Agnes. But surely she was dead too, to him. He had seen the newspapers. She had, after all, been nothing more than a German agent. Or become one. He remained desperately sorry to have forced that on her, after heaven knew what traumas, but now they were far more enemies than ever at the time of their first meeting. As for destroying her family, was he not now engaged in destroying her country?

At times it was difficult to believe the Allies were ever going to get to Germany. Logistics played a part in the endless delays; there was simply not enough petrol and diesel to go round all the varied and enormous Allied armies, and each army commander, from Montgomery through Bradley to Patton, had his own axe to grind. Politics also interfered with strategy, as when it was decided to launch yet another invasion, this time on the Riviera, a diversion of men and troops, from both Italy and the West, that could have no effect at all on the ultimate defeat of the German armies. But the biggest handicap under which the Allies suffered was the command structure, a weakness which Hector, on the fringes of the staff, was well placed to observe.

The problem was Eisenhower. The Supreme Commander had revealed the greatest powers of decision in opting for launching the assault on 6 June, despite the current bad weather and the unfavourable forecasts for the coming weeks; indeed, only a fortnight after the lodgment there was a gale of such severity that the artificial harbour – codenamed Mulberry – erected off the American beaches had been destroyed. Fortunately there had been another one off the British beaches, and this now had to be used for the landing of all men and materiel until the capture of Cherbourg. Thus no one could doubt Eisenhower's commitment or determination. Equally, he had revealed in North Africa and then in Sicily that he possessed the ability to harmonize his general officers, a very mixed bag of varying nationalities.

Once in France, however, these two basic virtues became serious liabilities. He was of course beset by political considerations himself. But he also began to reveal a hatred for the German enemy and all it stood for which began to resemble something approaching paranoia, and certainly induced tunnel vision. Hector reckoned a good commander had to hate his enemy while actually fighting him, but he should never allow personal feelings to cloud his judgement. In his determination to please the American media, to keep his generals happy, and to fight the enemy wherever possible, Eisenhower decreed that the Allies should advance on every front at once, their goal the Rhine. Of course the Germans were outnumbered, short of materiel, and harassed by constant air attack, but they were still a great army, and Eisenhower's decision negated the basic principle of warfare: choose your point of attack and concentrate on that as much power as possible. Even in World War One, that nadir of military history as regards generalship, neither Joffre nor Haig nor Foch had ever advocated an attack on the German lines the whole length of the front from the Channel to Switzerland. No wonder, Hector thought, that their successors were running out of fuel. Sadly, there was no risk of their running out of men.

Thus while the British and Canadians surged up the coast, making, with strategical correctitude, for the seaports, and above all, the gigantic port of Antwerp, that would so dramatically shorten their lines of communication, the Americans advanced in three huge prongs, splaying out across France like spread fingers, aiming, it seemed, at all reaching some point on the German border, from Belfort to Cologne, at the same time, pausing only long enough to allow a French army to liberate Paris, as was considered to be politically necessary.

Paris was liberated on 25 August. Ten days later the British captured Antwerp, with its port facilities intact. "This is actually about the most decisive victory of the invasion, after Day One," George Brand told his nephew as they had a drink together. "Even if we still have to clear the Scheldt. But it won't get much press. By the way, there's someone been asking for you."

Hector had spent the last few days trying to coax more fuel out of a dwindling stockpile. But having Antwerp was obviously going to relieve the situation, once the river was cleared; the Germans still held the islands forming the north bank. Now he frowned. "Who?"

"Chap called Davison," George said, raising and lowering his eyebrows.

Hector was so surprised he couldn't speak for several seconds. "Wasn't he the chap who was knifed by his Swiss miss who turned out to be a German agent?" George asked.

"Who's supposed to be dead," Hector said grimly.

"Seems she missed. He's a friend of yours, isn't he?"

"Chance would be a fine thing," Hector remarked.

But he was curious, both to see Davison again and to learn something more about what had happened, so met the American, as requested, in a waterfront estaminet. "It's been a long war," Davison remarked.

"I'm surprised they still let you take part in it," Hector said.

"Ah, but I'm on our side now," Davison said, and grinned. "Actually, I always was. But it wasn't something my bosses wanted publicized. Quite the reverse."

"In that case I owe you an apology," Hector said. "Just how did you survive?"

"I survived by spending nine months in hospital while they put my innards back together. There were times a lot of people didn't think I was going to make it."

"Including you, I presume."

Davison drank beer. "I didn't know anything about it, most of the time. I guess you know what it's like. Only I didn't have any beautiful nurse waiting to join me between the sheets."

"From what you have just said, it seems to me that Agnes did mean to kill you," Hector said.

"I don't think there is any doubt about that. She even photographed me lying there, apparently dead. They found the camera with bloody fingerprints all over it. I presume that was to prove to her masters that she had done the job."

"What are your feelings about her?"

"I enjoyed her company."

"That's a remarkably broad-minded statement."

"Shit, Brand, she was doing what she had to do. I know something of what she went through, what her family went through. Her sole aim in life was to keep her mother and sister and brother alive. To do that she'd have gone to hell

and tried to knife the devil, if that's what her bosses wanted."
He pointed. "You got her into that mess."

"Don't you think I am going to live with that for the
rest of my life?" Hector asked. "But . . ." he frowned. "If
Agnes was told to kill you, and then taken back to Germany
and touted as a heroine of the Third Reich, what is the
Third Reich's reaction going to be to the fact that you are
actually alive?"

"Well, hopefully they won't find out until we get there.
We haven't made a song and dance about my survival."

"If they were to find out . . . ."

"It'd be curtains for Agnes, in the nastiest possible way.
I know that. What I wanted to tell you was, once we get
across the Rhine I aim to go looking for her. You game?"

"Would your intention be to save her or execute her
yourself?"

"I'm not into executing dames."

"Are you trying to tell me that you still love her, after
what she did?"

Davison signalled for another beer. "Some diseases are
incurable. You only knew Agnes the girl. I knew Agnes the
woman. I want to find her, Brand. Yes, I want her back.
I *know* she was acting under orders. She and I, we had
something. I want that back too. But I may need a little
help, as this has to be totally unofficial. You're the only
person I can trust."

"I have a job to do."

"And you're not interested in what happens to Agnes,
any more."

Hector sighed. "Yes, I'm interested," he said. "Keep
in touch."

God, to know what to do! The only hope for his marriage

was never to see Agnes again. But as Davison had reminded him, he had placed her in this impossible position in the first place. He had taken a young girl's life and he had twisted it inside out – and he had known what he was doing when he had done it, had remained supremely confident that he could adjust everything once he was out of Germany. Now he was going back, having anticipated never seeing her again. Would that not be best, whatever she had to suffer? What an unimaginable thought!

Suddenly haste was everything. He gave his complete backing to Operation Market Garden, the scheme by which Montgomery aimed to cross the Rhine by means of parachute drops behind the German line. But that was a catastrophe, partly by bad luck, in that one of the drops landed in the midst of an SS regiment recuperating, and partly by bad management, for which the staff had to share the blame. "They'll hold it against us," George Brand said sombrely, as they watched the survivors of the Airborne Division filing past, after a dangerous crossing of the River Lek. Two thousand men came out; seven thousand remained behind, either dead or in German hands.

"A costly venture," Montgomery told his officers. "But it had to be tried. Well, gentlemen, let us turn our attention to Antwerp." The idea had been that had the Arnhem attack succeeded, the Germans remaining west of the Rhine would have been in an untenable position. Actually, they were, in any event, but they still held strong positions on Walcheren and South Beveland, islands which controlled the estuary of the Scheldt and thus the approaches to Antwerp. Having possession of the great port wasn't of much value when ships seeking to use its facilities could be sunk by gunfire from the shore. It took over a month to secure the approaches, and then the British Army went into winter quarters, as did the Americans farther south.

"I think we could all do with a spot of leave," George suggested. "I'm arranging a rota. Would you rather go now, or over Christmas, Hector?"

"Do I have a choice?"

"You do, seeing as I'm arranging the rota."

"I would rather not be on it," Hector said.

George frowned. "You'd have sufficient time to go up to Drumbooee, you know. But you don't want to do that. May I ask you a personal question?"

"I suspect you're going to do that anyway, Uncle."

"Is your marriage definitely over?"

"I hope not. It's just that I'd rather see the end of this first."

"Even if the end might not be quite as close as some people are hoping? You are still corresponding with Jocelyn?"

"I am, yes. We write about the boy."

"And there is no one else?"

"No," Hector said. "There is no one else." That was the first time he had ever lied to his uncle.

"And what do you suppose Jocelyn's reaction will be to the knowledge that you don't want to go home for Christmas?"

"Jocelyn will never know I was given the opportunity, sir. Unless you tell her."

George let the matter drop, and Hector duly replaced various officers as each in turn went home to his loved ones. Staff duties were light enough during this quiescent period; the British armies lay north of the Meuse River, the Americans south of it; they had just finished an autumn campaign which had taken them right up to the German border at St Vith, and everyone anticipated that as soon as the weather improved they would be on German soil, and the war would have entered its final phase, certainly in the West. But the way the Russians were advancing suggested it would have reached the end in the East as well. "It's a matter of who gets to Berlin first," Hector told his assistant, and looked up in surprise as the door opened. "Good God!"

"Surprise, surprise!" Louise said.

He hadn't seen Louise since they had embarked at Southampton. She had been laid low with seasickness during the Channel crossing, and then, as fighting close to the beachheads had remained severe, the ATS had not been allowed ashore until things had settled down, by which time he had been far inland with the advancing army. He gazed at her insignia. "Promotion?"

"Full commander. I have been busy."

"I can imagine. Oh, this is Captain Robertson."

Louise gave the captain a dazzling smile. "My pleasure. I've come to see if my darling cousin will take me out to dinner."

"At the mess?"

"No, not at the mess."

"Well, there's nowhere else much in this village."

"There are restaurants in Liège," she pointed out.

Hector requisitioned a jeep, and they drove the fifty-odd miles to the city. "Aren't you glad to see me?" Louise asked. "Or have you been having it off with all the Belgian bits?"

"I have been having it off with nobody," Hector told her. "And yes, I am glad to see you. Just how did you know where to find me?"

"Daddy told me. He said you needed cheering up. He says you have a problem, about Jocelyn."

"I don't think you are the one to ease it."

"In ten days' time it will be Christmas," she reminded

him. "Just let's have fun. You'll feel a lot better after you've had some fun."

He didn't think she was right, but he did feel like having some fun. And it appeared she knew, and was known, at a very good restaurant in Liège, to which she directed him through masses of soldiers and civilians, not entirely controlled by almost as many MPs. "They're all letting their hair down," Louise explained. The restaurant she had chosen provided a very good meal for a place only recently liberated from German rule. It was past ten when they emerged to a still-crowded street, and Louise gave a squeal of pleasure. "For God's sake, there's Buster!"

"Eh? Buster who?" Hector peered at the approaching group of American officers.

"How should I know? We never got past Buster. Buster!" she screamed, and was swept into the mammoth's arms to be kissed. He was a big fellow, several inches taller than Hector, who was 6ft 1in.

"Baby doll," Buster said. Presumably Louise, who was 5ft 10in, came into that category. "Long time no see!"

"This is my cousin, Colonel Hector Brand," Louise explained.

"Well, pleased to meet you, Colonel," Buster said. "You have *some* relatives! Say, you guys, come and meet this Limey colonel." His companions, who had hung back, hurried forward. Names swirled around Hector's head, and his hand was pumped time and again.

"Say, Lou, you partying?" Buster inquired.

"Where?"

"Malmedy. It's only twenty miles or so. And it's gonna be a ball."

"Then I'm partying."

"You, Colonel?"

"Well . . ."

"Of course he's coming," Louise said. "He's my transport. We'll follow you."

"You got it." Buster kissed her again, and he and his companions hurried to their jeep, which was parked just in front of Hector's.

"Just how well do you know this character?" Hector asked, as they left to a screaming of tyres and a great deal of slithering on the snow.

"How well does one know anyone in a war?" she asked. "Don't tell me you're jealous."

"Having not seen you for several months, I imagine that would be pointless. I hope we get through this without broken necks."

"The British," Louise said, "have entirely lost the art of enjoying themselves. I am not, of course, including myself in that."

Malmedy was crowded with soldiers having a good time; the women were also having a good time, and it was obvious that a large proportion of them made a profession of it. The party to which Buster led them was only one of several, but champagne was flowing as well as beer and spirits, and a gramophone blared for people to dance to. The noise was tremendous. "Anyone would think it was Christmas Day," Hector remarked to one officer he found wedged against him in the bar – he had no idea where Louise had got to. "Instead of nine days short."

"Look at it this way, buddy," the American said. "Christmas may never come."

Hector had had several drinks and dances and had still not spotted Louise before he next remembered to look at his watch. It was two in the morning, and he was on duty at eight! He fought his way through the throng and spotted his escort; he no longer considered himself hers. Louise was in a corner leaning against Buster and doing some very heavy petting. Apart from their mouths, which seemed glued together, Lou's skirt was around her waist and Buster's hands were beneath it, while her hands were between them. They weren't behaving very differently to several other couples, but maybe the others didn't have any place to go or cousins around. "Sorry to bother you, Buster," Hector said.

Buster took his mouth away from Lou's to blink at him. "Don't I know you?"

"Absolutely correct, old man," Hector said. "I came over to say goodnight, and thanks for the party."

"Oh! Right. Sure. Great to see you, man."

"I'll be taking Lou with me," Hector explained.

"Shit!" Louise commented.

"Come again?" the American inquired.

"The young lady," Hector explained. "My cousin. She's coming with me."

"Now listen up," Buster said.

"Push off, there's a dear," Louise said.

"I also happen to be her commanding officer," Hector said, stretching a point. "Come along, Lou."

"Well . . ." Louise made a face.

"You're not going with this guy?" Buster was scandalized.

"He can be very tough," Louise said.

"I ought to punch you in the kisser," Buster told Hector.

"I feel exactly the same way about yours," Hector said, pleasantly.

They glared at each other.

"We don't want any trouble," Louise said, stepping between them. "It's been great, Buster, but . . ."

Hector was sure there was going to be a problem, but in the background the telephone that had been jangling suddenly stopped as someone answered it. Then there was a great bellow: "Krauts!"

There was a great wail of terror from the women, shouts of startled alarm from the men; most looked at the door, as if expecting gray-clad figures to come bursting in. "Somebody shut off that fucking music!" Buster bellowed. "What the hell do you mean, Si?"

"There's an attack through St Vith. Tanks. Thousands of tanks. All officers report to their units immediately."

"Shitting hell!" Buster commented. "They're licked. Don't you know they're licked, Colonel? How the hell can they start attacking."

"And just before Christmas, too," Louise complained.

"I don't think they know they're licked," Hector said. His brain spun in momentary indecision. All hell would be breaking loose at British headquarters as well. But as he was here, within fifty miles of St Vith . . . an observation on the spot is always worth a thousand long-range reports.

"We'll have to take a rain cheque," Buster was telling Louise, kissing her as enthusiastically as before and then releasing her. "See you around, Colonel. Look after the little girl." He was lost in the throng.

"Listen," Hector said. "I need the jeep. You'll have to find your way back to Liege. You'll get transport from there."

"Like hell. And how do I get there? You expecting me to walk fifty miles?"

"I have to see what's going on," he explained.

"So why can't I come along?"

"Because it could be dangerous."

"A bit of danger is just what I feel like, seeing as how you so rudely interrupted a great moment."

Hector reflected, but only briefly, on his uncle's reactions were George Brand to discover that his nephew had taken his daughter into a combat zone . . . not to mention a wild party in Malmedy! But time was passing. "Listen," he said. "If you come with me, you do exactly what I tell you. Understood?"

"Yes, sir, Colonel, sir!"

They roared into the night, with a great deal of company, every road in and out of Malmedy had suddenly become very crowded. But Hector's insignia as well as his pass as a British staff officer saw them through all obstacles. Yet it was slow work, and long before dawn, which was about eight in the morning, they encountered columns of retreating soldiers, mostly looking bewildered. *They* were the victors, so they had been told often enough. So how come they were retreating? Hector found a jeepload of MPs. "I'm trying to find out what happened."

"Seems the bastards have managed to concentrate a couple of tank armies, with support troops, Colonel," the sergeant said.

"And you didn't know about this?" Hector was incredulous.

"All this foul weather has been limiting vis," complained a corporal. "Our observation planes have been grounded."

"And now they've just let it loose," the sergeant said. "Kind of caught us on the hop."

"So where are they?" Hector asked.

"Not too far, Colonel."

"Do you know where they are going to be checked?"

"Nope. We just received orders to pull back."

Bloody hell, Hector thought. "And you estimate their strength as two tank armies?" Louise asked, intent on doing her bit.

"At least, ma'am. We gotta go."

They drove off to the west, leaving Hector and Louise

gazing at the line of infantrymen plodding behind them. "Do you think it's serious?" Louise asked. "Where can they be heading?"

"I'd say, Antwerp."

"Antwerp?" Now she was incredulous.

"So it's a gambler's throw," Hector said. "It has to be. The Germans don't have either the men or the material to beat us in a pitched battle. Even if they have managed to get together a couple of tank armies, which, frankly, I take with a pinch of salt, it has to be with a limited objective in mind. Antwerp is the only logical target. It would knock out the port on which we are relying for our logistical support in the invasion of Germany, and it would drive a wedge between the British and American armies, which could, given the Nazi way of thinking, lead to quarrels and a general breakdown of the Allied assault. And if what we're looking at is typical of the whole American front at this moment, it could certainly be a major and morale-boosting victory."

"So what do we do?"

He chewed his lip. "I need some more exact information. You game?"

"I'm always game," she reminded him cheekily. They drove into the night.

After an hour the lines of retreating troops began to thin, until suddenly the road was empty. This meant that the snow had managed to drift in places and Hector had to reduce speed. He braked, and switched off the motor, listened. All around him there was a great stealthy rustle, of large numbers of men. But overlaying it was the grind and rattle of armour, as yet distant, but coming closer. "No point in coming this far and not seeing what we can see." He drove a bit farther, to where there was a slip road leading up to a low hill. Using all his gears on the soft snow, he swung up and parked in the shelter of some bushes.

"Oh, for some hot coffee!" Louise complained, rubbing her gloved hands together. "How long do you plan to stay here?"

"Until something devolves." He got out and stamped his feet, stared to the east. The darkness was now beginning to fade, and the growl of distant traffic was growing louder.

"You know something?" Louise said. "I'm scared stiff. What happens if we're captured?"

He took a pair of binoculars from the glove compartment, used them to peer into the gloom. "These are combat troops. I imagine they'd have your knickers off for a start."

"There's a happy thought! But I'd rather not. I'd freeze. Don't you think . . ."

"Sssh!"

A jeep was bouncing down the road towards them.

"Do you know, for a moment there I thought we were the only people left in the world," Louise said.

"Sssh," Hector said again and pulled her into the shelter of the bushes.

"But that's an American vehicle," she protested.

The jeep came up to their turn-off, and checked. It was using hooded headlamps, but had easily picked out the fresh tyre tracks in the snow. "Coming this way," someone said, in German!

"Speak English, you fool!" snapped another voice. "Check up that rise."

"What the fuck . . ." Louise whispered.

Hector drew his revolver. "Lie down," he told her, staring into the gloom. Two men in the front, definitely, one of whom was just getting out. And in the back . . . he couldn't be sure. But that they were Germans in American uniforms could not be doubted. "Stay down, and don't move," he whispered. "No matter what happens."

She made no reply, while he listened to the feet approaching, then suddenly stood up. Presumably he was breaking his parole, as the German hadn't actually shot at him, but he was prepared to argue that one later, if he had to. The man stopped in surprise at the figure appearing in front of him. Hector levelled the revolver and shot him in the chest. Then he swung the weapon to the officer sitting beside the wheel, and fired twice more. The officer gave a shriek and tumbled out of the jeep, to spreadeagle in the snow.

Now Hector realized there were two more men in the back, both armed with rifles, and both climbing out of the vehicle. One actually fired, but the bullet was wide. Hector sent three shots at them, and one fell. Then the hammer clicked on an empty chamber. The German soldier was levelling his rifle. Hector hurled himself into the shelter of the jeep, landed with a crash that winded him, listened to the sound of pounding feet as the German ran up the slope, snow crunching beneath his boots. I've had it, he thought.

"Englander?" The German asked, stepping round the jeep, and grinning as he levelled his rifle. Then there was a sharp explosion, and he gave a grunt and half-turned before hitting the ground with a thump.

Hector sat up. "Where did you get that thing?"

"I always carry one," Louise explained, tapping her shoulder bag. "He's not dead." She levelled her revolver again.

"Wait." Hector knelt beside the groaning German. He had been hit in the back, in the vicinity of his kidneys, Hector reckoned, and didn't have long to live. "Listen, Fritz," he said in German. "Do you want to die?"

"No," the soldier said. "Help me!"

"Tell me what's out there. All of it. Quickly, now."

"Water," the man begged. "Water."

"When you tell me what's out there."

The man gasped. "There are two armies. The Sixth and the Fifth. Twenty-four divisions, ten panzers. You will not stop them."

Hector put his memory to work. "Their commanding officers," he said.

"The Fifth is commanded by General Dietrich, the Sixth by General Manteuffel."

"God!" Hector commented. "He's telling the truth. Two armies!"

"Water," the man begged.

"He's going to die," Louise said, uncorking her canteen.

"I agree with you." Hector watched the blood spreading across the snow.

"And you don't care." Louise held the canteen to the man's lips.

"Listen, five minutes ago he was about to shoot me. And you shot him. Remember? We have to get out of here," Hector said. "We need both to warn our people of just what is coming, and that there are Germans dressed as American MPs knocking about as a screen."

"What about him?"

"Leave him your canteen. His friends will be here in a little while."

"He's not going to survive a little while."

"That's up to him."

"I'm not sure I love you any more," she remarked.

"I'm not sure you ever did. You coming with me, or would you rather stay here?" Louise got into the jeep without a word.

The Battle of the Bulge was never as close a matter as some

commentators tried to make out. The Germans gained a lot of ground by virtue of surprise, and because of the low cloud which negated the Allied air strength. But even before the weather cleared, as it was bound to do, the thrust had been held by troops pumped in from the north by Montgomery, and from the south by Bradley. It had been a costly gamblers' throw, wasting some of the best remaining elements in the German Army. "However," George Brand told his nephew, "your part in bringing us that early information of the exact enemy strength was of considerable importance; you're getting a bar to your DSO."

"I shouldn't have been there at all," Hector protested.

"Of course you shouldn't, my dear boy. Certainly not with Louise. But you were. As Napoleon said, a lucky general is more valuable than a good one." He glanced at the younger man. "You never did explain just how Louise happened to be with you."

"I can only say I'm sorry. We went to a party in Malmedy, this thing broke loose, and I felt I had to see for myself what was happening. I tried to persuade her to come back up here, but you know what Louise is like."

"I do indeed," George agreed, clearly not having a clue as to his only daughter's true disposition. "And the important thing is that you got her out. It's had an effect, though. Do you know, she's asked for a transfer back to England."

"I didn't know that," Hedtor said.

"Getting caught up in the actual fighting must have been too much for her," George said.

"Absolutely," Hector agreed.

Louise, Hector reflected, although the daughter and granddaughter and great-granddaughter ad infinitum of soldiers, had never really understood about men and war. Even

Davison and his domestic problems had been off-stage, as it were. The idea that her sexually-attractive cousin, whom she had known and with whom she had played games all of her life, could also be ruthless enough to leave a man to die in the snow because he had a job of work to do had been totally abhorrent to her. He did not expect her ever to come knocking at his door again. But he wished her well.

Meanwhile, the Rhine. The Allies spent the winter recuperating from the German Ardennes counter-offensive, preparatory to a general advance in the spring. Now at last Eisenhower realized that he had to make a positive choice of fronts, and he went for Montgomery and the British in the north. Matters were complicated by the seizure of the bridge at Remagen by units of the 9th US Armoured Division on 7 March, before it could be blown. This first bridgehead allowed the Americans to pour across to the east bank, but the original plan was largely adhered to, and Montgomery's British and Canadian troops flooded into the north German plain. Not even the sudden and totally unexpected death of Franklin Roosevelt disturbed the Allied plans.

Now, with the Russians almost at Berlin and all the materiel of war dwindling on the German side, staff work became mainly a matter of marking off the miles covered, the men killed and wounded, and the supplies necessary for the next advance. Which was what Hector was doing in his caravan when his orderly announced that there was an American correspondent wishing to see him. "Well, glory be," he remarked, as Davison filled the small cabin.

"You did say to keep in touch."

"I did." Hector gestured him to a seat, poured two glasses of scotch. "How's your war going?"

"Couldn't be better. I bet you've been working pretty hard."

"You could say that," Hector agreed. "Any news of our girl?"

"Not directly. But I have a pretty good idea that she's at the *schloss*; Luttmann is general in command of the Munich area, and I know he made the *schloss* his headquarters."

"When are your people aiming to take Munich?"

"There's the rub," Davison said. "It has a low priority, compared with driving towards Berlin. But there's another point. Ike has got it firmly fixed in his head, planted there by various intelligence suggestions, that up in the mountains behind Munich, in the area around Berchtesgaden, the Germans are going to make a last stand, that they've prepared a massive fortress where they will go down in a blaze of glory, taking as many of our people as they can with them."

"Do you believe that? Is Hitler down there? Our information is that he's still in Berlin."

"That goes with our information, too. But Ike still wants to make sure of the rest of Germany before he tackles what could be a tough nut."

"You haven't told me whether or not you believe that's true."

"Personally, I don't. You don't create a fortress on that scale overnight. Work would have had to start a long time ago, and I'm pretty damned sure I would have noticed something going on when last I was there. However . . ." he grinned. "Ike wouldn't say no to some positive information."

"You have got to be out of your mind!"

"You reckon? Look, Hector, we know the German armies are really in a state of collapse. They may be fighting like the devil to hold back the Russians, but that's only because they're still hoping to negotiate something with us here in the west. You know as well as I that when it comes to contact with us they can't surrender fast enough. Now I reckon that if two officers, a British and an American, using a white flag, drove up to Schloss Patten to discuss possible surrender terms with General Luttmann, they'd let us in."

"And when Luttmann realizes we do not have any terms to offer?"

"I said the ploy would get us in. We may have to shoot our way out. But I have some ideas about organizing that."

"You *are* mad!"

"With Agnes in tow," Davison went on as if Hector hadn't spoken. "Otherwise, I reckon it's curtains for the girl. And her family. You game?"

There was no choice. He had got her into this mess. "I'll have to arrange leave."

"Don't take too long, old man".

"It won't be a problem," Hector said. "I was due for leave last December, and passed it up. Anyway, my immediate commanding officer is my uncle."

Davison raised his eyebrows. "I don't reckon you should tell him what we're aiming to do."

"I don't either," Hector said.

Friedrich Luttmann wearily raised his head as his adjutant entered his office. "There is nothing at all, Herr General," the major said. "Nothing from Berlin, nothing from Army Group West. We are completely cut off. And in addition, there is a news report that the Russians are in Berlin. Admittedly it is a Russian news report, but . . ." He paused, because Luttmann was staring at him as if he wasn't there. "Have you orders, Herr General?" he ventured.

"I have fewer than twenty thousand effectives in and

around Munich," Luttmann said. "And a civilian population I can no longer trust. So, I have three alternatives. One is to surrender when called upon to do so by the Americans. That would be the easy way out for our men, and I very much fear it is one they will take whether we authorize it or not. But that would involve my trial as a war criminal. And no doubt yours as well, Liesemeyer. The second alternative is to pull our people out while there is yet time, abandon Munich, and retire into the mountains for a last-ditch stand."

"The Wolf's Lair," Liesemeyer said, eagerly.

Luttmann sighed. "There is no Wolf's Lair, Liesemeyer. This redoubt in the mountains is a figment of a journalist's imagination."

"But the Americans do not know this, Herr General. According to prisoners we have taken, they are sure it exists. That is why they are not moving south with all their strength."

"They are not moving south with all their strength, Liesemeyer, because they wish to occupy as much of Germany as possible before the Russians do so. Here in the south we are always going to fall into their laps. And whether they believe the Wolf's Lair exists or not, the fact is that it doesn't, and in the mountains we shall be like flowers in a vase, cut off from all sustenance, slowly dwindling."

"But what is the third alternative, Herr General?"

"Why, to follow the fashion set by Generals Model and Kluge, and blow out our brains."

Liesemeyer gulped.

"When it becomes necessary, of course, Liesemeyer. At the moment it is not. We will continue to present a bold front, allow the Americans to worry about the Wolf's Lair, and tell our own people that the Russians have been defeated and massive armies are moving down to defeat the Americans and relieve us. After all, if we cannot find out what is happening in the east, the people are not likely to be able to."

Luttmann called his command car and drove up to the *schloss*. He remembered when he first came to Munich, as a young SS officer, how he had looked up at this castle and thought, what a wonderful place to live. He had never imagined then that one day it would be his, to all intents and purposes. Would it also be a wonderful place to die? But dying seemed an eternity away as the car pulled into the courtyard, to the invariable chorus of barking dogs. The sky was blue, the sun was shining, there was no sign of any enemy, and the castle, and its grounds, were totally undamaged; there was nothing around here worth bombing, at least when compared with other targets.

Sentries clicked to attention and he touched the brim of his cap with his swagger stick as he entered the house. Johann bowed and Thelma von Patten curtsied; he was allowing her to act as housekeeper in her own house. He nodded to them, went into the study, and poured himself a glass of schnapps. For all his somewhat flippant attitude when with Liesemeyer, he knew there were some serious decisions to be made. Although he had, by force of circumstance, become over the years a policeman, an interrogator, a torturer, and an executioner, he was at heart a soldier; his instincts told him to pull his men into the mountains and fight that last-ditch guerilla campaign Liesemeyer dreamed about. It was just coming up to summer and survival would not be that difficult for another six months; they had sufficient ammunition to last them that long.

But would his men follow him? He was too proud to face a mutiny, a catastrophe of scorn and rejection. The door opened, and he turned to look at Agnes. She was, as always, simply dressed, in a white blouse and black ankle-length skirt, and her magnificent hair was loose. She was quite the most beautiful woman he had ever known. And he owned her, body and soul. Or did he? She was a symbol of the doubts that were beginning to take over his mind. Agnes knew, as well as anyone, that the war was lost, that total disaster lurked just around the corner. A catastrophe that would involve her death as much as his; she was a wanted criminal in the West. But he rather thought she was looking forward to that, if she could ensure the survival of her mother. Only Thelma was left now. The brother had died in Russia, and Charlotte had died a year ago, officially of tuberculosis, but Luttmann suspected it might have been of lingering shame and despair, even after she had been rescued from the military brothel. "Schnapps?" He raised the bottle.

She came across the room, took a glass from the sideboard, allowed him to fill it. "How much do you hate me?" he asked.

She turned, a faint frown gathering between her eyes. She was used to his moods, which varied from boisterous good humour to dark and brooding violence. "All right," he said. "You do not have to answer that. I will ask you another question: has it occurred to you that we are living the last few days of our lives?"

"It had occurred to me, yes."

"And no doubt you have made certain plans."

"I have no plans to make."

Clearly she was lying. But he was not in the mood to beat her. He stood up. "Well, come upstairs and we will forget our sorrows for a while."

She raised her eyebrows. "Before lunch?"

"Why not? I feel like sex. Do you not feel like sex?"

She bit her lip. Luttmann had an idea she never did actually feel like sex, until it had begun; then she was very responsive. He went to the door, opened it, and frowned as he heard car tyres crunching on the gravel, while the dogs recommenced barking. He strode past the sentries onto the terrace, looked down at Liesemeyer. A very agitated Liesemeyer. "What is the trouble?" Luttmann demanded.

"Herr General!" Liesemeyer ran up the steps. "There are two officers in Munich, one American, well, he is actually a war correspondent, but the other is an English officer from Montgomery's army."

"Montgomery's army is in the north," Luttmann pointed out.

"I know this, Herr General. But these two are travelling under a flag of truce. They were actually captured some miles north of Munich, having passed through the American lines. They say they have a message for the commanding general. You, Herr General. They mentioned you by name. This message contains an offer to us for an honourable surrender."

"That is ridiculous!"

"Absolutely, Herr General. I think they are spies, sent to discover our strength and dispositions. Shall I shoot them?"

"They came under a flag of truce, Liesemeyer. It is time for us to honour these niceties, in view of our situation. But it would be interesting to find out just what these two scoundrels are up to. Have them brought up here."

"I have them with me, Herr General. But I thought it best to leave them outside the castle while I spoke with you. I will call them in now."

He drove off, and Luttmann looked at Agnes, standing at the foot of the stairs. "Very curious," he remarked. "I think we shall put off our pleasure until I have seen these two gentlemen, and decided what to do with them. Go upstairs and wait for me."

Agnes looked as if she would have said something, then inclined her head and went up the stairs. Luttmann took a turn up and down the hall. Terms for surrender! If it could be true. But the Allies had only ever implemented a policy of unconditional surrender since landing in Normandy. There had never been any offer of terms before. If only he knew what was happening in the outside world!

He watched the car drive in. It was a closed tourer. Four men got out, the two German guards, and the two foreigners. Luttmann stared at them, and felt his entire body stiffen. Liesemeyer fussed about them like a mother hen, escorting them to the foot of the steps.

"My God!" Luttmann said.

"May I present Colonel Hector Brand, of Field Marshal Montgomery's staff," Liesemeyer said importantly, "and Mr James Davison, of the New York *Globe*, attached to General Eisenhower's staff."

Luttmann stared at him, then at the two men, who were smiling at him, then glanced at the windows above his head; they were open, and they belonged to the master bedroom, where Agnes would at that moment be undressing. "Liesemeyer," he said. "You are a fool. Take them behind that wall and shoot them. Now!"

Liesemeyer goggled at him.

"Don't you think it would be a good idea to hear what we have to offer, Friedrich?" James asked.

Luttmann pointed. "You are supposed to be dead."

"I've a tough hide. You going to invite us in?"

Luttmann glared at him, then looked at Hector. "Shoot us, and you'll be tried as a war criminal," Hector said. "Our armies know we're here."

Luttmann glanced at Liesemeyer; Hector had to presume an unspoken message had been passed. Then the SS General smiled. "Of course, gentlemen. We must let bygones be bygones, eh? Come in, and we will discuss your offer."

He gestured at the door, and Hector followed Davison into the hall. Agnes stood at the turn of the stairs; she had been listening. Then she came running down. "Well, hello, little girl," Davison said. "You know . . ."

But Agnes was past him and into Hector's arms. "Oh, my God," she gasped. "Hector . . . !"

"True love," Luttmann remarked, delighted at Davison's discomfiture.

Hector held Agnes close. "Sweetheart," he said.

"How I have waited," she moaned, face pressed against his tunic. "Now . . ."

"Now these gentlemen have some business with me, Agnes," Luttmann said. Slowly, Agnes released Hector and stepped back.

"We'll be with you as soon as we can," Hector assured her.

Luttmann was gesturing them into the study, then followed, closing the doors behind them. Agnes remained standing at the foot of the stairs. "Schnapps?"

"I wouldn't say no," Davison agreed.

Luttmann glanced at Hector, who nodded. He poured, gave them each a glass, lifted his own. "To the defeat of Communism."

"I'll drink to that." Davison drained his glass.

Luttmann sat behind his desk. "Be seated, gentlemen." He waited while they obeyed him. "Now then, what have you got to offer me?"

"A chance to save your skin," Davison said. "We have come for the Patten family. However many of them are left alive."

"And in return?"

"We will offer evidence of your clemency in defence of the charges that will be laid against you as a war criminal, following the surrender of the Reich. That can only be a few days off."

"You mean you have not come here to offer me and my command special terms."

"Afraid not, General. Those aren't on."

Luttmann stared at him for several seconds. "You are mad," he commented. "Stark raving mad. I am going to hang you. And I think it may be a good idea to hang Agnes beside you. That will be amusing, eh? You can look at each other as you die."

"We thought you might adopt that point of view," Davison said. "So . . ." without warning he propelled himself from his chair and leapt across Luttmann's desk. Luttmann gave a startled exclamation and tried to rise, at the same time unclipping his holster. But Davison was already on him, throwing him to the floor with a crash. "The gun!" he bawled.

Hector ran round the desk and knelt beside the struggling men. He pulled Luttmann's Luger pistol from the holster. Davison had just hit the general a short jab on the jaw, and Luttmann was clearly dazed. The door burst open, and a guard ran in, took in the situation at a glance, and levelled his rifle. Hector shot him in the chest and he crashed backwards, striking the doorway and sliding down it.

His place was taken by Agnes, stopping in consternation at the chaos in front of her. From outside there came shouts of command. "Wake up!" Davison slapped Luttmann several times on the face, and Luttmann blinked as he shook his head to clear his brain.

"Agnes!" Hector held her close, while still directing the pistol into the hall. But the guard there had disappeared.

"He went outside," Agnes said.

"Mad," Luttmann said. "And you have killed one of my men. Gentlemen, this is going to cost you dear. Don't you realize that this building is entirely surrounded by my people?"

"That's where you come in," Davison told him. "You are going to tell your people to withdraw all the way back to

Munich, and you are going to give us a signed safe conduct to return to the American lines. With Agnes and her family."

"Why should I do that, Herr Davison?"

"Simply because, if you do not, we are going to kill you."

Luttmann sat at his desk.

"And don't try opening any drawers," Davison said.

"I do not keep another weapon in here, Herr Davison. But I am not going to do as you wish."

"The front door!" Agnes snapped.

Hector tossed the Luger to Davison, who caught it expertly, picked up the dead guard's Schmeisser and stepped into the hall. The front door was just opening, and he sent a burst of bullets at it. There was a cry from outside, then the door swung shut. "Is there another way into the house?" Hector asked Agnes.

"About six."

"Well, listen, round up your mother and Charlotte . . ." he checked at her expression.

"Charlotte is dead," Agnes said.

There was no time to ask how, or why. "But your mother?"

"Mother is upstairs."

"Then get her down here and into this office." Agnes ran up the stairs. "James, old man, you had better get your boy moving."

"Come on," Davison said.

"I will sit here until my men come for me," Luttmann said.

"You'll be dead."

"That is up to you."

Davison looked at Hector, who was still standing in the study doorway, covering the hall and the front door. "You reckon he's bluffing?"

"Let's hope so," Hector said.

"Herr General!" There was a shout from outside. "Are you all right, Herr General?"

"I am being held a prisoner," Luttmann called back. "You are in command until my release, Liesemeyer." He smiled. "You have a few minutes, gentlemen; it will take that long for Major Liesemeyer to absorb the fact of his new responsibility. But I must warn you: he is a man of limited imagination. His instinct will be to order a charge."

"Not with you in our hands," Davison pointed out.

"He is a German soldier, Herr Davison. He knows that where battles are fought, even limited battles such as this, lives will be lost."

"Beginning with yours." Davison stepped behind Luttmann, rested the muzzle of the pistol on his neck. "Tell him to get out, with his men, or die, now."

Luttmann never moved. His hands were flat on the desk. He certainly had guts, Hector thought. But Davison was stymied, Hector reckoned; he was not a cold-blooded killer, and he had expected his bluff to work. On the other hand, he was not looking as disconcerted as might have been expected.

Agnes came back down the stairs, almost dragging Thelma. The servants had appeared at the back of the hall, and she waved them away. "Get into the kitchen," she shouted. "Keep down. There may be shooting."

"There's an understatement," Hector said, pulling the two women into the room.

From outside there came the tramp of marching feet as Liesemeyer's men took up their positions. "Gentlemen," Luttmann said. "I strongly suggest that you cease this charade, before someone else gets killed."

"I agree," Davison said, looking at his watch. "You have just on ten minutes, General."

"You have less than that," Luttmann argued.

"Herr General!" Liesemeyer shouted; he was now using a loudspeaker. "My men are all in position."

Luttmann got up, walked to the window; Davison made no attempt to stop him. "Very well, Liesemeyer," the general called. "You may commence operations whenever you are ready."

"They'll kill us all!" Thelma wailed.

"That's a distinct possibility," Davison agreed, but he still did not look terribly worried, and he was still looking at his watch. "Five to the hour. Listen, General."

Luttmann's head jerked as there came the drone of several airplane engines. "You bastard!" Hector said, admiringly.

Davison shrugged. "I told you I had an idea on how we might get out. It only took one phone call. But I'd hoped it wouldn't come to this."

"Herr General!" Liesemeyer was shouting. "There are enemy aircraft approaching from the north-west."

"Attack, you fool!" Luttmann shouted. "Get into the *schloss*!"

"Trouble is," Davison said, "I told the boys, in the absence of a signal from me, to strafe the castle as well as any troops they might see. And I haven't been able to send that signal, General."

The front doors were thrown open, and men stampeded in. But Hector checked them with his Schmeisser, spraying the entrance with bullets which sent grey-clad figures tumbling to and fro. While now there came the chatter of machine-guns, followed by the crump of bombs. "Liesemeyer!" Luttman was shouting. "Get in here."

But there was no further attempt on the door; the Germans were seeking shelter from the attacking aircraft. "We have to get out of here!" Davison said. "We'll try the back. Oh, you're coming with us, General." He grasped Luttmann's arm and turned him round, but as he did so there was a much louder explosion and the entire castle shook.

"Come on!" Hector bawled, grabbing Thelma's arm.

Agnes was hanging on to the other one. Thelma began to scream incoherently as there came another crash, and part of the staircase collapsed in a cloud of dust. Davison, just pushing Luttmann through the door behind them, checked at the explosion, as did Hector, then there came a burst of fire from the pantries; some of the soldiers had after all got into the building. Hector dived behind the rubbled staircase, carrying the two women with him. Thelma had stopped screaming. But now they were separated from Davison and Luttmann by the width of the hall, which was covered by German fire. "Is there another way?" Hector shouted at Agnes. "You said there were six entrances."

"Through there!" She pointed past the dining room.

"Can you make it over here?" Hector asked Davison.

"Can you cover us?"

Hector nodded, looked round the stairs and fired a burst at the kitchens. The noise of the aircraft had momentarily died, but presumably they were turning for another run. Davison leapt to his feet, dragging Luttmann, but the general suddenly jerked away from him and rolled back into the study. "Forget him!" Hector shouted. "We've got what we came for."

Davison hesitated, then propelled himself forward. But the delay had been fatal: the Germans in the pantries had recovered, and he was hit by several bullets while virtually in mid-air. He turned round and crashed to the floor in a welter of blood. "James!" Agnes screamed, and abandoned her mother to run to James's side. Desperately Hector stepped out from behind the shelter of the stairs to give her covering fire, before himself kneeling beside the American, seizing an arm to help Agnes drag him to shelter.

The Germans in the kitchen had retreated, and Agnes and Hector had got Davison into cover, when Hector looked up and saw Luttmann. The general had, after all, another weapon hidden in the study, and this pistol was now levelled. Desperately Hector unslung his Schmeisser, while shouting at Agnes. "Luttmann!"

Agnes had taken the Luger from Davison's lifeless hand. She turned and stood up.

"Bitch!" Luttmann shouted, and fired. Agnes gave a gasp and her knees buckled. But she returned fire and her bullet struck Luttmann in the chest. He was dead before he hit the floor.

Then Agnes was on her knees, panting, her own blouse smothered in blood. Hector cradled her in his arms. "Hector," she whispered, "Hector, my love. I love you! I have always loved you. Only you. But I *owed* James. Please understand that."

"I understand," he said.

Her lips parted in a smile. "At least tell me you love me," she said, and died.

"I don't know whether you should be cashiered or congratulated," George Brand told his nephew. "Going in there, without permission . . ."

"I had leave, sir," Hector pointed out. "And I was not specifically forbidden to go anywhere."

"You went and got yourself captured. You could have been shot."

"I think that fellow Liesemeyer had that in mind, once the American aircraft had withdrawn. But before he could get around to it, news came in of Hitler's death and the surrender. Then he couldn't do too much for me."

"Hm," George said. "I'm not going to ask you why you went probing down there, Hector; I have my own ideas. The story is that you and Davison went off on your own to see just how true were those rumours of a Wolf's Lair packed with men and munitions for a last-ditch Nazi stand. So, as you discovered there wasn't one, I think we will settle for congratulations. Now, you have leave. I think you should go home to your wife."

"Do you think she wants me?"

"My information is that she does, Hector. But it might be a good idea to write her first."

It seemed an eternity since last Hector had stood at the bottom of this garden lane. It was his house, his garden, his lane. But did he really belong here?

The door opened and the boy stood there. He stared at the gaunt figure in front of him for several seconds, then he asked, "Daddy?"

"Alan!"

Alan ran forward, and Hector swept him from the ground. "I wasn't sure you'd recognize me."

"Mummy has so many photos . . ."

Hector looked past him at Jocelyn, standing in the doorway. "Welcome home," she said. Hector carried the boy towards her, set him down, and took her in his arms. "I got your letter," she said. "I am so very sorry."

"About Jim Davison? Or Agnes?"

"I'm sorry about everyone who got killed in this war, Hector. I'm only happy you survived. But . . . what you feel . . ."

"We have a lot of time that needs making up," Hector said. "War does things to people, changes them. But they should change back, when it's over. Maybe Davison – and Agnes – made us both look at life a little differently. But maybe we'll benefit from that."

Jocelyn kissed him.